DISCARD

After the Feeling

After the Feeling

T.N. Williams

www.urbanchristianonline.net

Urban Books, LLC
78 East Industry Court
Deer Park, NY 11729

ISBN 13: 978-1-60162-805-3
ISBN 10: 1-60162-805-6

First Mass Market Printing October 2011
First Trade Paperback Printing May 2009
Printed in the United States of America

10 9 8 7 6 5 4 3 2 1

This is a work of fiction. Any references or similarities to actual events, real people, living, or dead, or to real locales are intended to give the novel a sense of reality. Any similarity in other names, characters, places, and incidents is entirely coincidental.

Distributed by Kensington Publishing Corp.
Submit Wholesale Orders to:
Kensington Publishing Corp.
C/O Penguin Group (USA) Inc.
Attention: Order Processing
405 Murray Hill Parkway
East Rutherford, NJ 07073-2316
Phone: 1-800-526-0275
Fax: 1-800-227-9604

PROLOGUE

GERMANI

October 11, 2007
9:58 P.M.

The fateful call came in.

The credits to a re-run episode of *Grey's Anatomy* had begun to play.

I didn't answer on the first ring.

I was too busy wallowing in aggravation and exhaustion as I devoured a plate full of grease-laden buffalo wings and mozzarella sticks.

My husband, Scott's, porn obsession was wearying me out. Nothing I said or did seemed to matter. My feelings of confusion, shame, loneliness and rejection were ignored by the man I vowed to love unconditionally; wasted on deaf ears like a bruised apple tumbling from a wind-blown tree.

Scott's attention was consumed by sexual images on his computer from the Internet, DVDs from the local sex shops, and those videos from

Pay-Per-View. It was more than I could handle. More than I knew how to deal with. Maybe if he acknowledged how bad things were, we wouldn't be at odds. Maybe. But he kept making excuses; justifying his actions at the expense of our family.

There's only so much understanding that a woman can give before . . . enough becomes enough.

It brought to mind a colorful logo I saw on the bumper sticker of a Yugo parked at the grocery store that read, SEX SELLS. Made me think it was too bad that same statement didn't come with a warning.

Sex kills too.

The phone's ringing interrupted my sulking.

I was willing to let that call go to voice mail, but curiosity compelled me to answer just from the phone number flashing across my television.

"Germani?" an anguished voice cracked after I answered.

The caller on the other end of the line was familiar, but sounded in worse condition than I felt. I couldn't put my finger on it. There was no other definition to describe the conversation beyond peculiar. When the caller made a shocking confession I saw warning signs and red flags go up all around me.

I put the caller on hold while I went to the bathroom to wash the remnants of my meal from my greasy hands. The caller needed better advice than I could give. I was clueless on how I'd help 'em when my own thoughts were all messed up. But I knew I had to do something. On the way back to the family room, I grabbed a New King James Version of the Bible off the bookshelf near the computer center and flipped through as I walked. I tried to find the right words amongst the pages as my mind drew blanks. By the time I made it back to the phone with Bible in clean hands, a busy signal blared through and the caller was gone.

My heart quickened as I thought about what to do next.

10:41 P.M. Blood.

There was blood everywhere when I made it to the caller's home. Deep crimson streaks that saturated vanilla satin sheets and rained burgundy droplets onto the Persian area rug beneath the bed.

I stood planted against the door frame like a wisteria vine attached to aluminum siding. I was too afraid to step in the room and too disturbed to walk away.

Music was playing. The eighties song, "Real Love" by a group named Skyy ended. An eerie silence penetrated the air for just a few seconds. The song began to play again. Somebody had put it on repeat.

Don't be afraid of the way you feel.

Fear came quickly. I was too late.

I couldn't think as my eyes stayed locked on the crimson streaks, mesmerized like a teenager on an acid trip. Dazed and stunned, my lips slowly opened as my brain processed. I was in the middle of a gory crime scene and somebody was dead . . . murdered. Suddenly, terror filled the once irritated space of my abdomen where aggravation was devoured by panic, and I screamed at the top of my lungs.

CHAPTER ONE

GERMANI

June 16, 2007

"Lord, I can't believe I agreed to this," I muttered with irritation. Rings of smoke blew my way as the three men at the table behind me whistled obscene remarks and cat calls at the stage performer.

I glanced back to match the voice to the owner of its lewdness as I tried to cough away the singe of my throat. I wanted to tell him to show a little respect, but my comment would be contrary to my environment. Instead, I sized him up. Gray sports coat, navy blue and gray striped silk tie, white button down shirt, simple mustache on pale skin, short auburn hair, professionally cut, every bit the representation of the all-American white male. A thick gold band adorned his ring finger, on his left hand; the same hand he smacked the waitress' behind with when she set a glass in front of him. I wondered if his wife knew he frequented black stripper joints with his coworkers, or if she was even slightly aware that he had a taste for chocolate. More than likely, it was a secret obsession. The allure of the forbidden could be an aphrodisiac, and he looked like he was high on something.

I diverted my eyes back to the table where I was sitting. I was trying to contain my growing annoyance, but it was becoming more difficult by the minute as I observed my surroundings. Most importantly, my husband was just as much a part of the sexual utopia as the other horny men in the club. I watched the pleasure and glee play across Scott's face, from the smile straining the corners of his lips to the smoldering gaze of undivided attention as he sat in the chair on the left of me. Attention that should have belonged to me instead of the stage before us. My only response was to let the anger and embarrassment simmer inside as I gritted my teeth.

I had no business sitting in the Playa's Lounge gnawing away at my enamel. My husband had no business foaming at the mouth over a stripper named Satin, and we, for sure, had no business being there together.

My skin crawled with each penance glance around the room. Shame mingled with irritation, slowly rising to full blown anger as I thought again about what I agreed to by coming to the Playa's Lounge.

Scott looked my way and the smile disappeared. He could sense my displeasure instantly. "Hey, are you okay?" He leaned toward me with concern in his eyes. He rubbed my back as I choked when another ring of smoke assaulted my already sensitive throat.

"Yes, I'm fine," I forced from my lips.

I had agreed to come. In fact, I was the one who insisted that I come. Even suggested that Damon and Cherish ride with us to the Playa's Lounge. Thought it would be better to indulge in his fantasy, instead of arguing about why he couldn't enjoy his evening the way he wanted to. It was his thirty-fifth birthday and I didn't want to ruin the night for him by acting uptight. I thought if I could handle the porn videos we watched regularly, then one night in a strip club couldn't be all that bad. As long as we were together, the environment shouldn't matter. That's what I kept trying to rationalize. But no matter how I tried to convince myself to relax, my mind and body wouldn't cooperate.

Scott smiled with relief and captured my lips, not recognizing that my words and my body language weren't in sync. "Good," he replied.

I leaned my head down toward my chest and coughed again.

Scott went back to drooling over Satin, who was removing the flimsy material that rendered her topless.

I watched Satin sashay across the stage and bend down. A short rotund man tucked a fifty dollar bill down the front of Satin's gold costume bottom. His chubby fingers held languid on the fabric beneath her belly button. A bulked up bouncer moved forward and the stripper's bottom was quickly released.

Things were far from good.

My fingers tightened around the silver links of my purse strap. I could feel the metal press an indention into my palm. I glanced at Cherish to gauge how she was taking in the scene, but to my disappointment, she was hugged up with her husband, and Scott's best friend, Damon, smiling just as hard as the men. I felt entirely out of place. Evidently I was the only one in the whole club that didn't think pole dancing was a suitable activity for married couples to be watching.

My co-worker, Daphne, had sent me an e-mail that Walter Beasley was playing at the Jazz Café for the weekend. Scott and I both could have enjoyed the smooth melody of a saxophone extraordinaire. Or if my husband needed hot and

spicy excitement, we could have gone salsa dancing at Latorres.

Just about anything would have been better
than us at the Playa's Lounge.

"Hey, man, check out that female over there.
She must be new. I haven't seen her in here before. Now that is what I call a fine specimen. All
that definition . . ." Damon's tongue hung from
his mouth like a dog in heat as he gestured toward a caramel sister with black and burgundy
streaked hair that hung to the middle of her bare
back in loose waves.

I tried not to grunt with disgust as my eyes
roamed in the direction he pointed to near the
bar. The girl had on two silver dollars covering
her chest and a neon green thong. I could do
nothing but close my eyes and shake my head.
This was what I agreed to, taking my husband to
lust over other women. I must have been completely out of my mind. I knew better.

Knots of guilt formed in my abdomen.

I cast my eyes on the Missoni lace stitch dress
I got on clearance from Nordstrom for seventy-
five percent off. When I picked up the sleeveless
cowl neck little outfit, I thought it was extremely
sexy. I was convinced that me in it, would drop
Scott's mouth to the ground and I'd have to help
him get his jaw back in place. When I first put it

on and strutted in front of him, he slid his hands down the soft wool from Italy as I twirled to give him a full view. He acted like I was the finest thing alive. How quickly that changed.

"You know who she reminds me of?" Damon asked Scott like wives weren't present.

Scott scrunched his eyebrows and squinted like he was trying hard to figure it out.

Damon licked his lips and grinned devilishly, "Tandy. That's who she favors . . . that girl from high school. You remember her. I know you do, because you had a hardcore crush on that girl back in the day. You drooled and stuff every single time she walked by smelling like peaches and cream from Vicki's Secret. I wouldn't be surprised if it was her. She seemed like she had a little freak in her back then. That female even sways those jumbo hips like Tandy."

Scott tilted his head slightly and looked the girl up and down before disagreeing. "I don't see it."

Damon stood up and pulled his wallet from his back pocket. "You're crazy. We just need to see her up close." He was intent upon proving his point. "I'll tell you what I'm going to do. Thirty-five only rolls around once. You deserve a birthday lap dance to make it memorable."

I was appalled. I bore my eyes into Cherish and willed her to check her husband. Once again, I faced disappointment. Cherish was staring absently into her glass of mandarin flavored Absolut vodka as if being disrespected was a normal thing. I understood being open. I came to the Playa's Lounge with the full intent of being open, but it wasn't that much openness in the plains of the Maharia Desert. I wasn't about to sit back and get humiliated, birthday or no birthday. Damon was out of line, and if I had to end this fiasco, then the ugly might come out of me.

Damon waved three crisp hundred dollar bills in the air and the dancer approached the table.

Money exchanged hands. Scott scooted his chair back in anticipation of her gyrating thick hips between his legs.

"It is not going to happen," I blurted out loudly, so insulted I couldn't contain it anymore.

"What?" Scott blinked twice at me like he had seen an apparition.

"Scott, I'm ready to go. This is not my type of thing. I tried to get into this for your sake, because I thought . . . I don't know what I thought. I don't know what I thought at all, but I'm not feeling this." I chuckled sarcastically as I waved the dancer away from the table. I rose from my chair, snatched my purse off the table and put the chain strap on my shoulder. "This whole raunchy, sordid little scene is more than I can take."

My husband rose too, obviously disappointed. He nodded his head. "All right, baby, we can go. It's no problem." There was no point in arguing about it in the middle of the club. Eyes had already diverted toward us.

Damon objected. "Whatcha mean, it's no problem? I just spent three hundred bones for a lap dance. It is a problem. That ain't refundable. I don't have money to be throwing away like that."

"Well, I suggest you call her back over here and let her grind on you, because my husband and I are leaving!" I snapped at Damon. I had to maintain my composure and act like the lady I was raised to be. Then again, if that were the case, I wouldn't be here in the first place.

"Somebody must be feeling insecure," Damon snapped back.

"Look, man, we're leaving," Scott cut in to diffuse the conversation before it became more heated. "Are you riding with us or catching a cab?"

"Oh, it's like that?" Damon asked, holding his hands in the air like he was the one offended.

I turned on my heels and walked out of the club. How Damon got home was of no concern. He was a real piece of work, but I didn't have to put up with him. That kind of ignorance belonged to Cherish.

I walked to the car in a parking lot across Davidson Street, barely waiting for traffic to clear. I didn't know what had come over me, whether it was purely irritation or something stronger. But like flies on mess, I had to get it off me.

CHAPTER TWO

SCOTT

My eyes deviated from I-77 to my wife. Germani had a wicked scowl on her bronze-toned face. Creases etched a map across her forehead. She looked like the Olmec stone sculpture we had seen on a trip to a little town in Veracruz, Mexico. The expression pinched her features. Made a fine woman look ugly, act ugly. I had never seen her veer from sophistication in public, rarely caught drama in private either.

"What is with you?" I asked as I reached over the armrest and clasped my fingers around Germani's left hand. It lay limply in her lap. I looked her in the face and squeezed her fingers, trying to get her attention. She glanced at me out of the corner of her eye. She then removed her hand from beneath mine. The hand went to the back of her neck where she rubbed like she had a painful crick.

I didn't understand the problem. Germani asked to go to the Playa's Lounge with me. We went. She asked to leave the club. We left. So, why was she blowing a cold drift through my 300C like a Siberian winter in June?

Giggles reverberated from the backseat. I looked up into my rear view mirror. Damon was whispering into Cherish's ear. It must have been something good to make Cherish cup Damon's cheek and pull his head closer to her face. I watched him whisper, her giggle.

If I was a lesser man, I would be envious. I'd covet the intimacy that should have belonged to me. My wife didn't even want me touching her, yet, the two lovebirds behind me were acting like they were on a backseat rendezvous. That was supposed to be me hugged up with Germani, buzzing sweet nothings against her lobe.

"Happy birthday to me," I mumbled under my breath as I pulled into the Ballantyne subdivision.

Damon and Cherish's place was a three-story brick front with an immaculate lawn on a corner lot. I often wondered why he needed that entire house with just the two of them. I kinda figured it was a trophy palace for the business partners he entertained. It definitely wasn't for accommodating his estranged family. His mother, two sisters and brother weren't allowed within two hundred feet of him.

I turned into the driveway and said, "All right, man, it's been real. Thanks for coming out to celebrate my day with me."

"For sure. We need to get together again and do something with just me and you. Hang like we used to do. Manly stuff; uninterrupted." Damon patted my shoulder as he got out of my vehicle. I chuckled, remembering the trouble we got ourselves into doing manly stuff before I changed my lifestyle.

Germani snapped her head our way. She evil mugged him and then me. Damon didn't notice, and more than likely didn't care. The comment was yet another reason for Germani to be mad at me. A brotha can't win for losing. I can't even laugh without it being a problem. Some things shouldn't be that serious.

The ride home was silent and I was cool with it. If she wanted to be mad, let her. She would calm down if I didn't feed into her attitude. When we made it to our modest bilevel home, she jumped out of the car and stalked up the front entrance before the garage door could go all the way up.

"What the . . ." I said to myself, baffled as I cruised the car into the garage. "Oh, she is seriously trippin'." I cut the car off and sat there for a minute. I didn't do anything wrong.

When I made it into the house and up the stairs, Germani had her arm twisted up behind her back, wrestling with the zipper.

"Here." I walked behind her and gently pulled the zipper to the middle of her back. The bareness of her back, with its creamy soft skin, made my masculine impulse kick in. I brushed my lips against her shoulder as the garment fell to the floor.

Germani mumbled, "Thanks." She picked up the dress that poodled at her feet and walked around me like I was a piece of the furniture.

I watched her stiff movements as she walked around the room like a lost sheep. She was working overtime to show her peevishness. I sat on the bed and began unbuttoning my black silk shirt. I was waiting for her aimless quick strides to cease.

She opened the closet door and hung up the dress. Then she pulled that same dress back out of the closet and tossed it over the chair with the hanger still on it. Germani opened drawers and pulled nothing out, and then she slammed them closed. She scuffled through another set of drawers. A light blue lace nightie appeared as she snatched it out and tossed it over her head. She closed the drawers and stood, making circular motions with her hands like it was some kind of yoga self therapy. I had seen her do the same moves to a video she watched before she went to work each morning.

"We are not going to be like this, Germani. Let's clear the air and discuss this before we go to bed," I stated calmly as I stripped down to my boxers while I was still on the edge of the bed.

Suddenly, she stopped and pivoted around to look at me. Her frown was prominent. "Do you feel the least little bit of guilt?"

"Guilty about what?" I asked incredulously.

She popped her tongue against the roof of her mouth. "Yeah, that's what I thought. We . . ." Germani swung her index finger between the both of us like an out of control clock pendulum. Her head matched the stride of her finger, ". . . . don't have anything to discuss." She stomped to the bed, snatched the covers back and jumped in. She bumped against me with her feet until I was on my side of the bed. The comforter rose up to her chin as she wiggled to get comfortable.

"Whoa. Wait," I said as I noticed the corner of the comforter that was left for me to sleep under. I couldn't let the night end that way. Besides, it was my birthday and I deserved some tender affection. I rose from the bed to turn off the bedroom light. My wife was still beneath the covers as I looked over at her before darkness covered the room. I slipped back into the bed next to Germani. I tugged at the covers until the barrier she created was gone. I nestled my body against hers and placed my hand on her thigh.

"No!" she snapped like I was trying to steal her loving.

"Fine." I removed my hands and lay on my back. She was about to take me to her side of anger. I was too tired to be mad about nothing.

I stared at the ceiling and took myself to an earlier portion of the evening. I had taken the day off and spent the morning with our three-year-old son, Elijah. After dropping him off at my sister, Sharon's house to spend the night, I picked Germani up and we went to enjoy a Gullah Island cuisine at a restaurant called Mert's Heart and Soul on North College.

Sharon was due in August with her first child and wanted some hands on training with our son before hers got here. She never really wanted kids, but her husband, Corbin, convinced her to have one baby. He came from a big family and wanted at least one child of his own. He told her that he would do most of the work. I think Sharon was testing Corbin to see how true to the word he really was. Personally, I thought she should have done her parent testing before she got pregnant, but I guess we would have to see how all that worked out.

It was at Mert's that the discussion about the Playa's Lounge came up. I was waiting for the right time to mention it, because I hadn't been to that strip joint since we got married over four years ago. Damon talked constantly about how the spot had gone through a major renovation. New management had hooked the place up and I wanted to see the improvements with my best friend. I knew Germani wouldn't see it that way. She would think I had ungodly intentions. I was surprised when she said she was all right with me going. That is, as long as she went with me. At first, I was apprehensive about the idea of my wife sitting in the Playa's Lounge with me, but I knew Cherish went with Damon all the time and I had seen other couples there. But boy, oh boy, if I would have known she would get to acting the way she had, the topic would never have came up. I drifted asleep with regret on my mind.

"Scott." I could hear her voice, but my sleep induced coma wouldn't let me respond. "Scott!" The voice came more firmly as I felt my shoulder being nudged.

"Yeah," I responded as I lingered between slumber and consciousness.

"We need to talk," Germani said.

Talk. Talk. My body didn't feel like cooperating with a conversation, but I could tell from her determined voice that she needed to be heard. If it would bring peace and a conclusion to her irritation, then talking is what we would have to do.

I sighed as I pulled my eyelids up and reached for my watch on the nightstand. My pupils needed to adjust to the lack of light as I tried to see the time. It took a minute for my vision to come into focus, but I still had to squint to see the hands of the watch. The big hand was on the four and the little hand sat above the ten. Seconds ticked by and it was still too early in the morning for me to think.

"Can we have this conversation in a couple more hours?" I asked as I turned on my back and tried to stretch away the fatigue. I glanced over at Germani who was sitting with her back against the headboard. "We are getting up for church at eight. I can set the clock back to seven thirty if need be. Baby, I'm tired and I'd be more coherent in the morning."

"You were going to let her grind on you, weren't you?" Germani asked. She still had an attitude.

"What are you talking about? Who? What?" I was tired, clueless and trying not to be irritated.

"Tandy or Tandy's look-a-like. Whichever way you want to call it."

"Tandy? You mean that stripper?" I arched myself up on my elbows and became fully alert.

Germani sighed like I was automatically supposed to know what she was talking about. "Scott, don't play like you don't know what I'm talking about. Of course, I'm talking about the stripper. You certainly didn't mind when Damon shelled out money on your behalf. I'm kind of glad I went. Now I know what after hour activities you're really into. God only knows how far that sexual exchange would have progressed if I hadn't been there to intervene."

I waited for her to pause as I let her words sink in. Her interpretation of the night was all wrong. "Germani, I was not going to take a lap dance with my wife sitting right next to me."

"Oh, so you would have taken the lap dance if I wasn't there?"

There she goes, trying to twist my words all up. "No. I didn't ask for a lap dance and I didn't want a lap dance. It all happened so fast. I didn't think that Damon was serious about paying that girl. I would have called his bluff."

"Money exchanged hands, Scott. There was no bluff."

"Damon and I joke around like that. It didn't have to go that far."

"Once again, money exchanged hands. I thought you had more respect for me than that. Heck, I thought you had more respect for women period. Do you know how that made me feel? I've never felt so devalued. Like we . . . like we didn't have morals." Germani sounded hurt as her voice cracked.

I sat all the way up and reached over. She allowed me to embrace her. I needed to calm the storm. "Oh, baby, I'm sorry you feel that way. I didn't intend for it to be that way. You shouldn't have gone."

I could feel her pull a little away from me, but I held her within my arms. "*We* shouldn't have gone," Germani stated as the acid in her voice disintegrated.

"We shouldn't have gone," I agreed. I still didn't see it her way, but I cared more about getting some peace and some sleep more than I cared about being right. Especially about something that went on in a strip joint. I was hoping this would be the end of the conversation.

"I need to feel respected by you, Scott . . . all the time. That whole scene was jacked. We're supposed to be Christians. What kind of mess is that for us to go to a strip club on Saturday and then go to church the next morning? Didn't you feel the least bit out of place? Why did you need to go to a strip club anyway?"

"But, Germani, you wanted to go to the strip club."

"No, I wanted to be with my husband on his birthday. Clearly, I wasn't thinking when I agreed to the rest." She adjusted the covers before continuing. "Am I not enough? Are you going to take Elijah to those places when he grows up—"

"Germani, I said I was sorry we went to the Playa's Lounge." I had to cut her off, because she was taking the conversation to a whole other level. It wasn't that serious.

"But I want you to understand how I felt."

"You already told me how you felt. Can't we just kiss and make up? Maybe make love?" I said, kissing her neck as I stroked her arm. I wanted a repeat of the lovemaking we shared the night before.

She wiggled like she was fighting the feeling. "I don't want to make love right now. Can we pray?"

I lifted my mouth from a comfortable place. "Yes. We can do that. You want to do it or you want me to say something?"

Germani sighed. "You go."

I didn't know what to say. Her thoughts weren't the same as mine. I prayed for what I wanted all night. "Lord, Father in heaven. I ask that you restore peace in my home and our hearts. My wife is troubled and I don't want to be the cause of her frustration. Mend what is broken and give us strength. Lord, I want to thank you for bringing some resolution on this night so we don't carry discord into tomorrow. In your Son's name, I pray. Amen."

It was short and sweet, but I know the big man heard me. My wife finally relaxed and we spooned as we fell asleep.

CHAPTER THREE

GERMANI

I didn't sleep a wink last night and it was becoming increasingly difficult to hear what Pastor Mackenzie was preaching about.

After our pre-dawn discussion, I had laid awake and listened to the hum of slumber coming from my husband's lips. I couldn't get comfortable. My mind had stayed conscious as I remained in his arms. Scott made the conversation last night seem simplistic. He completely disconnected my words and the emotions attached to them. First, he devalued me and every other woman in that raunchy club, and then he disregarded me in our own bed.

I wanted to let it go like he said. I wanted to settle into our closeness like our night wasn't scarred and the cove of his arms was my shelter. But I couldn't. He allowed me to vent just enough to appear like he wasn't completely self-absorbed. That wasn't acceptable. All of last night's activities were unacceptable.

I redirected my attention back to Pastor Mackenzie. His voice boomed across the room. "Unification is necessary for the body of Christ." He paused. "Church, I don't think you heard me. Unification is necessary for the body of Christ." Pastor Mackenzie strained 'necessary' like its four syllables were separate words.

Deliverance Temple was a small church by today's standards. A white building on the Eastside of Charlotte only housing about three hundred seats, it made the church more of a family atmosphere. Everybody knew who was a member and who wasn't. The pastor also knew who all his members were and didn't hesitate to make himself available whenever necessary. Pastor Mackenzie was a man who knew the Word and taught it with fervor.

I nodded my head and tried to focus with both hands occupied; highlighter in right and ballpoint pen in left. My instruments of learning were angled in preparation and my notebook lay flat in my lap beneath my Bible. I waited for the pastor to instruct the congregation on which chapters the message was coming from. When he spoke, I put the bottom of my high-lighter in my mouth while I flipped pages of my Bible to the New Testament. I had to keep blinking. Every time I looked down at the Bible, my eyes became heavy. I took the high-lighter out of my mouth and put it back in my hand after finding the page I needed. I suppressed the urge to yawn and rolled my neck from side to side. Scott briefly glanced at me. He had his arm resting against my back on the pew.

Pastor Mackenzie further stated, "In Ephesians four, verses thirteen through sixteen, the Word says, *'til we all come to the unity of the faith and of the knowledge of the Son of God, to a perfect man, to the measure of the stature of the fullness of Christ; that we should no longer be children, tossed to and from and carried about with every wind of doctrine, by the trickery of men, in the cunning craftiness of deceitful plotting, but speaking the truth in love, may grow up in all things into Him . . ."*

I could hear those words as my head drooped and I drifted into unconsciousness. Sleep felt so good I didn't even try to fight it. It wasn't until my mouth dropped open, a sliver of drool left my lips and descended to my Bible that Scott tapped me on my back. My head jerked up and eyes popped open. The highlighter fell to the floor. I reached under the pew in front of me to grab it. I sat back up and wiped at the wet spot soaking my page, but didn't bother looking at Scott.

Pastor Mackenzie was still preaching. "Just because this chapter says *speaking the truth in love* doesn't mean you have a license to gossip, congregation. You see, we like to get things twisted and dog out people when they're down. The first thing we want to say is, 'I'm just telling the truth.'" He perched his lips, rolled his head and put his hand on one hip like he was imitating somebody he knew personally.

I was trying hard to stay awake. When Pastor Mackenzie moved across the pulpit, my eyes followed. I knew if he stood still I would be gone; my eyes would drop back down.

He scanned the church like he was seeking out the gossipers. He waved his Bible as he walked the full length of the pulpit. "People, we have got to learn that the words that we speak from our mouths can be lethal. We can break somebody's spirit with these lips. Love in truth is saying to your fellow sista or brotha that you don't agree with their lifestyle and know a God that can meet all the needs they seek out in the street, but you will love them where they are in the meantime. It is by showing them how good our God is to us even when we are going through."

My eyes became heavier and heavier.

Scott whispered in my ear, "Maybe you should go to the bathroom and try to walk it off."

He was right. I needed to get my blood circulating. I handed him all my stuff and stood. Luckily we were on the end of the row. I wouldn't have to interrupt anybody who was sitting down.

I walked into the lavender and sage bathroom with its array of colorful plants that would put a greenhouse to shame. The space looked like it would infuse energy, but it did nothing to make me less tired. I went into a stall, closed the door and laid my head against the cold steel partition. I could hear several other women come and go, but I didn't move. My mind kept going back to how disrespected I felt the night before.

I didn't realize how uninhibited Scott was until after we were married. I should have put a halt to the direction our sex life was taking the first time he asked to watch a sex tape. It was our wedding night; one of many nights I would make a compromise to please my husband. Submission. I thought I was doing my part in our marital contract. Scott explained that he just wanted to enhance our sensual union. He convinced me that anything we did in the privacy of our room was well . . . our business.

The experience at the Playa's Lounge was an eye opener for me. Watching a pornographic video was one thing. The movies didn't have the same effect as being at the Playa's Lounge. Maybe it was easier to be desensitized by a television. But watching the gyration of naked female bodies and lewd participation from men. . . . seeing that up close and in person was a bit much. A wake up call.

That one experience let me know that things in my marriage needed to change. I couldn't keep accepting what I knew wasn't right. I couldn't keep allowing Scott to use porn as foreplay to our intimacy, and we definitely wouldn't be going to anymore strip clubs. That was a first and last time for me.

As I finally left the bathroom, I had my mind set. I would just have to get Scott to see things my way.

I didn't know how long I was in the ladies room, but benediction was ending as I approached the sanctuary doors. I waited outside for Scott to appear in the crowd. When he saw me, an awkward expression crossed his face. "Did you fall asleep in there?"

"Hardy ha ha. What time am I picking up Elijah?" I asked as I took my Bible, notebook and purse from his hand.

"My sister probably won't be out of church until around three o'clock. As long as you call her first, I don't think it matters."

Scott headed to his car and I walked to my Cougar. We had driven to church separately because he had to be at work at two o'clock. His job as manager at Car Care was eight miles from the church, but also in the opposite direction of where we lived. He wanted to transfer to a location closer to our house than the forty-five minute commute, but the request was denied. He worked in a high crime area and the boys in charge didn't want to let him go.

My phone began to vibrate in my purse.

I shoveled it out and checked the caller ID. *Private.* I was inclined to not answer with all the hang-up calls I had been receiving from private lines. Couldn't nobody be calling private and want something good from me.

"Hello," I answered.

"Hey, Germani," the man said pleasantly, but I wasn't pleased as I recognized the voice. I could hear hollering of profanities in the background.

"Who's that?" Scott questioned as he watched my apprehension in answering. We were almost to our cars, but I had stopped short in the parking lot when I saw the screen.

"Mekhi," I stated dryly.

"Yeah?" my cousin asked, hearing me call his name while I talked to Scott.

"I was talking to Scott. He asked who was on the phone. You know I just got out of church, right?" Mekhi found the most inopportune times to contact somebody.

"Look at this mess. What is wrong with you? Don't ignore me. Look at what you did, Mekhi," the voice screamed in the background from Mekhi's line.

"What's going on, Mekhi?" I didn't really want to know, but the sooner the problem was revealed, the sooner I would be able to get off the phone. I was sure that his girlfriend was the one going off like a siren at the fire department. I was also sure that Mekhi had done something to make her that mad.

"I need you to come get me," Mekhi said without answering the question.

Getting him was not a good thing. There was no telling what I would be walking into.

I spoke loudly into the phone to combat the hollering on the other end. "I said what is going on?"

Scott furrowed his eyebrows with concern as we began walking again and approached his 300C. My car was on the other side of his. I used my remote starter keyless entry, while I debated whether I should go get Mekhi.

"Shell is over here clownin'. I need you to come scoop me before something pop off." Mekhi must have gone into a different room. I could finally hear him clearly.

"I'm on my way," I reluctantly told Mekhi before ending the call. I then explained to Scott, "They're having a crisis over at his place. I'm going to swing over that way and see what's up."

"They always got something going on over there," he groaned disapprovingly. "You need me to go with you? Mishelle can get a little wild."

I looked at the time on my phone. It was a quarter to two. "Yes, she can. I'll be all right though. Mishelle is probably kicking him out again."

"You sure?" he asked, like he needed to protect me.

I smiled at my husband gratefully. "You better get to work before you're late."

Scott was neurotic about punctuality. To him, late meant fired. He didn't feel he could ask his employees to be on time if he wasn't leading by example. That was probably another reason the company heads didn't want to transfer him. He didn't abuse his position and his employees respected him.

Scott checked his watch and nodded his head as he jumped into his car. I got into mine as well. Scott rolled down his window before pulling off. "Call me if you need me."

"Have a good evening at work, I will see you tonight." His concern warmed my heart and made me want to set aside my irritation about our disagreement.

I turned on my car and drove out of the parking lot behind Scott. He went left. I veered right. I headed toward Sugar Creek, not knowing what to expect once I got there.

CHAPTER FOUR

SCOTT

Car Care was running a sales promotion to stay in line with the competition. For the month of June each store was giving various discounts for repairs with any of the automobile repair shops working with the store. Business was booming.

The only problem arose when my employees decided to take unscheduled extra days off for their own recreation. Granted, I considered myself to be a lenient family-oriented boss, but some of the excuses I had been hearing were on the ridiculous side. When I came into work this afternoon, three people had called in sick. One from the morning shift and two from the evening, which put me in a bind, because I only had one other person, Craig, in the building with me to handle the crowd of customers standing before me. Anybody in retail would know that customers didn't care if you were short staffed. They wanted to get their purchase and get gone.

"I need to return this." A short pudgy man with baby dreadlocks in gray dirty overalls stood before me and plopped his bag on the counter.

I pulled the item out of his Best Buy plastic bag and examined the product. Besides a few smudges from a finger imprint, the part seemed to be in good condition. I looked inside the bag for the receipt to go with the product. When I didn't find it, I set the bag aside and asked kindly, "Do you have the receipt on you for this item, sir?"

The man patted his overalls and then dug his hands inside the pockets. When his hands came from his pockets, they were empty. He took the bag and shook it upside down as if expecting the receipt to appear. A scowl came across his face and he frowned. "I must have lost it."

"Okay, give me just a second," I said as I ran the item number etched into the metal. I had to make sure that it was our product. After clicking the numbers into the system, the verification popped up.

"This is a Crankshaft Position Sensor for a 2004 Kia Sorrento with four wheel drive. Priced at $127.50 with tax. It has a one year warranty."

The man nodded his head as confirmation. "Yeah, that's it. I got the wrong part. It was supposed to be for a 2003 Sorrento. That one won't fit."

"Well, because you don't have your receipt I can't give you a refund, but I can do an exchange for you and get the sensor for a 2003."

"I just bought that sensor two days ago. Can't I get my money back?"

I hated when people acted like they didn't know the store's policy. NO RECEIPT, NO REFUND was in big bold letters on both sides of the glass entrance door. I pointed at it and he briefly glanced that way. "I'm sorry, sir. If you want to go and see if you can find the receipt, I would be more than willing to give you your money back, or as I said before, I can give you a sensor to match the 2003 Kia Sorrento."

The man appeared to be getting irritated as his lips above a nappy goatee formed a straight line. "Man, I was just here. Torrance helped me out. I'm a regular customer. I know you ain't gonna make me go through all that. Plus, I called a junk yard and they have one of these available for $45, but I can't get it if you don't give me my money back. How about you let me talk to your store manager?"

He had named one of the employees who called in sick and we had a lot of regular customers. I knew I didn't recognize him and there was a growing line of other irritated customers standing behind him. Craig was ringing people up as fast as he could from his line, but there was only so much that two workers could do.

We needed to wrap this up before customers started leaving and giving Car Care a bad reputation for poor customer service. "I am the store manager. Torrance is not here today, and even if he was, I would still need a receipt because of the amount of the purchase. If you don't want to exchange the item, then I can put your item back into its bag. I have more customers to assist."

"Fine." He snatched the sensor and the bag off the counter. He crammed the sensor back into the Best Buy bag.

Once again, I apologized. "I'm sorry I couldn't be of more assistance, but if you find that receipt, please come back and get your refund."

The man huffed as he shoved the glass door open.

It took close to an hour to help the remaining customers. Thankfully, only a few left, even with the long wait.

Customers came in spurts and there were a few browsers. I left Craig to take care of them

while I went to call my missing employees. Craig
came in at seven that morning and besides a
half an hour lunch, worked straight through. It
was almost six-thirty in the evening. I didn't like
any of my staff working more than twelve hours.
I would prefer them to not work over seven
hours a day, because Car Care didn't want to
pay for benefits. As long as I kept my employees
at under thirty-two hours a week, the company
wouldn't breathe down my back.

I decided to call my supposedly ill employees
and see if I could convince one of them to come
in to relieve Craig of his duties.

I went to the back office, sat in the mesh office
chair and flipped through the employee log. Sara
was the first person I dialed. Craig told me she
said that she twisted her ankle and needed to stay
off her feet for a day or two. A nineteen-year-old
vocational training student, who aspired to be
a mechanic, Sara primarily worked weekends. I
think she took the job to meet men. I found her
flirting with the customers on more than one occasion. As long as her persuasions weren't overt
or offensive, I left her alone. She memorized the
product lines and worked well with all the guys.

The phone rang five times before going to
voice mail. I left a message and went on to the
next employee.

I then spoke with Richard who stated that he had a stomach virus, everything that he ate kept coming back up. He sounded genuinely ill.

Lastly, I called Torrance. He answered on the third ring. "Hello," he said with his strong Brooklyn accent.

He didn't sound sick. "What's going on with you, Torrance? Craig said you called in sick, but he didn't say what was wrong."

"I didn't tell Craig I was sick. I told him that my mom wasn't feeling well. Her and my aunt took the car to the emergency room. She said her head was hurting. She has high blood pressure and diabetes. She needed to be checked out. They still haven't got back. I'm stranded."

"Why didn't you catch a cab or bus?"

"Man, I don't have any money like that. I'm broke. I've got one dime and one quarter in my pocket right now. You know Car Care ain't paying me enough to keep my pockets lined. I help my mom out with whatever I got. In fact, I just filled up the tank yesterday, so I thought I was good to go. Scott, man, you know I don't be missing work on purpose. Them chicken heads be chasing me for child support." Torrance, a twenty two-year-old with a hard edge, had four kids mothered by three women.

"Torrance, didn't we already talk about your terminology for the women you have children with. You know how I feel about that."

"I remember, but you're not able to see it through my eyes. If it walks like a chicken head, talks like a chicken head and hits my pocket like a chicken head, then I got to call it like it is. There are worse things I could call them."

That boy was still young and I hoped his perception would change. I was determined to help him out with that as time went on. He was the newest hire working a little over four months.

"I'm going to leave my cell number with you. Next time you get stranded, call me. If we are working the same shift, I will come pick you up. All right?"

"That's cool," Torrance responded.

I proceeded to give him the number quickly. I hung up the phone and went back on the floor to help Craig. Another crowd was forming. People love sales. I mentally prepared myself. It was going to be a long night.

CHAPTER FIVE

GERMANI

Some things were just uncalled for.

I tried to explain to Momma that Mekhi was a product of his own misery and maybe he would stop the madness if we weren't enabling him. Momma didn't want to hear my opinion or objections, because we were the only family he had to depend on.

I got what Momma was saying, but I didn't agree with her. Ever since him and Mishelle have been together, I haven't wanted to be bothered with him. I still loved my cousin, but the predicaments he puts himself in were just plain stupid.

Mekhi reminded me of Uncle Frank, his daddy and my father's older brother. Uncle Frank was evil and ornery. I used to hate holidays at Uncle Frank's house because of how bad he treated Aunt Pat. He once threw a whole pan of cornbread dressing in the garbage on Thanksgiving and cursed Aunt Pat out in front of all their guests. He had said the dressing was dry and bitter. He made Aunt Pat cook another one from scratch before anybody could touch the rest of the holiday meal. Momma helped cut up the bell pepper, onions and celery, while Aunt Pat cried herself through another batch of cornbread. I remember wishing that somebody would make Uncle Frank be nice to Aunt Pat; that people shouldn't act that evil.

Aunt Pat, Mekhi's mother, passed away of pancreatic cancer that next year. Uncle Frank took it hard. I thought Aunt Pat died so quickly because she gave up on life, didn't want to live with ornery Uncle Frank anymore. Uncle Frank never remarried. After Aunt Pat's death, Daddy would send for Mekhi during the summer months no matter where we were stationed. That was, until my father was declared missing-in-action during an assignment in the Air Force. Then everything in our family changed.

Mekhi and I were close back when we were younger, both united by a loss of a parent. I didn't realize that the sins of his father would be passed down to Mekhi.

The front door was wide open as I made it to the house. Mishelle's high pitched vocals were bouncing off the walls like an opera singer in

Mezzo Soprano. I was expecting a glass to shatter. I followed the shriek into the front room. The closer I got to her voice, I could smell mildew.

Mekhi was sitting on the blue loveseat with a calm façade. Mishelle's tiny frame leaned imposingly over him, her acrylic nail pressed against his forehead.

"You're so stupid, I can't stand you. I don't even know why I'm with your sorry tail." Mishelle's breathing was heavy as she yelled. "You ain't a man. You're a weak little boy perpetrating like a man. A real man would take care of business."

"Move your hand, Mishelle," said Mekhi as he tilted his head to the side.

Her hand moved right along with his head as she continued to spit out insults. "You are a waste of oxygen and space. I should have made you a one-night stand. Somebody more important should be dwelling up in here. At least then I wouldn't have to deal with your sorry tail."

I could see the anger rising in Mekhi. His nostrils flared. "Get your finger off my forehead, girl."

"Or what?" Mishelle pressed into him harder. "What are you going to do?"

His hands balled into fists at his sides. "I'm not playing with you, 'Shell."

She removed her finger and lowered her face to his. "What? You want to hit me? Come on and hit me. Do I look scared? You can jump stupid if you want to. There's some numbers at Forsyth Correctional Center waiting for you to come back and claim them," Mishelle dared him.

Mekhi became volcanic. His body vibrated with anger. He rose up six foot four with 270-pounds and Mishelle's five foot two, 120-pounds stood against him. Her midget rivaled his mammoth build. She may have been little, but she didn't believe in backing down.

As I looked on, I didn't want to become debris left after their explosion. "All right, ya'll need to calm down," I said, making my presence known.

They both looked at me like I had walked out of a foreign film.

"Do you see what this fool did to my house?" Mishelle ranted as she pointed to a large hole in the ceiling. Clumps of plaster lay on the carpet directly beneath the hole.

I saw the result, but didn't know the cause.

As if reading my mind she said, "This fool broke my water pipes, let water rain down on all my furniture, and then he left the house. Didn't bother to call me at work and tell me what happened or nothing. I come home and there are wet towels every dang on where." Mishelle had her hand on her hip as she flayed the other hand toward a pile of towels brimming over the top of a laundry hamper.

"I didn't break the pipes, they burst on their own," Mekhi interjected.

"That's what your mouth says, but you still the reason I have a big hole in my ceiling. How am I going to explain that to Section 8 housing?" Mishelle asked Mekhi as he looked at the pile of rubble dumbfounded. She snapped her hand like she was dismissing him. It looked like her rage was waning; her fuse dying out. "Don't answer that. You don't care. I already know that."

"Where are Camry and Lexus?" I didn't mean to sound insensitive, but my concern was with the kids, who were too often witnesses to their parents' blow-ups.

"They next door at Twanda's," Mishelle responded before turning her attention back to Mekhi. "I pay the bills. I clean the house. I do everything. All you do is watch the kids. You're just a glorified babysitter."

Mekhi threw his eyes up at the hole. "And all you do is guilt trip me. I shut the water off as soon as I heard the pipe blow. I had nothing to do with your old broken down walls falling apart. I told you I was handling it."

The fuse reignited. Mishelle hollered with attitude rolling from her head. She stomped across the room to the basket sitting against a wall. "Oh, you handled it. Yeah, right. Then you kick down my crib and you haven't put three pennies on rent."

"You don't pay rent either, Section 8 does. You only work part-time at Family Dollar."

"So what if I only work part time. At least I have a job. I'm one up on you."

"You can't clown me about not paying rent. I help out around here. I was handling. I don't care what you say," Mekhi said as he picked up a leather duffel bag like he was ready to go.

"You have got some nerve." She reached into the laundry hamper and pulled out a dripping wet flowered hand towel. "This is handling it?" Mishelle threw the towel at Mekhi, hitting him in the face. Before the towel could hit the floor, another towel went flying into the air and then another. All aimed at Mekhi's head.

I watched Mekhi drop the bag and take incensed steps toward Mishelle. I rushed over to him before he could get to her. The air became still. I stood directly in front of him like the rock of Gibraltar, praying that my spirit woman would block Mekhi taking a chunk out of Mishelle's behind.

"You wanted me to come get you. Don't do anything stupid," I warned.

The crease left his forehead as his face went blank. "You're right. I've been in enough trouble anyway."

"Yeah, get gone, troublemaker. You're not welcome here anymore," Mishelle said tauntingly as she came up behind me and swung a towel at his face. It hit him right below the eye. Water splashed on us both.

Mekhi's nose flared as he gave Mishelle an angry stare. He shoved me aside and rushed into her. I fell against the rectangular coffee table as I tried to brace my fall. By the time I got up and turned around, he had Mishelle penned against the wall. His hand held her by the jaw as she dangled several feet off the ground at eye level with him.

"Oh, Lord, Mekhi. Please let her go," I pleaded with him as I used both of my hands and pulled at his thick unmovable arm. The veins in his lifted right arm bulged against his skin as he stared into Mishelle's teary eyes.

I used all my strength to try and remove his arm, but he was too strong. "Dang it. Mekhi, stop it. We've been down this road before. It's not worth some more prison time. You can't raise your kids from inside a block cell."

His teeth gritted, but he slowly lowered his arm with Mishelle's head sliding down the wall. He let go of her jaw as her feet touched the ground.

"One day your mouth is going to get you killed," he told Mishelle as he grabbed his duffel bag.

"I hate you, Mekhi," she cried.

Mekhi backed out the front room with his eyes intent on Mishelle. I followed. He walked out and I was grateful to God that things weren't worse.

Mekhi muttered to me when we were both outside after leaving Mishelle's house, "Thanks for coming to get me. I'll get the rest of my stuff while she's at work tomorrow. Mishelle's liable to throw my clothes in a plastic bag on the front stairs."

If he was looking for understanding, he wasn't going to get it. My right arm hurt from where I fell against the coffee table when he pushed me.

"Do not call me anymore for your junk. You two got way too many issues." I checked my sore arm for bruising. "I'm not going to keep dealing with your mess, if you don't find a better way to deal with it yourself," I warned as soon as Mekhi got into my car.

He didn't have anywhere else to go and he wasn't staying with me. Recently, Momma sold the three-bedroom house on East John Street to downgrade to a two-bedroom loft off Gleneagles Road. She had only lived in the new place for two and a half months and was enjoying her empty nest. I had to take him over to Momma's condo. Even with less space, she wouldn't mind him being there. Mekhi had a way of making Momma feel sorry for him since Uncle Frank was in a nursing home with multiple sclerosis.

Mekhi looked ahead with a mean mug on his face. "You just don't know."

"I know it don't make any sense to be acting like that. Why didn't you leave before things got crazy?"

"That's why I called you. I was trying to get out of there before I lost my temper. I tried to ignore her until she calmed down, but she wouldn't shut up. Now, you were there and you saw I was trying to be civilized while I waited for you to come get me. But Mishelle likes to push things to the limit." Mekhi looked out the back window like he expected Mishelle to becoming down the street.

Excuses. He knew he could have avoided the drama.

"Mekhi, you weren't forced to stay. It's not like you didn't have your cell phone on you. You should have started walking out the house when she started cussing you out. You knew nothing good was going to come from your sticking around. In fact, you should have been down the block before you dialed my number. I can't keep rescuing you, for you to turn around and go right back into it. You aren't married to Mishelle. It's not like you're obligated to be with her. You haven't been out of prison five months yet for domestic assault and already there have been two big blow-ups between you and Mishelle. Only five months of freedom." I put my hand up and flashed five fingers at Mekhi representing his time on parole.

He looked at me and shook his head.

"I don't care about no marriage papers. We have kids together. I just want to be around to watch them grow up."

"Camry and Lexus are not gaining anything positive from seeing you and Mishelle acting crazy. You won't get a chance to see them grow up if you keep doing what y'all been doing. You're going to end up locked up permanently."

Mekhi rubbed his bald head. "I really have tried to do better since I got out. I thought because I got saved in prison and started living for

Christ that Mishelle wouldn't get under my skin like before. All them times she was visiting me things were nice. We talked about all the things we were going to do different after I got out. I thought the time apart did some good for the both of us."

"Well, you were wrong." I glanced at him sideways. Mekhi was delusional if he thought Mishelle changed that quickly and once he got delivered from his anger like he claimed, then he wouldn't go back to the one person who provoked him.

I sighed. "Being around you and Mishelle is dangerous. You pushed me down trying to get at that girl."

He winced. "Oh, dang . . . Germani, I didn't mean to do that. I just was so mad at the way she was treating me that all I saw was red."

"Yeah, uh-huh," I mumbled as I drove down Independence past the sign for Steve and Barry's. I grabbed my phone, which sat in the cup holder, then went to Momma's number on my cell and pressed the button of my Bluetooth.

I didn't want to get all the way over there and find out she wasn't at home. Momma was supposed to give me a spare key, but the front locks frequently jammed and she still needed to get somebody out there to replace them.

She didn't answer when I first called. I hung up before the voice mail could come on. Momma wasn't always the most expedient in answering her phone. I dialed the number again. It seemed like it took her forever to answer, but she finally did.

"Mom, Mekhi got kicked out again. He needs some place to stay." I was exasperated as I got within a couple blocks of her house.

Mekhi mumbled something to himself.

Momma was quiet.

"Hello. Are you still there?" I said into the phone.

"Is he with you right now?" she asked.

"Yes. I'm on the way to your house as we speak."

"I'll be waiting," Momma replied warmly.

I rolled my eyes as I pressed a finger to my ear and turned off my Bluetooth.

Mishelle could kick him out every other day and Momma would make sure he had somewhere to lay his head.

Instead of constantly being rescued, Mekhi needed to get his life together. His emotions were out of control. He needed to do something constructive with his time. Let that girl go before his temper and excuses got him into trouble that neither Momma nor I could get him out of.

CHAPTER SIX

SCOTT

"I wish you would let me die. Please, just let me die," my niece, Alexis cried, knocking an empty water pitcher to the ground as a nurse tried to stick the IV needle in her skinny arm.

"Don't talk like that. You don't really want to die. That's the pain talking. The nurse is going to give you some relief, but you have got to stay still," her mother and my sister, Beverly said, patting Alexis on the thigh while she sat in a chair alongside the bed.

Beverly, Sharon and I had come to the hospital three hours ago after Alexis complained of chest pain. It was the first Monday I had off in weeks and I thought I was going to get to spend some time with my wife after our bad weekend and Mekhi calling her with his drama.

"I don't think Matthew likes all this noise. I hate when he gets under my rib like this." Sharon leaned on the chair arm and rubbed her eight-month pregnant belly. She and Corbin had already named their unborn son.

"Nurse Coleman, no disrespect, but you're going to have to hurry up and do something. Alexis has been poked for the last fifteen minutes and the IV still isn't in. We've never had this much trouble getting her hooked up before," Beverly explained.

The more the nurse tried to hold her arm steady, Alexis pulled away in resistance. Her peach-toned complexion turned bright plum as she used all her strength to fasten her arm against her side, the injection site hidden from the nurse.

"Leave me alone," Alexis said defiantly.

At twelve years old, people assumed she was three or four years younger due to her squeaky voice and thin frame. The sickle cell disease delayed her growth.

The nurse apologized as she slowly poked at Alexis' skin. "I'm sorry this is taking so long," she explained to Beverly, "but your daughter has small rolling veins. Every time I think I have it, the vein moves." She turned her attention to my niece. "Alexis, I realize you are uncomfortable, but you're going to have to keep this arm in one place."

"Can't you sedate her and then put the IV in after she falls asleep?" I suggested, wishing I could do something to bring my niece relief. Her face was soaked in tears. I grabbed a box of Kleenex from a table by the closet and handed it to Beverly.

The nurse shook her head, while a brown ponytail swung against her neck. "No. Dr. Sanchez needs her to be awake for an MRI and some other additional tests. We have to make sure she doesn't have pneumonia from her sickle cell crisis. That's the biggest concern. I can't get it."

"Lexie, stay still," Sharon demanded as she waddled over to the top of the bed behind Beverly. She grabbed Alexis' flailing arm and held it against the white sheet. "You are acting a fool. Stop twitching and let this nice nurse help you."

Sharon had the patience of a jackrabbit. On occasion, she could handle Elijah because he was a quiet child, but Alexis had a strong personality that irked Sharon.

"Uh-uh, I just want the pain to stop. I don't want—" Alexis' voice ceased as she lost consciousness. Her body suddenly and violently began to spasm. The brown of her eyes rolled back as her head jerked on the pillow.

Sharon stepped back from the force.

Beverly and I both stood up saying simultaneously, "What's going on?"

Nurse Coleman pressed a call button. "I need some assistance in here. This patient is having a seizure. Stat." She abruptly shifted the pillow from beneath Alexis' head and pushed the bed down until Alexis lay flat. We watched her body rise and fall. The vibrations shook the whole bed. Seizures weren't uncommon for Alexis, but we had never seen one this bad.

A doctor, along with three other people from the medical staff, rushed into the room. Sharon came and stood with us. Beverly grasped my arm as she looked at her daughter.

"We're going to have to get this under control. I need for you three to step out of the room," the doctor said as the small space became over-crowded with people.

We knew the routine and walked into the hall. Beverly threw her head up to the ceiling and wailed, "I shouldn't be her only parent dealing with this."

Sharon and I exchanged looks.

Bad choices breed bad results.

Alexis didn't know her father even though she was his namesake. At seventeen, Beverly had thought Alex Haworth was the 'one' just like every other young woman with high expectations of love. But I should have known what that brotha was up to when she introduced him to me at an

A & T frat party. Back then, Beverly and Germani were dorm roommates. I had taken them with me to the party. I didn't want my sister going to frat parties by herself. I also liked being around Germani. She had a boyfriend and didn't see me as anything other than Beverly's big brother. I wanted to be more to her and found how easy conversation came between us. Germani and I were sitting against a wall talking when Beverly brought Alex over by us. My mind was on Germani and not where it needed to be.

I'll give it to him; Alex stuck around longer than I expected. Two years longer than any of us expected; even was there through Beverly's entire pregnancy. Alex vanished out of her life when Beverly told him his child was sick and Beverly needed him to add Alexis to his health insurance policy. Her Medicaid physician kept misdiagnosing Alexis, and Beverly wasn't going to let her child get passed over because they didn't have good medical coverage.

We all carried the sickle cell anemia trait. Our mother had it and it was passed down to her from her father. The trait in itself was harmless, but when two people with the same trait had a child, it could be detrimental to that child's health. Beverly didn't realize that both her and Alex were carriers of the sickle cell trait until the test results came in after routine testing during Alexis' birth. For some reason, there were no signs, but it seemed that the disease took a seriously hard toll on Alexis' body. She had been in and out of hospitals since she was eight months old.

"Did you call Mom or Daddy and let one of them know that Alexis is back in the hospital?" I asked.

Our parents had gone back to Baton Rouge, Louisiana, where they grew up, to take care of Grandma Edna after her stroke. Daddy was trying to convince his mother to move to Charlotte, but Grandma didn't want to leave Louisiana. She wasn't giving up her house.

Beverly responded, "Not yet. I wanted to wait and see what all is wrong. Her doctor was talking about all the long-term complications and how we may need to take a more aggressive approach. And you know what that means."

Levine Children's Hospital was a state-of-the-art facility dedicated to the health and well-being of small, sickly kids. Yet, I didn't have a whole lot of confidence in their ability, because they couldn't cure Alexis. All they could do was drug her until she didn't realize the pain was there.

The medical team rolled Alexis out of the room and stopped in front of us.

The doctor was a short, chunky man with dark hair that was balding in the middle and a contrast to his young face. "We've got her stabilized, but I'm going to take her down for the test now to see if there is a reason for the grand mal seizure she just had. We'll give her regular physician a call for further orders. You can go back in her room and wait for us to finish."

As we all walked back into the room and sat down in the cushioned chairs surrounding Alexis' empty bed, Beverly confessed "I finally saw him."

I knew who she was talking about as soon as she said *him*. I remarked in shock. "You were able to get in touch with Alex? I thought you said he moved away to some part of Minnesota and his family acted like they didn't know where he was at."

"That's true. Most of his family isn't even from here, and the only people I knew were his cousins that stayed near the Microtel Inn. They don't care about Alexis, so I wasn't going to waste my time contacting them anymore."

Sharon frowned at Beverly, filling a cup with ice from Alexis' pitcher on the side table. "How did you end up seeing him? Was he in town recently or something?"

"Because I am desperate to help my child, I found his information through the public records office in the City of St. Paul. He bought a house there. They have the deed on file for the mortgage company. Alex owes twelve thousand dollars on the house. I checked the market for his area in Macalester-Groveland. Those houses go for between $250,000 and $400,000 now. Amazing that his house is almost paid for, yet I can't get the $54,657.88 he owes me in back child support."

She shouldn't be keeping track of what he owed. If he didn't want to pay, no calculation on paper would make the money appear.

Sharon asked as she chewed on chipped ice, "Why would you waste your money flying all the way out there on some wild goose chase for him and he has never done a thing for Alexis?"

"I went to St. Paul after Alexis' physician first told me she may need that bone marrow transplant. He said that a family member could be a good match, and he asked me all kind of questions about her paternal background. I don't know squat-ditty about Alex's side of the family. Therefore, I had to go find out."

Beverly continued talking. "Anyway, I showed up on his doorsteps. Saw his wife, Selma, the two kids, both boys, and his dog. One of their boys answered the door. I think I scared the heck out of Alex when he saw me standing there." She chuckled thinking about it. "He was scared stiff. I didn't give him time to deny Alexis. I took a picture of Alexis with me and showed it to his wife, and explained what was going on. Right there in front of Selma he told me that Alexis wasn't his problem and he wouldn't be paying for a mistake from twelve years ago. Once I explained that I knew about the worth of his home and I was more than willing to take my cut of child support in a lump sum out of his property value if he wanted to be a butt about it, he changed his tune."

"He was a butt back then too. You shouldn't expect that to change," Sharon said as she tipped the cup of ice up into her mouth again.

"And that's the man I chose to make a baby with." Beverly let out a despaired yak. Her misery for present circumstances and disgust with the former relationship only deepened with her daughter's illness.

Withholding my opinion of Alex, I had to know. "So I take it he is willing to be tested as a match for Alexis."

"Yes he is. It's a shame that I have to bribe Alex to man up to his responsibility. I wasn't thinking at all when I got with him, and now, our daughter is paying for it."

I wasn't going to let her wallow. "Beverly, you can't keep beating up on yourself. You didn't do this to Alexis."

She shook her head, "I'm not in denial, Scott. This is my fault. I knew we had the trait. I just didn't believe it could happen to me or my child; like I was invincible or something."

Sharon rose from the chair and gestured toward the room with a toilet. "I got to use the bathroom. Do you think they will let me go in here?"

"There's nobody here to stop you," I told her as she wobbled to the bathroom holding her bladder.

I turned back to Beverly. "Alexis is going to be okay. You have got to stay prayed up about God healing her. Especially with the way she has been talking lately about dying."

Beverly began to tear up. "Scott, she is always saying that she doesn't want to live anymore. I don't know how much fight she got left. I really don't."

"It's going to be all right. If we have to be her strength and hold her up when she can't hold herself, then we will," I assured Beverly.

The orderly wheeled Alexis back into the room. "We're all done. This young lady was a real trooper." As he put Alexis into the bed, I moved the covers back. Beverly quickly wiped her own face.

I could tell some medicine was working from the glazed serenity in Alexis' eyes.

"Swiss Miss stirred up," I told her in the phrase we created when she was six years old to describe the doctors trying to treat the oddly shaped blood cells flowing through her veins. It meant her system had to be mixed and shaken to get it right, just like the hot chocolate milk she drank all the time.

"Yeah, Uncle Scott, Swiss Miss stirred up." She gave me a slight smile as the orderly lifted the rail on her bed.

I knew my niece and she had enough fight in her to get through, and with God's help, she would.

CHAPTER SEVEN

GERMANI

I searched through the bathroom pantry for the scented body oil. It had been a while since I used the bottle.

"Ah-ha." I found the Ocean Body and Bath oil behind Elijah's bubble bath. I pulled it out, took the cap off and inhaled the intoxicating fragrance of watermelon and cucumber mixed with lavender and rosemary. The smell always did something to me. Made bad days seem tolerable.

I discovered the brand while searching online for a gift collection to give my mom for Mother's Day. The company, *Carol's Daughter*, popped up in the search engine. I recalled seeing an article about that line of products in a magazine. Jada Pickett Smith and Mary J. Blige adorned the pages of the website as obvious endorsers for its credibility.

I purchased Mango Melange Shining Star for my mother and the Ocean Collection for myself. I must admit, I was impressed. It kept my skin silky smooth, plus the body oil had multiple intriguing uses.

Pattering barefoot from the bathroom after my shower, I quickly maneuvered around the bedroom to make the environment sensual before Scott came home from work. Scott and I hadn't spent any time making up with me having to go rescue Mekhi on Sunday and Scott getting called to the hospital for Alexis yesterday. He usually made it in by 10:30 P.M. when he worked the evening shift.

I folded the bedspread and lay it on the floor next to the bed. I removed the burgundy and cream striped sheet set and replaced it with a white, more durable, cotton one. I then sprinkled lavender talc from the headboard to the bottom bedpost for a pinch of extra freshness.

Scott's favorite lingerie on me was a sheer deep red negligee that flowed to my ankles and split up both sides to my hip bone. I slinked into the nice little number that covered my pear shape and confidently twirled in the mirror. I turned to look at my backside. My definition wasn't as well formed as that stripper Damon had paid, nor were my breasts as large as the pole dancer's, but I could hold my own. That was all physicality anyway. What Scott and I had was much deeper than that.

I heard the door close and slowly walked out of the bedroom to meet Scott on the stairs. The split level design of our home placed merely four steps between the upper and lower level. The distance was short, but I expected the effect to permeate his mind indefinitely.

A moment of delight coursed through my veins when I saw his weary frown turn upside down. That was the look I needed.

I took his hand and guided him to the bedroom as I seductively unbuttoned his pants. "I want you to stand here and follow my direction," I instructed. "First, remove every . . . single . . . thought that's not centered on me in this moment. We are going to have a special night free of anger, sadness, discord and negativism." I pulled his polo shirt over his head while he stood as prostrate as a mannequin on display in a department store.

After his lithe beige colored skin was free of clothing, I instructed him to lie face down on the middle of the bed, while I hiked up my negligee and kneeled on the bed over him. I proceeded to give him a massage that started with his scalp. My fingertips gently pressed in circular motions against his buzz cut. Extra attention was given to tension areas like his temples, the muscles in his neck and above his shoulder blades. Slow movements gravitated downward until I covered every inch of his anatomy. I trickled a small dollop of oil in my palm once I got to the soles of his feet and began to knead my way back up again.

"What brought this on?" Scott asked from his now relaxed position as I stroked lines on his spine.

"Without going into too much detail, I was reflecting on Mekhi and Mishelle. Their version of love is crazy. Scott, every time I leave their house I am drained. It's like my energy is sucked dry by that drama. I can't imagine us being that way. Three days ago was your birthday, and I agreed to something I knew I wouldn't like and it snowballed on me. I felt I needed to rectify the situation. Let it go. It's not worth the effort to stay angry. Life's too precious to stay angry unnecessarily. I truly was hurt about the other night."

"Baby, you shouldn't have been hurt—"

I cut him off. "Maybe not, but I was."

"I'm sorry you felt that way."

"It's over and done with. We need to focus on the now. When you walk through those doors downstairs, you should always feel welcome. I prefer to feel good and flow in the positive." I had stopped working my magic and continued to kneel next to Scott with my elbows perked on his back while I spoke.

Scott turned on his back and pulled me on top of him. "I'm the lucky one, Germani. Believe that you are a special kind of lady." A smile formed on his face. "Maybe you should meet me at the door with lingerie on every night. I could get used to this."

I smiled back. "I bet you could. I'll see what I can do to fulfill that request."

"Yeah, you do that." His gaze became smoky as he pressed his lips against mine. He pulled the lingerie off me, letting it drop alongside the bed. Our lips reunited like a lover's return after a long hiatus. I found myself falling deeper into the feeling of him. We slipped into a seductive world composed of just us two.

"Want to put in a video?" he asked as his hands made me weak.

"I don't want the sex tapes this time. I want to focus on me and you without any other distractions. We don't need those props for our pleasure. We should be enough," I said against his ear, determined to be the center of his attention. I slid my hands up his arms until our fingers became intertwined, allowing my husband to take us to the next level.

My eyes opened when what should have happened didn't. "What's wrong?"

Scott looked just as mystified. A scowl formed as he pressed his hand between the middle of us. "I don't know."

He opened his mouth like he planned to talk. He closed it and wrapped his arms tightly around my waist.

I could feel a repetitive request brewing in his mind, but as long as it didn't come from his mouth, I continued to work my womanly magic and dissipate the option. That is until I looked into his face.

Frustration glimmered in his eyes. "Baby, I need the visual stimulation."

His comment doused me like a car crashing into a water hydrate. My sexual confidence clipped into shreds like carrots through a food processor.

I repeated what I said earlier. "I don't want to watch a porn video." My words were curt, even though I wasn't trying to have an attitude. My stand on the subject had to be clear though.

"Why not? We've been watching videos as foreplay to our intimacy." His voice was pleading, "You know that's what I'm used to doing. It's a big part of our arousal."

He made our intimacy sound cheap, fleeting and worldly. "No, Scott, it is a big part of your arousal. I just went along for the ride. I don't need to see other people in action to feel connected to my husband." I knew my words sounded crude, but he needed to understand my point. I flounced against my pillow, dejected. My desire for intimacy lost.

Scott uttered inaudible words under his breathe.

I softened my voice. "I don't have to be entertained by movies or books or stage plays for that matter, to make love to you. We could be in a cave in the middle of Timbuktu and all I'd need is you."

"You're upset that I asked to do what we've been doing?" Scott questioned. His inquisition was flat. Scott acted like I didn't make sense.

"Change is good for a healthy relationship."

"Baby, if it works, why change course now?" he reasoned. "If this were an airplane, me the pilot and you the copilot, we wouldn't dismiss the flight plan before we reached our destination. We would discuss it after landing." He jokingly cupped my chin and kissed me. Him and his corny interpretations.

I took that to mean I interrupted the flow of the night, which was probably true, but I felt how

I felt. "No, I need us to be one without the over-the-top additions."

"Our making love is over-the-top?" Scott asked, astonished.

"No, not the loving making. The foreplay is a bit much and I sometimes feel guilty after we do what we do."

"There is nothing wrong with two married people finding creative ways to enjoy each other. Your guilt is self imposed and unnecessary torture. The videos only heighten the adventure we already have in us." He placed his leg atop mine and caressed my chest.

The realization sickened me. He didn't want me. His desire revolved around a fantasy on a television screen or in a stripper's club.

I refused Scott's advances as his lips moved across my body. My arm went up as a barrier, pushing him to his side of the bed. I picked up my red negligee off the floor and clothed my nakedness. Thoughts of Eve in that garden flashed through my mind. I wondered if she felt my kind of shame when truth met her on the ground of Eden.

"Where are you going?" Scott asked. I could hear a touch of aggravation in his voice.

"Downstairs. I'm sleeping on the couch," I replied as I once again clutched emotions I didn't want to feel. My frustration controlled me.

"What happened to removing all negativism, anger, sadness and discord? We're supposed to be basking in the blessing of our union."

My words sounded fake coming from his mouth. "Too late," I grumbled, my tone sated with sorrow. I walked to the hall closet and removed a thin, tattered, brown blanket to sleep under. Maybe my perceived notion of a blessed union was an illusion. The Bible said dwell with those equally yoked. If that was true, then I was going to need more than prayer.

CHAPTER EIGHT

SCOTT

The humidity steamed my skin like an outdoor sauna. Sweat circles formed from my armpits all over my teal Rocawear shirt. I could barely think, let alone tee off on the eleventh hole of the driving range at The Golf Village. Damon bought time at the golf course during one of the hottest months of the year. August had ninety-degree weather that felt more like 110. I wiped wet beads from my forehead and leaned on my club. My sixty-four-ounce icy Gatorade bottle was down to a corner of liquid. We had been out on the course for over two hours and the heat was making a brotha tired.

Damon didn't seem bothered by the smolder-ing heat as he swung his club into the golf ball and it flew high up across the green. We both watched that ball until it hit the ground several feet from its intended hole. The flag on the metal pole swayed, giving the impression that there really was a breeze. But if that was the case, I sure wished the breeze would come touch me. We began walking toward the flag pole. I surveyed the surrounding area for shades of color. Damon and I were it. Specks of brown in a sea of white.

"Nice," I said, realizing how skilled Damon was becoming as we eyed his golf ball.

He looked down at the ball then smiled at his near triumph.

"How do you do it, man? Swinging like that in this heat? I'm about to pass out myself. I don't know where you get your tolerance, but shoot." That's all I could say. Breathing was becoming a problem. I felt like an asthma patient without an inhaler.

Damon bent over with his club held firm. He appeared to be studying the golf ball as he aligned the iron behind it. "Determination. It's all about the drive and determination. Anything can be accomplished if you want it bad enough and you mentally prepare to get it. Like in Darwinism; only the strong survive. The weak whither away like dust into the ground, quickly forgotten. I am where I am today because I don't allow weakness to emanate my mind. I focus on a goal, research the methodology of pursuit and gain what I want. Let's discuss this game for a moment. I don't like golf, but it has the perfect advantage." He stood and shrugged like it was an obvious fact. His expression was one of indifference.

He could have fooled me about not liking the game. Damon had been on a golf course every Saturday morning for the past nine weeks. I only came to see the allure because he seemed so devoted to the craft. And considering how hot it was and my dislike for the game, we could have found an equally displeasing sport to play indoors. One that didn't shrink my lungs like I was smoking three packs of cigarettes a day.

I wasn't about to pick up golf as the new black man hobby.

"I play golf for the networking opportunities. The majority of the physicians I deal with enjoy this sport. In order to develop a rapport with my clientele, I have to become equipped in what they know. It's just as much about *what* you know as it is *who* you know. I have to be seen as an equal in order to develop the trust factor. Maybe manipulate a few things in my favor. Once I gain someone's trust, everything else is easy."

It sounded like a waste of energy. "Oh. Different strokes for different folks. Impressions mean a great deal more to you than to me. I'm not going to fabricate me to impress somebody just for financial gain. Manipulation for equality. Nah, I'm not interested. "

"Negro, pul-lease. Who you fooling? Don't hate my game because you can't play it. Besides, I like making money, and connecting with all the physicians for other activities generates a significant amount of funds to play with." Damon popped his shirt like he was fanning his chest. I could see sweat drip down his neck. It was a surprise that he hadn't called it quits. Damon wasn't one to allow himself to get funky; for no amount of money.

"Don't you think it's time for us to resign the clubs for the day? This heat is killing me."

"State of mind. Partner, it's your state of mind. Let me just finish this hole." Damon practiced swinging the club without actually hitting the ball.

"You already have a significant clientele. You're covering all of the Mecklenburg region and the surrounding areas, visiting doctor offices seven hours a day, Monday to Friday, selling prescription drugs and giving away samples. Burnout is going to creep up on you and knock you flat on your butt."

"I've had to get through harder times than balancing my work schedule. I got too much fortitude to go down. That is the main thing the hood taught me. If you stay where you're at, you'll never go anywhere. Just like Darwin's theory, I was smart enough to learn from my environment. If you want to be poor, stay around poor people. They don't mind having somebody to stay lazy, unfocused and stupid with. If you want to be rich, you got to step up your game and get connected to people with the right means. The best way to get somewhere is to step on or over the less inspired to get what you want. Pursuit. Position. Possession." Damon lightly tapped the golf ball and it rolled into the hole.

"I hear you, man. Do your thing. I can't be mad at you for doing you." I wiped at more sweat dripping on my forehead. "Since meeting Germani, my family became a priority. I like money, but I love my wife and son. I'm blessed without all that you talking about."

"Blessed is what you call it. Broke is what I call it. I guess that's why you are living check to check. Waiting on your blessing from God." He chuckled sarcastically.

He didn't used to be overtly egotistical. When Damon became the top performing sales representative for Pharm Access, his life perception altered. All of a sudden, acquiring money became his main focus. The more he got, the more he obsessed about having more.

"Don't hate on me, and I won't hate on you. I'm out." I put my iron back into the golf bag I had rented from the golf course shop. "You coming or are you giving me your car keys?" I said. It was too hot to be talking trash. Damon was my boy, but he could work a nerve when he put himself on an invisible pedestal. I tried not to take it personal. It wasn't like I was slumming. Germani and I did all right financially. Our combined incomes allowed us to do what we needed to provide for our family, plus have a little extra for entertainment. We traveled to countries throughout the world when the budget allowed for it. That was more than some could say.

Damon may be living high class now, but I remember back in the day when we sat on his front porch, eating Spam sandwiches and drinking grape Kool-aid out of mayonnaise jars.

"All right. I'm done," Damon picked up his equipment and he sniffed himself as he followed me off the course. "You want to go by my crib and get a quick shower, then maybe hit Outerbounds Sports Bar and grab some eats?"

"We can do that." Until he mentioned it, I didn't realize how hungry I was. Germani stopped cooking after our last argument two weeks ago. She went grocery shopping every other week on a Friday. Yesterday, I noticed that all the fresh meats and produce for meal preparations were replaced with microwavable garbage. She knew I stayed away from processed food. My momma didn't raise us on TV dinners and I wasn't going to start eating them now. I could tell my wife was trying to make some kind of crazy point, but she didn't have to do it at the expense of my stomach. It was bad enough that she had taken the sex away. Depriving a man of his food, too, was unnecessary torture.

On the ride to the house, Damon played a recent CD by Brian McKnight. "She Used To Be My Girl" blared from the speakers as we turned off Polk Street in Pineville. The air conditioner came on. It soothed my hot flesh like ice on a sunburn.

I pulled my cell phone off my hip and looked at the blank screen. Germani hadn't called. Not even once. I probably should have expected it, but I was hoping that one day, she would wake up and throw away her attitude problem. Each time I tried to smooth things over, she gave me the cold shoulder. Even walked around me like I didn't exist a couple times. I resigned myself to let her stew alone over whatever issue she had. She and Elijah were already gone this morning when I woke up. She didn't leave me a note to tell me where they were going or nothing. Another reminder that bliss wasn't living at the Wilson residence.

I placed the phone back on my clip and sighed. "Women."

Damon glanced over at me. "Trouble at home?"

I hesitated about how much I wanted to tell Damon. "Little bit," I replied. Germani was wearing me out with her hostile demeanor. It'd be different if I understood the problem. Then I could rectify the situation; but psychic ability didn't run in my family.

"What's going on?" he asked.

"I'd rather not say," I paused. "You know how you get about women."

"What you trying to say, I can't be a sympathetic ear?"

Damon looked offended, but I knew better. My friend had many qualities, but sympathetic wasn't one of them. His logic was hard-edged and unemotional.

"You couldn't find sympathy on a crossword puzzle."

"We boys, though. I've never said anything that wasn't true."

"I know, but I don't know." I was in a state of conflict. I was learning in church to take things to God, but His response time was challenging. Some answers I needed quickly and God didn't work on people time.

"Talk man," said Damon. He slowed the car and moved toward the side of the road as an ambulance zoomed by, sirens screaming.

We pulled back onto the road.

"Does Cherish ever take you through drama just 'cause she can?" I had a vague idea about Germani's issue with me; I just didn't know what to do about it.

"I must admit, I can't complain. Cherish is a dime piece. She doesn't give me any kind of grief. My wife knows what boundaries not to cross. I rule. She follows. It's that simple." Damon was gloating.

I shook my head. "It's not that simple. Not for me. Germani wants to change me and I think she is upset that I have things that aren't up for change. Namely, sex. She knew I was a freak when she married me. I've been watching porn since I was ten years old. Germani watched it with me. Even incorporated some of the positions into our love making. Now, all of a sudden, after five years of doing it, the good stuff is off limits. Ungodly is what she called it. Ain't that a trip!"

Damon's eyebrows crunched together. He looked just as shocked as I felt. He used his palm to turn the steering wheel, placing us onto Mallard Creek Church Road. One side of his mouth twitched. His disapproval was obvious. "That's messed up, Scott. Over some movies?" he questioned like he couldn't believe it.

"Over some movies," I confirmed as we pulled into his driveway. "And now she has cut me off from the goodies. She might as well have put a pillowcase over my head and cut off my air supply." It was nice to get the frustration off my chest. Only a man could relate to another man about a subject like sex. Men are physical creatures. I don't care how saved a man becomes, sex is still important.

Damon took the keys out of the ignition and sat for a minute. "Wow. You are dealing with some stuff."

We got out of the car and removed the golf bags. "You wearing panties now . . . Hanes Her Way?" he joked. Damon was having a field day with my problem. "Seriously, aren't you the head of your household?" he asked as we entered his house and walked through his entryway, stopping at the carpet to take his tennis shoes off.

"Suppose to be," I responded.

"See, I told you to be careful with all that religion and niceties. Church will have you acting like a little punk. You need to get your manhood out of Germani's purse and attach it back where it belongs."

We headed up the spiral staircase and into his master bedroom. A sixty-inch flat screen television was on the wall directly across from the king size Mahogany four-column bed that Damon threw his car keys on. The room was massive with twenty-seven feet of professionally decorated space. Damon strolled into his walk-in closet.

I stood at the bay window and looked down on the patio and in-ground pool.

Damon came out of the closet and handed me a folded beige Lacoste polo shirt. "Your wife running you because you let her. Get a grip on your emotions and show Germani who's in charge. Cherish knows her place and she can be replaced if she crosses the line of respect."

Damon made Cherish expendable. Germani was my heart. Another woman couldn't step into her shoes.

I unfolded the shirt and checked the size. Damon was only maybe ten or fifteen pounds heavier than me, but my shoulders were broader. "This is not football. I'm not trying to trade up. I want a solution for my current problem, in my current relationship. Thanks for looking out, but I'll find a way to fix things with my wife."

"Do what you got to do." Damon shrugged and went to his attached bathroom. I went to the guest bathroom down the hall thinking up a resolution. Whatever was done, Germani would have to meet me halfway.

CHAPTER NINE

GERMANI

The balls of my feet were aching like I'd walked barefoot down a beach on ridgy stone. The warm bubbling water of the foot spa soothed the sharp pain caused by wearing too many uncomfortable but fashionable high heels. I needed to invest in shoes with supportive soles.

"Don't you get tired of being around dead people?" I asked my best friend as she sat in the chair next to me talking about her latest autopsy.

Autumn practically lived in the morgue as an assistant medical examiner. She had graduated from medical school only a year ago and was still morbidly fascinated by the causes of death.

"I just can't get over how diabolical people are. The killer bonded that seventy-five-year-old lady's mouth and nose shut with super glue. He probably stood there and watched her suffocate to death after he raped her. He's probably a serial killer, because his method is signature. It was too precise to be the first time he'd done something like that."

I cringed at the image she put in my head as I watched a technician skillfully paint the long, awkwardly curled nails of a young lady, at the nearby nail station, in blue topaz as a first coat. A yellow triangular pattern was airbrushed on top of the blue. It made for an interesting, flashy design. The girl looked to be in her late teens or early twenties. Just the right age for daring self expression.

I wondered how she drove her car, cooked, cleaned or answered her phone with nails that extended at least seven inches. It seemed that nails like that would disable a person from their daily function. Then again, determination had no bounds.

Yousei, one of the female nail technicians, finished with another customer and came over. She pulled Autumn's feet from the thermal basin and patted them dry with a cloth. She gently massaged foot cream onto Autumn's skin.

We came to Ming's Nail Salon twice a month for a spa treatment. I had discovered the location after receiving a coupon packet in the mail with a few of their promotions. I clipped out the duo special, where we purchased a pedicure and the manicure was free.

They had me as a lifetime customer from the first time I stepped into the serene Asian-style environment. Not only did Ming's have excellent interior design with the accents of bamboo lamps, silk shoji screens, copper vases and natural looking grayish green and bronze color scheme, but the nail technicians specialized in outstanding customer service. I felt special each time I came back. The whole staff of eight knew me and Autumn by first name.

I decided to change the subject before Autumn went deeper into detail. "Have you ever felt like you blocked your blessing or stifled your anointing?"

I was trying to stand by my convictions, but it was harder than I thought it would be. The days seemed longer since I declined watching sex tapes with Scott. I dreaded interaction with my husband because I knew what he really wanted to do. If I remained aloof, he wouldn't approach me sexually. On the flip side, the longer we walked around each other like immigrants at U.S. border patrol, the harder it was going to become to successfully live together.

"You know . . . trying to undo some garbage that you created, but the efforts seem in vain when you work to make things right? Get caught in the cusps of wrong, even when it is obvious that wrong is wrong?" I asked Autumn while Yousei airbrushed her toes with French tips. My heart felt heavy with indecisiveness. I looked down the row and another technician was finishing up. I would be next for my pedicure. I needed to be pampered.

Autumn stared at me, "What's going on? You're sounding real philosophical."

"I went to the Playa's Lounge with Scott on his birthday," I confessed.

As her eyebrows rose, her mouth formed a circle. She was clearly shocked by my admission.

I should have allowed my embarrassment to be enough to shut my mouth, but I kept talking anyway. "It was the most degrading experience of my life. I felt spiritually out of order and physically out of place. My skin crawled and there wasn't a bug in sight. There were plenty of snakes in that spot, but no bugs."

"And your husband was one of them?" Autumn asked the question slowly as if she feared insulting me with the truth. I couldn't be mad at her for speaking what we both knew. Honesty could destroy just as quickly as it could build. I just had to discover where my reality was taking me.

"Don't get me wrong. I agreed to go to the Playa's Lounge. So I can't act like I was forced to be there. I had no idea Scott would show his all natural that way though. The straw that broke the camel's back was the lap dance. Can you believe he was going to take a lap dance from some half naked hoochie, while I was sitting right next to him?" I paused while waiting for her reaction. I expected her to be just as appalled as I had been when it happened. I wanted her to co-sign my frustration.

Instead, her eyes cast downward. Instead, her lips merged together into a singular railroad track. Her effectual silence neglected the confirmation I needed because of my suffering, my irritation and my continued angst.

Autumn must have scrolled through a dozen thoughts in her head. The silence got larger and longer, extending a mile.

My technician, Oaku, had come during our conversation and was painting my toes a vibrant color of red as she tried to act like she wasn't listening.

When Autumn finally acknowledged my question she said, "So, what are you going to do now?" She put the ball back in my court without answering, like I felt she would.

I didn't know what I was going to do. That was the problem. If I had my own resolution, then I would've never mentioned the subject to her.

I stated as much. "That's why I asked you. I need advice."

"You don't want my advice," Autumn stated in a matter-of-fact tone.

She had been my prayer partner since before I was married, even before I knew Scott existed. Prayed for me back before I was saved and prayed with me after I discovered how awesome God really was. Autumn was there when I trusted no one else in my business. Her unbiased straight-to-the-point commentary always made me feel she had a direct connection to the Higher Power.

Autumn hadn't given me significant advice since I married Scott. Although she thought Scott's nose was wide open for me, she was opposed to my less-than-honorable reason for our nuptials. I had an ulterior motive for wanting the marriage. My best friend was certain that I'd regret my decision to go forward with the wedding. Until now, I'd proved her wrong.

"What you allow is what will be expected. That's the problem women have. We lower our standards and then get mad about the lack of respect. If you set a firm foundation in the beginning, one not built from deceit I might add," Autumn gave her I-told-you-so look, "you don't have to worry about things crumbling at your feet later. You've known the power of God for quite some time. You are familiar with the ability to discern demonic forces, especially if they are in you. I'm not married, but I'm sure God wouldn't want you to willingly let your husband stray you from the love of Christ. The enemy will use those closest to you, who are weaker in their Christian walk, to lure you away from God."

"Nothing can separate me from the love of God. I may lose favor, but not His love," I said confidently. "My concern is pleasing God and pleasing Scott simultaneously."

Yousei finished with Autumn's feet. The salon was still packed, so Yousei moved on to the next customer. Autumn thanked her before she stood up, admiring her pedicure, and slipped her feet into her sandals. She placed the magazine on the spa chair. "If your husband's not living right, you have to spend less time pleasing Scott and more time pleasing God. If you focus on God, pray about the lust demon ruling in your marriage, God will work out the rest."

I knew she was right. I had to get my mind focused. Scott would have to take a backseat to God. The Lord said He would never forsake me. He also said to meditate on His Word day and night. If I gave God His due, then maybe Scott would start to see things my way.

"Maybe that's all I need, improvement of my prayer life." I pondered that thought and instantly felt my load of frustration lifted.

I reached down and rubbed the smoothness of my soles. Oaku had done an amazing job on my feet. She had the magic touch in those fingers of hers. The sharp pain was gone. They felt like satin. I slipped my feet into a pair of blue denim low-heel mules. Autumn and I walked to the cash register to pay for our manicures and pedicures.

"That and get some blessed oil. Cover every surface that may be tainted, including your door frames, the televisions, and—" Autumn handed the salon hostess her MasterCard, "rub oil on Scott's forehead while you pray for his deliverance."

She was trying to give me a death wish. "Scott's not going to let me do that." That decision was as far from wise as one person could get.

Scott thought that my former church was a cult, and it was the same one Autumn still attended. He got spooked all three times that he visited with me. Scott declared apostolic shouting to be chanting and Holy Ghost dancing to be voodoo. His Catholic upbringing skewed his perception of the Holy Spirit. He said it didn't take all that for God to hear you.

It was one of very few arguments that we had. I wasn't happy about leaving the church that I'd grown spiritually in because it challenged his belief system. It wasn't until my former pastor suggested that I go with my husband to a church we could both be comfortable in, but for us to pray about the decision. I didn't know what I was praying for. My husband wasn't going to be happy with any church I picked, and I doubted my spiritual hunger would be fed at a synagogue. Out of obedience to my pastor and self-sacrifice for my husband, I prayed anyway.

It took a while, but eventually, we ended up at our current church. The non-denominational fellowship center catered to both my and Scott's interests. It wasn't as live as my former church and we didn't use blessed oil, but when the Spirit of the Lord showed up, He showed out. Plus I saw a change in Scott. But was that change enough? That was the million dollar question.

CHAPTER TEN

SCOTT

The desire awoke me in the middle of the night. It surged through me intensely as I dreamed. Sexual images emerged that were as real as Germani who slept on her side next to me; ones in which pleasure sated my need. I delicately touched my wife's soft skin as I pressed my lips to her neck. I inhaled the sweet smell of her. My eyes closed while I pressed against her curves and thought about us making love. Yet, I couldn't get completely aroused, just like the last time we tried to be intimate.

I didn't want to chance the development of an argument if I woke her up and asked for porn foreplay again. Instead, I slipped from the bed, needing a release. Just because she decided to give up our sexual ritual didn't mean I had to. If only she could allow things to go back to the way they used to be.

Of the things I could do wrong in our relationship, watching porn with my wife should have
been minor. I didn't smoke, drink, cuss, hang
out all night nor cheat on Germani. Damon
kept suggesting that I get a mistress, but as far
as I was concerned, one relationship required
enough work. I wasn't the cheating type anyway.
I just wanted to be with my wife and enjoy sex-
heightening movies together.

Obviously, what I wanted was of no impor-
tance to Germani.

I tiptoed down the hall to the computer room.
I had an extensive adult DVD collection, but
could watch nothing in the living room. That
television faced the stairs and I didn't want to
take the chance of Elijah coming down while my
movies were playing. The one in the bedroom
would surely wake up Germani and she didn't
need to know what I was doing.

I closed the door of the computer room and
rushed to the desk like a kid after the ice cream
man. I pushed the button to turn the computer
on and my giddiness escalated as the Internet
browser appeared. I hadn't skimmed an online
porn site in years. With a sex life as active as ours
had been, who needed a computer? Germani had
been more than willing to entertain all my fantasies. Even created a few of her own.

I tried to recall the sites I used to explore, but my mind drew a blank.

I glanced to my right as I tried to jog my memory and there was a Bible sitting on the desk. I looked at the Bible, and then looked at the computer screen. I could feel guilt creeping up inside of me.

Bible . . . Computer.

Computer . . . Bible.

The brown leather bound book felt heavy as I slid it across the desk and palmed it. I wondered how Jesus resisted that temptation in the desert. He had to be a seriously disciplined man. "Lord, forgive me," I muttered as I tossed the Bible in a drawer and quickly shut it.

My sexual desire won out. Compared to all the drive-by shootings, car jackings, parents drowning their children, spouses decapitating their mates, the ridiculous and unnecessary travesty of war in Iraq, my little sin was inconsequential. If Germani wasn't trippin', it wouldn't be a sin at all.

I clicked from one porn site to the next, fascinated by all the new virtual reality options. My senses almost overdosed on the visual stimulation. Reminded me of my introduction to adult entertainment.

We were two rambunctious twelve-year-olds, Damon and I. Damon brought over a couple of movies from his mother's stash. I thought he was going to get in trouble, but he assured me that his mother wouldn't mind that the movies were gone. Damon said that his mother let him see adult movies whenever he wanted to. She would rather he learned about sex watching it at home instead of experimenting out in the streets. If it was anybody else, I would bet money that they were lying. Most parents I knew, including mine, weren't that liberated. But I knew Damon's mom, because she was dating my Uncle Gabe. He was the fun uncle that would let us get away with just about anything. Damon's mom also had a different parenting perception.

My parents bought a new VCR and let me get the old one from the family room. It made loud whizzing noises, especially when the rewind or fast forward buttons were pressed. The picture quality appeared grainy as if dust had settled inside the component and it had no remote control. To a ten-year-old, it was prime electronic equipment. None of the other kids in the neighborhood had the luxury of their own VCR in their bedrooms. My house became the hanging spot. We snuck in all kinds of stuff we had no business watching. Once I got a hold to those porn movies two years later, I graduated myself to adulthood.

Traded Disney for Del Rio.

From then on, I was hooked—a habit I formed over twenty-two years ago.

I remembered the frustration and hurt I saw in my wife's eyes the last time we tried to have sex. When I couldn't rise to the occasion. Maybe I could give it up. Maybe I needed to pray about it. Reopen that drawer and pull the Bible back out.

Maybe . . . just maybe. But not tonight.

CHAPTER ELEVEN

GERMANI

The verse for the day on my Christian calendar had a saying that perplexed me. It read: *The sluggard will not plow by reason of the cold; therefore he shall beg in harvest and have nothing.* I wondered if that applied to me. Probably. I felt convicted. A different version of that meant a lazy man doesn't eat. I hadn't cooked in weeks. Not out of malicious defiance, as Scott would like to believe, but more out of weariness. My doubts about my marriage were wreaking havoc on my ability to perform basic household duties. I cleaned regularly and made sure Elijah was fed. The least Scott could do was cook a few meals once in a while. If I wasn't appreciated, why put forth the extra effort? Okay, maybe I was exuding a little defiance. I wasn't perfect, but I wasn't lazy either. Maybe that verse wasn't applicable.

I chewed on the straw from my Dairy Queen mocha latte as I visually scanned the application for the second time. The words jumbled together. Name melting with address, employment history becoming abstract print. I shuffled the papers, widened my eyes and tried again.

Focus . . . Germani . . . Focus.

Abraham and Sons needed to fill a machine maintenance technician position; preferably, by the end of the day on Friday. If the company I worked for, Job Track, wasn't able to come through, they would post the position in the jobs section of the Sunday newspaper, costing us a significant residual from their contract and jeopardizing a working relationship. Abraham and Sons expected us to follow through, and usually, we did. We hired the majority of their industrial and clerical staff. I was fast running out of decent candidates to fill the position though.

Mitchell Camden's qualifications matched the company's profile from our database. He was the first one I called because of his twelve years of experience in the industry, but after relocating from New Orleans following Hurricane Katrina, he was still having a tough time finding something that suited him. When Mitchell came in for dexterity testing, I pitched the benefits. The job sounded promising. A long-term position would close his gap of non-employment. An eight-month contract. What more could he ask for? Money. Mitchell asked for a higher wage. He thought he had room for negotiations as he requested five dollars an hour more than offered by the company.

I warned him that he may want to rethink his demanding stand. We weren't a permanent placement agency. Job Track specialized in temporary employment and he hadn't worked in close to a year. Mitchell didn't take the hint. The company said no. Now I had to keep looking for other applicants and the options were thinning like an eighty-year-old man's receding hairline.

Daphne, our petite freckle-faced administrative assistant, appeared in the doorway of my cubicle. "There's a man here to see you."

Couldn't be for me.

I leafed through my black date binder.

Tuesday, July 5th at 11 A.M. was blank.

A scowl formed on my face. "I don't have anybody scheduled with me this morning. Did he give you a name?

"No. He said you would know him."

People always try to front like they have connections that don't exist. "He is mistaken."

We exchanged knowing glances.

"Get a resume from him and tell him that I will call him if I find a position to match his skills." I removed a business card from the holder on my desk. I handed one to Daphne, then thumbed through the stack of cards. It was getting low. I needed to order more.

Daphne took the card and nodded her head. Auburn curls bounced against her shoulders. She was used to walk-in clients claiming to have interviews with the agency. The trend was predictable. People will lie their way through just about anything. Misconstrue a situation to meet their purposes.

Within minutes, Daphne waltzed right back in my area. "He doesn't have a resume and he won't leave." One eyebrow arched as she looked at me suspiciously.

"What do you mean he won't leave? He has no choice. This is a professional environment, not some free hangout spot. See, that's why we need security." I picked up the phone to dial John's extension. He was our staffing manager and everybody looked to him when clients clowned, which didn't happen often, but it did happen. A former marine with combat military training, he retired after twenty years of service. John's charming, yet aggressive personality commanded attention and demanded respect.

"John's on vacation," Daphne said.

My hand slowed as I punched the third of four digits.

"He won't be back for two weeks. He went to Mackinaw Island in Michigan." She finished as she watched me with a curious stare. "The guy out there doesn't look dangerous, just determined."

I sighed, "I guess I'll have to take care of this myself. Is he out in the lobby or in a testing room?" I jaunted around my desk and stood next to Daphne. I couldn't be sure of his location and wanted to handle things accordingly. Preparation, if there was a scene. We didn't need commotion in the lobby. That's bad business. Seeing that Daphne didn't fear our intruder or the possibility of him going Virginia Tech crazy, it was probably safe to take him into one of the testing rooms.

"Lobby," Daphne replied as we strolled down the hall and around a corner.

Daphne fingered him as he pulled a "Tips to Employment" brochure from the floor spindle. His bald head bowed as he read.

My erect professional posture immediately eased. A relieved breath escaped my lips. "Mekhi?" I asked, although it was more of a what-are-you-doing-in-my-place-of-business statement rather than a question.

My cousin looked up from the brochure innocently smiling.

He was too big to be playing coy.

"It's about time. Your gatekeeper refused to let me walk back on my own. She was posted up like this is Homeland Security." He placed the brochure back on the spindle.

"This is my cousin, Mekhi," I said as Daphne stood by waiting for an introduction. "Well, maybe if you had told her your name, some of your time would have been shaved off your unexpected arrival. Next time, call before you show," I told Mekhi as I escorted him back to my cubicle

He stopped at the entrance. "You don't have your own office. With a door?"

"No."

Mekhi bit the inside of his cheek as he looked up and down the row of cubicles. "These things don't have any privacy."

What did he need privacy for? My co-workers didn't care about his conversation. He had nothing to worry about.

"State your business," I said as he sank into my client chair.

I sat back in my chair and rolled in close to the desk.

"I need to borrow your car."

I had automatically assumed he was already in a vehicle. "How did you get down here?"

"Bus. Route Eight. Took me fifty minutes to get here," he complained.

"Why do you need my car?" He had used it before, but loaning out my car wasn't habitual.

"I got to pick up something."

"Something like what?" His game of mystery, annoying me when my temperament was already compromised, didn't work in his favor. Mekhi only beat around the bush when he doubted my understanding of his need or situation.

He leaned closer to my desk. His voice dipped several octaves. "I got to go pick up my replacement food stamp card."

My pitch rose like a Ferris wheel on the upswing at an amusement park. "Food stamps? What are you doing getting food stamps? Boy, what is wrong with you?" I scolded. "Your feet should have never stepped in a welfare building. You are not that deprived."

I eyeballed his white, red and black Rocawear jersey, the nicely pressed matching black jeans, and Mark Ecko Crest Watch. Clean white Nike tennis shoes peeked out from the other side of my desk.

Mekhi glanced down, ashamed. He rubbed his hands across his jeans. "Things are kinda tight for me right now," he explained. "I'm trying to make due. You know how hard it is for a black man out here."

I cocked my head to the side and pursed my lips. Once again, no reason would justify a healthy able-bodied man standing in line for a hand-out.

He further explained, "Mishelle hipped me to it. When I got out of prison, she took me to fill out the application so we'd have more food in the house until I could get back on my feet.

"Uh-huh." I wanted to run down the laundry list of other things Mishelle had him doing that weren't in his best interest.

"Mekhi, you could have used that time to find employment. I don't know about you, but to me, application means job and work. Your applying for food stamps should have never been an option. A lazy man is supposed to be hungry." I referred back to the verse I learned earlier. I felt a sense of pride from being able to share the scripture I learned.

His nettled gaze told me he didn't like my comment.

"Donate your plasma at the Red Cross or somewhere, they pay for blood. An even exchange. You give, you get in return. That is more dignified than taking your overgrown behind through a welfare line."

"You act like I want to live this way. Ain't nobody hiring felons." He clapped his hands in sync with his measured words. "Believe me, I've been looking. I stay on the hunt. Both you and Scott work in management and neither of you can hook a brotha up. Now can you?"

"I . . . well, um," I stuttered, knowing he was right. Our company had a strict policy about criminal backgrounds. I could barely get a person with a misdemeanor employed, let alone someone with felony assault charges.

"But I do know a guy who is looking for some part-time help unloading trucks. He called last week. We don't really specialize in that type of thing, but he may still be hiring. Here is the address. Go check it out." I scribbled on a piece of yellow tablet paper, opened a top drawer and pulled out my car keys. "Have my car back here before this building closes at five."

He smiled as he jumped from his chair. "I promise."

He tried to pull the keys, but I held on with fingers looped around the ring. "Mekhi, you deserve better than hand-outs from the welfare system and you might want to stop taking advice from Mishelle. You feel me?"

"I feel you," he said, nodding in agreement as I released the key ring.

I hoped he did. I sure hoped he did.

CHAPTER TWELVE

SCOTT

The undeniable smell of food greeted me as I entered the threshold of my house. A home-cooked meal appeased my appetite. Chicken pot pies don't give off that aroma. I followed the smell like an obedient servant to hunger. The house had been void of anything remotely requiring preparation beyond the removal of plastic or compression of microwave buttons. Food fixed in five minutes or less. I'd forgotten what it felt like to eat the real deal.

Germani stirred a pot on the back burner of our electric stove, already dressed for bed in a hot pink short pajama set. She didn't turn as I walked into the kitchen; probably didn't hear me come into the house. She was completely engrossed in her cooking as she dipped a serving spoon into the pot and tasted the contents. She picked up the salt shaker, sprinkled a dash in the concoction and slowly stirred clockwise.

"What's this, a special occasion?" I asked as I stood next to her and lifted a lid. A steamy cloud rose from the low simmering pan of smothered chicken with brown gravy and Vidalia onions.

"Not really. Eating garbage everyday gets old after a while."

She strolled over to the refrigerator and reached inside to get a stick of butter. I could see juice, milk, eggs and what looked like a fully stocked refrigerator from my view. A welcome change.

I took that to mean she was no longer on a silent war path. The caustic environment changed. I could relax a little.

"Are you going to eat with me?" I lifted the lid of another smaller pot. French style green beans.

She turned off all the burners and opened the oven. "I'm not all that hungry, but I'll eat a little something with you. Can you hand me the pot holders?"

"Sure," I walked to the far edge of the 'L' shaped countertop and slid the flowered mittens we used for kitchen towels off the shelf. I put the mittens on my thick hands and removed the tin baking pan from its rack.

"Thanks." She continued to give me minimal conversation as she rubbed over the top of a dozen golden dinner rolls. I didn't know what kind of mood she was in. No smiles, but on the upside, she wasn't frowning either. The vibe didn't feel negative. She'd cooked, so I wasn't going to question her mood.

I watched her fill each of our plates with food. Mine was stacked, while hers had a single chicken drumstick, three tablespoons of mashed potatoes and a dab of string beans.

"That's all you're gonna eat?" I asked, pointing at her plate atop a placemat. We sat down at the glass, round table and Germani lowered her head to pray. I followed suit.

Raising her head she responded, "I ate a ham sandwich and a bowl of grapes with Elijah."

Elijah had to be sleep. It was well after ten at night.

She propped her elbow on the table and placed her chin in her palm. "How was your day?"

"It was okay." I dug my fork into the mountain of potatoes and swirled my utensil in gravy before bringing it to my mouth. I took in a couple more forkfuls, grateful for the meal. "The inventory numbers are off. Totally inaccurate. The calculations don't add up on paper. Our system usually computes the product line minus the amount of items purchased. Takes me a couple of hours to add the bottom line."

"Merchandise doesn't disappear into thin air. Think it could be a computer glitch?" Germani asked, poking her drumstick with her fork.

"That's my hope. It's going to be a headache to scan every item in the back room of the store and break down the numbers by manual application. Shoot, I've only had to do that two other times, and both times, the calculations were off because something was placed in the wrong location and not counted."

"Hummmm."

"If our company had more updated registers and tracking equipment, this wouldn't be a problem. It could take months to get this figured out."

The miscalculation made me edgy. Several hundreds of dollars in car parts had vanished. I didn't want to startle Germani by confiding my fears.

"This is delicious, baby. After working fourteen hours, this was exactly what I needed to come home to. Thank you. Thank you. Thank you." I took another bite and let my expression say it all. I truly was grateful, and if I could keep this momentum going, our relationship may be in a much better place.

Her lips extended slightly, but then she got a far away look. The kind when something has been on the brain all day. I didn't ask what it might be. If she wanted to talk about it, she would tell me. And to be quite honest, I didn't want to hear about anything that was going to change the element.

"I went to Bible study this evening." She watched me like I was supposed to respond to that.

"What did you learn?" I asked.

"Pastor Mackenzie came from the Book of Proverbs."

"Proverbs. That's the one mainly written by King Solomon."

"Yeah. That's right." She acted shocked, like she didn't expect me to know that.

I might not be a theologian with an advanced degree in the subject, but I knew a little something about the Bible.

"In fact, Pastor said that there was much debate over whether the son of David, King Solomon, had penned the whole book or just pieces of it. Pastor Mackenzie's lesson was based on Proverbs 12:4 which read: *An excellent wife is the crown of her husband, but she who causes shame is like rottenness in his bones.* He told us that our actions and words have more power than we realize. If God gave woman the ability to bring forth life, wouldn't we also have just as much power to bring forth death? In today's society women are honored for being strong and independent, but sometimes, independence can breed spitefulness or indifference. Women have the ability to build a man up or tear him down. Women like to be right and we tend to do things or withhold things to prove our point.

"Pastor can't stand to hear women say they don't need a man for nothing, because it was God's design for us to need each other. Woman was created from a rib to be a helpmeet, which basically means for women to help men meet God's plan for life. Pastor clarified that he wasn't talking about women allowing themselves to be used by beaters, leeches, or cheaters. Men in those categories haven't reached manhood yet. He spoke for all the men trying to do the right thing. On no occasion is belittling a man acceptable in God's eyes. Shame brings about destruction." Germani summarized her version.

"It sounds like Bible study got real deep," I replied.

"It did, but the whole point of Bible study is to go more in depth into a biblical perspective. He made all of us women in class think about the reason we do the things we do. If the purpose of doing is because of what we gain by our actions, we end up losing anyway. We are to revel in our men's accomplishments; encourage them despite their failures."

While Germani talked, I polished off my meal and sucked fragments of chicken off the bones. I wasn't leaving a smidgen behind, nothing but gristle remained. After close to a month without a decent meal, I savored every last morsel.

She paused as I got up from the table and placed my plate in the sink. I poured a tall glass of sweet tea from the refrigerator.

"I forgot to get you a beverage," she apologized.

"Don't worry about it. I was so hungry I didn't think to get myself something to drink." I gulped the cool liquid.

Germani was still picking at her food.

"Do you mind?" I asked before taking her plate from the table. She shook her head.

I began to rinse the dishes and put them in the dishwasher while Germani sat in the chair quietly watching. "Continue telling me what you learned," I encouraged.

She got up from the table, pushed both our seats in and removed Tupperware from the kitchen cabinets on the side of the refrigerator.

"We haven't exactly been enjoying life lately. The lesson taught me to do things in kindness despite what I may be going through mentally. I must admit my actions were a little spiteful. Just a little bit." She pinched her fingers close together.

At least she admitted her angst. Obviously, her attitude was more than a figment of my imagination. I kept to myself and let the storm ride out. I didn't like walking through my house waiting for Hurricane Germani to pass over.

"I'll try not to take you on a roller coaster of my emotions, but I don't like feeling like a piece of tail. There is a difference between sensual intimacy and straight raunchiness. We need to find a way to work through this whole porn loving thing."

"We only have a problem because you're making it into one," I remarked as I dried my hands and playfully snapped the waistband of her cute little shorts while she was bent over in the refrigerator rotating items around to make room for the Tupperware.

She stood up and turned around. One container still in hand, her eyes slanted as she frowned. The frustration was on the rise again, but she kept it at a reasonable level. "It's deeper than that. I need you to take this seriously. I'm not going to keep doing what I've been doing when I know how wrong it is."

I felt like Keith Sweat, whining in a love song. "I'm sorry. I'm so very sorry. If you don't ever want to watch another pornographic movie and experiment together again, then we don't have to. I promise you that we will never have to watch or do anything that makes you uncomfortable."

I didn't know how I was going to hold to that promise, but I loved her enough to try.

CHAPTER THIRTEEN

GERMANI

"You know Richard was blowing smoke up our rear end," Stewart, my recruitment partner, said with his strong Southern accent after we left our meeting at Plas-tech. They were in the middle of a merger with an unknown corporation and we went out to discuss plans for the ninety temps we had placed there. Richard, Contract Divisional Manager, assured us that our temps wouldn't be affected by the upcoming changes, but we knew better. Whenever there was an acquisition, somebody lost their job.

Stewart wanted to make a stop at The Grape Wine Bar and Bistro to pick up something to drink for a date who was cooking for him that night.

As we pressed through throngs of weekend shoppers at the Northlake Mall, I thought of Scott. He had just promised that we would both stop watching porn last week. I didn't even know that he was into the Internet porn until a few days ago when I did a search for a gumbo recipe. Once I saw the first porn pop-ups, it wasn't hard to pull up URL entries on the computer we shared. There were thirty odd viewings listed before he made the promise to stop; five viewings after. What was the point in him making a promise that he wouldn't keep? How reliable was his word? Why did Scott pick porn over me? Question after question that wouldn't have resolved anything. I guess a little piece of me had given up on the subject. I didn't know what else to say to Scott that hadn't been said already. The porn pop-ups jabbed at my sexuality as a reminder that my husband didn't want to be intimate with me . . . with only me. My womanly pride was wounded. I missed being touched and caressed by my husband. I missed us making love. Scott wasn't the only one with needs and desires.

"I shouldn't be long. Meet you back at the Macy's entrance in about half an hour?" Stewart asked, looking at his watch.

"Works for me," I agreed.

I went to Borders Books and perused the aisles for a title that would catch my attention. Strolled from Biographies down to Christian Fiction around the corner to the Inspirational section.

My attention was caught by a book about the discovery of a divine plan for sexual and emotional fulfillment. The title . . . *Every Woman's Battle*.

"Germani?" a voice as familiar as ice cream floats on a hot summer day called my name.

I instantly felt buried emotions revive themselves as I looked into hazel eyes that once captured every essence of me. A smile grew across my face, one that shouldn't have been there.

"Tre." I wanted to be enraged, but my smile remained intact. I conjured up hurt, but the pain of old wounds stayed buried.

I placed the book back on its rack as I soaked in his appearance. The stone-washed jeans and tan T-shirt hung loosely on Tre's medium frame. His simplistic style of dress hadn't changed.

He hugged me. As my chin touched his neck, I inhaled the scent of his cologne: Perry Ellis 18. The same brand he wore back when.

"How have you been?" he asked with a wide grin on smooth mocha skin. He'd cut his goatee off since the last time I'd seen him.

I wanted to tell him that it was none of his business how I was doing, but I couldn't deny my joy at his presence. He always had that effect on me; could make my heart do double-dutch. Somehow, marriage didn't change that or maybe it was the state of my marriage that was the problem. Maybe if Scott and I were on better terms, I'd be able to block the feeling rising in me.

"I'm doing well. Life is good, better than it ever has been." I embellished a little, but hoped I sounded convincing. I wanted him to think I was okay even if I wasn't. I couldn't have the first man I ever loved, an ex-boyfriend, realizing my life didn't turn out as well as I expected.

"I heard you were married," Tre said as his eyes locked with mine.

Tre's and my relationship had ended six years ago when he joined the Peace Corps for a three-year assignment. It dissolved on a bad note, one that took a serious toll on me. I started seeing Scott one year later and married him six months after that. It was easy to do. His sister, Beverly, was my college roommate and Scott used to come visit her every other weekend. Scott and I became close friends and he stuck around when Tre left me. I knew I wasn't over Tre, but Scott soothed the rejection I was feeling at the time.

A woman with a double stroller came down the aisle and tried to get past us blocking the way.

"Excuse us," Tre said as he instinctually pulled me to him as she went by. Being that close to him felt too familiar. I took several steps back as soon as the aisle cleared.

"Scott is his name. We have one son, Elijah. What about you? What have you been up to?" I asked, controlling that slight tremor in my voice.

"Well, I can't say that I have the pleasure of sharing my life with a mate, but I've been busy. The organization I work for is still focused on relief efforts in Darfur. I just recently came back to stay for awhile."

His peace work was a point of contention for us. I didn't comment because I didn't want to sound bitter.

"Found anything interesting to read?" I asked.

Tre read avidly. He was so many firsts for me. Tre introduced me to the biographies of Coltrane in Jazz and Nietzsche in Philosophy. He gave me a lot of knowledge from the books he used to pick up.

His hands were empty. "No. At least not what I was looking for. I just wanted to say hello when I saw you standing in this section. I'm going to get out of here."

I said hesitantly, "Oh, okay. It was good seeing you."

"You too." He headed toward an exit and I wished he had stayed to talk just a little longer.

CHAPTER FOURTEEN

SCOTT

Cut-N-Up barber shop on Eastway Drive was packed with brothers on Friday. I brought Elijah with me so we could get hooked up at the same time on either Wednesday evenings or Friday mornings, based upon my time off.

There were five barbers on hand and all of them were busy.

Deon handled the heads of young boys and placed a booster seat in the chair as I lifted Elijah up. "Want the usual?" he asked me as he picked up a set of clippers.

"Can you taper the sides a little more this time and curve the line by his ears." I pointed to Elijah's head as I gave Deon instructions.

Steve, the owner of the shop, turned the television volume up on *ESPN* as a picture of Michael Vick flashed across the screen.

"Why they messing with Mike? They know that ain't necessary. Don't nobody care about dogs fighting like that," Steve said as I sat down to wait for the next available barber.

The Vick coverage had been all over the news stations since the dog fighting story first broke.

Joe responded, "Well, you know what it is. Discrimination.

Michael Vick is popular. He was the first African American quarterback pick taken number one in the NFL Draft back in '04. The Atlanta Falcons signed that boy on a $130 million dollar deal, plus $37 million just as the sign on bonus. Nobody's ever been offered that much money to play football before. And they gave the deal to a black man. You know that somebody was going to start looking for some dirt on that brotha."

The customer sitting in Joe's chair added to the conversation. "Yeah, somebody was mad he had all that money. They brought the Feds into it too. What do the Feds have to do with dog fighting? Nothing until Michael Vick. He didn't even live in that house."

Steve responded, "Evidently, he didn't have to live there. Mike admitted to funding the gambling ring for the dog fights. He kind of set himself up for the rest when he started talking. The NFL said they want their money back for signing him on. They said he knew he was into some illegal stuff when he signed that contract. He's supposed to give back twenty million of the thirty-seven he got for the sign-on. And he lost all his endorsements."

Joe pointed his clippers at Steve. "No. What happened was he got bad legal advice. He might as well have had a public defender instead of that attorney of his for all the stuff he lost. That cat wouldn't have got paid if he was my lawyer."

"Too bad Cochran is gone," the customer added.

Joe placed his clippers on the stand behind him and brushed off his customer's cape. "He needs R. Kelly's lawyer. Those sexual charges have been pending since 2002. Now that's what I call some good legal defense. Whoever he has is seriously earning his pay to keep R. out of jail."

"It's not too late. Mike better call Robert and get the hook up," Steve joked.

Everybody in the shop laughed.

Next to my chair was a table full of reading material:

Maxim, swimsuit edition of *Sports Illustrated* and *King* magazines. I looked over at Elijah who had his head bent while Deon trimmed the back of his hair. I picked up a *King* magazine with Kim Kardasain in a bikini on the cover, but I wasn't all that interested in reading it.

There was such a steady stream of people coming through that I didn't notice when Doug, from church, sat down next to me.

"Hey, Scott. I didn't know you got your hair cut here," he said as he glanced at the *King* I was holding.

I tossed the magazine back on the table. "Yeah, my son and I come here every couple of weeks. You know how it is. Got to keep a fresh cut."

"True. Taylor is at the shop up the street getting her hair together too. Me and the wife are going to the Comedy Zone in Greensboro tonight. She keeps complaining that I don't take her anywhere. She sees me everyday at home, but evidently, that's not enough. I hope they funny, since we driving an hour and a half to see this comedian she heard about. Have you been to the Comedy Zone before?"

"No. Germani and I haven't been getting out too much lately, because of our work schedules. Not a whole lot of quality time in the evenings."

Doug opened a folder and pulled out a flyer. "I don't know if you heard the church announcement, but we're starting services for Angel Food Ministries next weekend. We are desperately in need of volunteers if you can spare a couple of hours on that Saturday morning."

I was hesitant. "I don't know. It's not going to be an all-day thing is it?"

I didn't want to get locked into an ongoing obligation that I knew I wouldn't commit to. I knew some of those people who spent every day of the week doing church stuff. That wasn't my type of thing.

"No. We are just trying to increase our community support.

Let people know about the positive things we got going on at the church. I think Pastor Mackenzie is expanding outreach for the Church Without Walls programs. We don't have enough men representing the good things we are capable of doing. Let the media tell it, black men aren't doing anything positive. We can't let that continue to be the perception. The children's center will be open if you want to bring your son." Doug smiled as he gestured toward Elijah, who was almost finished.

I took the flyer from him. Volunteering for one Saturday sounded doable. I made the schedule at work, so I could take that day off and Germani could probably go with me to lend a hand. "I'll be there. What time we need to be at the church?"

Doug gave me all the details.

A couple of hours at church couldn't be all that bad, now could it?

king about the military made me think
Daddy as well. I wondered where we'd be
dy were here. The longing never left me.
ys hear people say boys need fathers, but
do too. I had only a few significant times
my father that I could recall. For two years,
y was stationed in Colorado Springs when
were able to enjoy him like never before.
's where I gained my most memorable expe-
ce with my father.

was seven years old. A city surrounded with
ding cliffs and picturesque mountains pock-
d in crisp clean air, we snow sled in the winter
d went swimming in the warm months. On
e coldest days, I often fell asleep on a recliner
uggled up with Daddy next to the roaring
place. Daddy had taken a position as a Mili-
ry Recruiter so he could come home at night.
e loved us, but he was never happy doing that
rt of job. The thrill of foreign land and chal-
nging assignments lured him back into Special
rces.

My fore long memories froze the expression
a my face. I caught myself staring across the
om at an eight by ten brass polished frame
ith the picture of a youthful, but stern William
eckford in his uniform with his radiant bride
sed at his side under an archway. The pho-

CHAPTER FIFTEEN

GERMANI

Momma called me over to look through some
kids' clothes she picked up at the Salvation
Army. I had already created three piles. The 'yes'
pile, the 'absolutely not' pile and a hill of clothes
that were in good condition, but not adequate for
my son. Her bedroom was a nice size space, but
she had it cluttered with things she didn't need.
An old record player that hadn't worked since
1975, hat boxes stacked underneath the bed and
in two corners of the room, and a portable ward-
robe closet full of her church coats and dresses,
that wouldn't fit into her regular already overstuffed closet, took up the whole wall next to her
Bombay dresser and mirror.

Thin streaks of gray were beginning to show
through the hard green rollers of her black hair
rinse as she leaned over me to grab something.
Momma didn't like to go to the hair salon; in-

stead, once every two weeks, she would press and curl her own hair. She also had a cabinet full of Dark and Lovely jet black hair color products she used.

"What's wrong with this?" Momma asked as she held up a gray overall set. The white shirt attached had little dancing panda bears covering the ribbed material. She couldn't just let me pick out what I liked; she had to rummage through all the discards.

"Maybe you didn't notice the awkward shaped hole in the buttock." I took the outfit from her hands and showed her the gaping hole.

"Oh, child, that's nothing some thread and a needle won't fix. The outfit only cost me fifty cents and it's good material for the winter months. Didn't I buy you a sewing kit?"

She knew I didn't like craft projects, especially ones that required me to stitch something without the aid of a sewing machine.

I stuck three fingers through the hole and waved at my mom. "Yes, mother, I still have the sewing kit at home. It's going to take more than thread and a needle to get me to put this on Elijah." I threw the overalls back into the absolutely not pile where they landed atop a pair of faded navy blue corduroys.

"I'll sew it myself. You ju times." Momma grabbed th the discarded pile again. H air like she was too through you add up all the money you and Kid's Depot in compariso the thrift store, you would see I wasting. The clothes you buy are ger after you wear them once."

I endured the same lecture re like clock work. She would find s thought was ideal for Elijah, I'd rej tion and she'd go on a tangent abou ing habits. My respect ranked too her to mind her business. Instead, I skilled enough to listen and tune her same time. She had bought so many cl discount stores over the years, that I had room for them. It just meant that I the clothes I didn't want at a later date.

My mother wasn't broke, she was fruga came slow after dad went missing. She'd pennies ever since they brought that A flag in place of Daddy. The military comp for my father's honor couldn't cover all From her job on base as a civilian office Momma scraped money together for us tain.

Thir
about
if Dad
I alwa
girls
with
Dad
we v
That
rien

I
win
ete
an
th
sr
fi
ta
H
s
le
F

o
r
w
B
p

tographer's powder blue background didn't do justice to the glowing couple.

"I still miss him too," mom said, reaching into my thoughts.

My father was a Senior Master Sergeant in the United States Air Force on special assignment in the Hashemite Kingdom of Jordan. Reportedly, his plane disappeared in the desert on route to Sinai. The radar picked up no sign of the aircraft. Eight crew members and the pilot were missing. Daddy wasn't coming home.

"Do you think Daddy would have liked being a granddaddy?" I asked as I stuffed the discarded pile of clothing back into a white tall kitchen bag and looked at Elijah rolling his toy truck around on the carpet.

"I'm sure that he would have loved being a granddaddy. He would have loved all three little ones, regardless of whether they were his own. Now that Camry, I don't think he'd be as devilish as he is now if William were alive. The other day, I came out of the bathroom and I heard him cuss at Lexus. Nearly burned my ears right off my head. They were playing in the TV room and Lexus was screaming, 'Stop, Cam-Cam.' I guess she and Camry were tug-a-warring over some toy.

"I got to the room right when he called her the "B" word and demanded she give him his toy. Then I witnessed him snatch the thing out of her hand. I tore his little behind up and made him gargle his filthy mouth out with undiluted vinegar. And yes, I know I taught you and Mekhi to never hit kids while you mad, but that great-nephew of mine is going to have me catch a child abuse case." She whispered the last part of the sentence so that Elijah wouldn't hear.

"Oh, Mom." My mouth dropped open. "He gets it from his parents. If Mekhi hadn't called Mishelle that word, Camry would never have known the word existed. Or he may have known what the word was, but he wouldn't be able to get away with using it. Cussing is a regular activity over in their home."

"Don't get me started on that. I'm just glad that Mekhi changed his vocabulary and attitude when he came from prison." Momma pointed her finger at me and exclaimed, "I'll tell you what, if Mekhi and Mishelle don't get a grip on that little boy right now, they are going to have heck to pay when he's older. Your daddy would have had that child strictly disciplined. Camry would have been scared to talk without being told, let alone cuss. Y'all knew better. Lord knows I wished he were here." Mom's voice seemed to wail as anguish covered her face and she waved one hand in the air with closed eyes.

Elijah stopped playing with his truck and looked up at Momma like she'd lost her mind. I shuffled through the other clothes on her bed to keep the evening from becoming a crying fest.

"Whew. I had to get that out. I reconciled long ago that God must have had reason to take my William away, but when I've seen his brother deteriorate from multiple sclerosis, watch Mekhi on his own destructive warpath and Camry acting downright disrespectful . . ." She took a deep breath, but didn't finish her thought.

Momma stood from the bed and smiled. "Mekhi is on the right path. I guess I need patience for this situation and for my great-nephew. Camry will be all right. This family will make sure of that."

Momma tried to be the mother Mekhi no longer had and the father he didn't see.

"That reminds me, I want to take Camry and Lexus to the church carnival on Friday. Is Mekhi over at 'Shelle's, so I can see if they already have plans?" I asked.

"No, he only goes over there to pick up the kids. He's in the room." Momma gestured toward the room across the hall. She checked the time on her nightstand. "Has a foul mood too.

'Shelle probably said something to get under his skin. I don't say nothing to him when he gets reclusive. You can go talk to him if you want. It's time for *Deal or no Deal*."

The world stopped on its axis when her show came on. No matter what was going on around her, she was going to watch the bald headed Howie Mandel. The apparition of winning a million dollars made tangible.

"Mom, can you get Elijah some juice and take him into the living room with you?"

She grinned at my little man and held her hand out. "Come on, baby, let's go get us a quick snack."

I went across the hall as they walked toward the kitchen. I knocked, but Mekhi didn't answer. Instead of knocking louder, I let myself into the room. Mekhi lay on a weight bench in the corner of the bedroom. His arms were in mid lift of a set of dumbbells.

"Can I come in?" I asked as I eased the door closed.

"I don't care." His tenor voice grunted as he brought the weights back down to his chest.

"Having a rough day?"

"A little like."

"'Shelle?"

"'Shelle," he confirmed dryly.

I didn't want to ask what happened because it was usually the same story on a different day. Mishelle pissed Mekhi off. Mekhi clicked out on Mishelle. Or visa versa. The attitudes would be gone by morning and they'd be blissfully re-united all over again.

"We're having a carnival at the church on August tenth. Do you think that Camry and Lexus can come with me? I'm sure they will have a fun time. Last year, I took Elijah, but he was too little to really appreciate it. I think the clowns scared him."

"They don't live over there anymore. Mishelle moved out yesterday." He sounded like he didn't have any say in the decision.

Mishelle's parents had bought that house for below market value when Camry was born. It was a foreclosure property the bank was desperate to get rid of. When Mishelle applied for the housing voucher program, her parents received a Section 8 check for rent and gave her half the money back for living expenses. Her rent was less than my phone bill. Due to her having a different last name than her mother and stepfather, she was able to get away with the arrangement. I was surprised that she was leaving her nice little set up. "Where did she move to?"

Mishelle had only put him out two weeks ago. I didn't know how she could have planned to move so quickly.

"She moved in with some cat she barely knows. Said she met him at the Groove Club a few months back. I have limited knowledge about the cat and she's got my kids in the house of some stranger blowing promises in her ear."

I didn't know if I was relieved, shocked or disgusted. They had been on the bad side of love for so long that I didn't expect for it to change. Even when Mekhi was locked up, Mishelle was there to visit him every weekend. Mishelle had unexpectedly moved on awfully fast.

Mekhi sucked on his teeth. "Talking about she finally got a real man. She knows that stuff gets to me. I've been spending every day since they opened that prison gate trying to get it right. Trying to make up for all the wrongs. I haven't hit her one time. As bad as I've wanted to, I've kept control of myself. And she dogs me. What am I supposed to do with that?"

I could feel vibrations on the floor as he dropped the weights on the rack above his head. He grabbed a towel and wiped the sweat from his brow.

I sighed as I searched for my tact. Needed to speak with an unbiased view, but I couldn't.

"You're trying to stay in the wrong place with the wrong woman." I let the words fall from my lips, knowing he wouldn't be receptive.

Mishelle wasn't the problem. Mekhi not letting go was.

"She said since I couldn't take care of my children, maybe I need to relinquish my parental rights. I'm a man, Germani. I have no problem hustling to take care of mine. Before I got these aggravated assault charges on my record, I had no problem getting a job. 'Shelle was deep in my corner when I kept money in her pocket. Then I hit a bad stroke of luck with this criminal record, and she has no love at all. Nags me when I'm there and complains when I'm not. Now she's trying to use the kids like they pawns. All I want to do is be there for my family."

"You can't make her want you. Camry and Lexus will be your family whether Mishelle is your woman or not."

"It won't last. We're still in love with each other. Eventually, 'Shelle and I will be back together," Mekhi said confidently.

I didn't say anything else. My cousin was so far gone over Mishelle that he couldn't think straight. Whether he acknowledged it or not, I had an irksome feeling that things were bound to get worse with their situation.

CHAPTER SIXTEEN

SCOTT

My employee from work, Torrance, called me this morning at home. He needed a ride to work; said his car wouldn't start. He thought it was the battery, but his cousin had already tried to jump it and the engine still wouldn't turn over. I told him that he could use one of the mechanics we worked with to take a look at it, but he said he already had somebody to work on it.

I pulled up to the address in Charlotte's housing project off Tryon. I had his house number on a slip of paper I ripped off an envelope. I thought I had passed his address and slowed down in search for his number.

A flash of red passed by my eyes as I looked up from the paper. Suddenly, a crunching sound exploded under my tires. My wheels screeched to a halt. I didn't know if I should put the car in reverse and see what I had run over or stay still.

My tongue felt like paste. I jumped from the car and ran in front of my vehicle to check and see what damage was done.

Two small children were nearby. There was a turned over tricycle on the ground. A little boy, that looked to be about two years old, lay beside it. The other, a girl with two long ponytails dangling on each side of her face, who looked to be in kindergarten, had her arm wrapped around the little boy's arm as she picked him up from the ground.

"Is he okay?" I asked the little girl about the whimpering boy. A steady line of tears flowed from his eyes, skin darkened by his flushed face.

Oh my God; did I hit him without realizing it?

"He fell," the little girl told me as she consoled the boy, who must have been her brother.

A sigh of relief escaped me as I saw that my car was at least two feet from where the bike lay with a crushed two-liter Sun-drop plastic bottle beneath the wheel.

"Dominic, knee hurt?" she asked as we noticed his skinned leg. The boy stood up and walked with a limp.

I set the bike upright then held my arms out to see if he would let me pick him up. The little boy reached up to touch my outstretched hand and I lifted his lightweight compact body into my arms.

His sister stared at me with doe eyes. A cross between suspicion and uncertainty played on her chubby face as she eyed me up and down.

I held my free hand out for her to grasp, but she simply stared at it like I had fungus growing.

"My momma told me that we're not supposed to talk to strangers." Her voice was loud and clear as she watched me.

I searched the area for a distracted parent. An elderly woman sat in a lawn chair placed in front of her door. Her gaze followed me as I stepped over a small patch of grass between the parking lot and the sidewalk. Five teenage boys bumped against each other as they threw a basketball around a makeshift hoop and court.

"Where's your momma at?" I stopped on the sidewalk and sought direction from the little girl.

Her index finger pointed at the apartment three doors down. I looked back at my awkwardly parked car and hoped a police officer didn't come by and give me a citation while I took the children to their mother. Between my front end and the bumper of my car, I was blocking three other vehicles. I had to make it quick.

The little girl opened her front door and trotted in. I stood at the door, the screen slapped against my backside. Dominic, as she called him, remained in my arm. Dry streaks of tears covered light brown skin. He looked comfortable, so I let him stay where he was. I also felt guilty that the little man had hurt his leg.

A woman with black, naturally curly hair pulled back into a clip, high cheek bones, full pouty lips, green eyes and skin the color of smooth sandstone stomped toward me with an angry scowl. She was so fine I had to stop myself from staring.

"Who are you and what are you doing in my house? With my child?" she demanded. The glare of a protective woman slammed into me as she snatched her son from my arms. The little girl crept up behind her and peeked at me.

I automatically stiffened.

All I could do was defend my reason for being there. "I almost hit your son. I was driving down the lot." I paused. "I was looking for an address when your son and daughter came from behind a parked car on their bicycles right past my car. Fortunately, I was able to stop in time, but—" I held my hand up and out. I tilted my head letting my body language tell her that stuff like that got kids run over.

Her angry glare went from me to Dominic and the sister I had no name for. Her attention set on her daughter. "You know I told you to stay on the sidewalk. All I asked was for you to watch your

lidn't know where you were.
e an Amber Alert put out on
l the seat tilted back with one
the steering wheel like it was

loing?" I pointed to his com-
a my seat.
r whip?" Torrance asked with-
ng to budge.
I opened the driver's side door
rrance to move from my seat
r side of the car. Lisa stood in
waved at me like we were old

ed Lisa go back into her home.
le. "So that's why you had the
you running something over
it with the sexiest thing on the
nodded his head without wait-
firm or deny. He seemed to be

the street. "It's not what you
married."
ed out his lips. He didn't be-
ody tryna holla at her fine self.
from Cuba. Is it true? Cuban
cinky kinda loving."

brother for a little while. What were you doing in the middle of the parking lot? You . . . know . . . better." She verbally chastised her daughter as she jotted her index finger at the child. "Do you realize how dangerous that is? You know better than that, don't you? Don't you? Answer me, Cheyenne."

Cheyenne quickly shook her head as tears spilled and her lips quivered. "Yes," her small voice said.

The air seemed to thicken.

"Stop all that crying and go to your room. Stay there until I come get you." Her voice roared as she held Dominic against her chest. He had begun to cry again.

I knew I needed to get out of there.

"I'm not sure what you were doing while they were outside, but . . . um . . . they really need an adult to supervise them. You can't expect children as young as yours to be responsible. Maybe you can entrust one of your neighbors to look out for them when you're busy," I advised.

She rocked as she talked. "I don't trust everybody with my kids. Besides, Cheyenne is not your average six-year-old. She is smart enough to know right from wrong."

People took too much for granted. Assumed safety was an automatic. If somebody snatched up both of those kids, she would feel differently.

Unsupervised children went missing all the time. I guess my face must have said something because she went hard on the defensive.

"Don't look at me like that. I am a good mother. I take care of my kids. You come in here trying to tell me how to parent and you don't know a thing about me. While you talking, you probably have a bunch of your own kids you're not taking care of. You can't judge me."

"Whoa, lady, all I wanted to do was let you know what was going on with your kids. I'm sorry if you took it the wrong way." I started walking toward the door. I wasn't expecting all the angry commentary when I stepped in, and was definitely ready to go by then.

Her emotions changed yet again, from anger to guilt. Women kill me with that.

She said before I touched the doorknob, "My name is Lisa. I was only busy for a minute. I tried to put together her bedroom unit and didn't want the kids running back and forth through the room. I should have waited until they went to bed to complete the chifferobe."

She seemed more like an overwhelmed mother instead of an unfit parent. Something inside urged me to lend a hand. I didn't know why. I couldn't explain it. I guess I felt sorry for her. Thought about my sister and what Beverly had to go through as a single mother.

"I'm
obe tog
Her
"It w
evening
do the j
She
"I don't
thing. V
"Noth
I would
wife und
Just a
car horn
"I did
hicles in
"I got to
She p
lowed m
"No st
to decide
"No st
and glan
was park
Torran
pressed h
fore he sa

"Scott, man,
I was about to h
you." Torrance h
hand on the top
his car.
"What are you
fortable position
"Let me get yo
out even attempt
I responded as
and waited for T
and go to the oth
her doorway and
friends.
Torrance watc
He chuckled a li
300 parked like
here. You kicking
block?" Torrance
ing for me to co
proud of me.
I drove out t
think. I'm happi
Torrance pus
lieve me. "Every
I heard she wa
women into tha

Torrance's mind stayed in the gutter.

All I could do was shake my head at the boy. "I already told you that I don't see every woman as a conquest. Lisa seems like she's going through a lot."

"I heard from Lemon, who's kicking it with a girl who works in housing, that Ms. Fine's man got busted on some Federal charges. They repossessed the house they were living in and all the furniture. They wouldn't even let her get her kids' clothes out the crib. Then they deported her man back to Mexico."

"See what I'm saying. Even if I didn't have a wife, what I look like trying to use her when she already having a hard time? Plus, she's got two kids. I don't roll like that."

Torrance ignored my point. "She's vulnerable. She should be easy booty."

"I have more respect for women than that. I grew up in a house with sisters. I would hurt a man over any one of them. Dogging women don't make you a man. That stuff ain't cool."

"You make it sound like a bad thing. If she's consenting, then it shouldn't be nothing but pleasure. Women know whassup if you holla at them."

"I can respect that she's not trying to listen to somebody who just wants to get in her panties."

Torrance rolled down the window as we passed three girls on the sidewalk. "I like them shorts you got on," he shouted out.

I could hear the girls giggle as I kept driving.

CHAPTER SEVENTEEN

GERMANI

"Mommy, can we watch *Ratatouille*?" Elijah came into the kitchen and asked.

"Do you remember which button to push?" I replied as I scraped out the hardening grits from breakfast. The children wolfed down the pancakes and country ham, but picked over the little bit of grits I had put on their plates. I thought everybody liked grits.

"Yes, ma'am"

"Okay. Go ahead."

Elijah went back into the room with Josiah, Lexus and Camry. I had the children overnight after taking them to the church carnival. Mekhi's kids had spent the night on several occasions, but it was the first time Josiah got to stay. Nicole had attachment issues and didn't trust her son with just about nobody after a recent divorce. Elijah and Josiah often played together in the toddler room at church, in which I spent two Sundays a month monitoring the children's care. I had been around Nicole enough to gain her trust. She knew I was just as protective over Elijah. Compared to the twenty to twenty-five children that were regulars in the toddler's room, watching the four was like a cake walk.

Elijah broke my concentration when he walked back into the kitchen and patted my leg while I rinsed plastic cups. "Mommy, Camry won't help me find *Ratatouille*. My movie is missing."

His eyes began to water. Camry was always being mischievous. The oldest of the bunch, he liked to be the bully.

"Is Cam in there being mean to you?" I wiped Elijah's face after drying my hand on the front of my robe.

"He won't let me watch *Ratatouille*," he repeated. "I don't like the naked people. They're making scary noises and hurting each other."

"Naked people? What naked people?" I went from the kitchen into the family room where the children lay on blanket pallets made for them the night before.

Josiah and Lexus were lying on their stomach with legs fanning the air. Camry sat up close to the television on Scott's ottoman. His cheeks were about to burst from the grin spread across his little face.

My mouth dropped as I realized what he was fixated on. Actually, the sound of sensual moaning caught me first, and then I looked at the screen. Two women and a man were performing erotic acts on each other.

I don't know which one was bigger, my mouth or my eyes as I realized what they were watching. I rushed across the room and turned the DVD Player off. The *Ratatouille* disc sat on top of the black box.

I turned to look at Camry, who was no longer smiling. "What do you think you were doing? Didn't nobody tell you to put that movie in there. I should whip your little mannish behind."

The adult movies should have been in a box on the top rack of the storage room where I had placed them to get them out of our bedroom and far out of reach from little prying hands. Yet, I knew Camry had a knack for getting into unusual places; messing with stuff he had no business touching. I couldn't figure out how he got to the box without my knowing it. Especially considering he would have to pass by me in the kitchen in order to even make it to the storage room. I was pretty certain none of the children were out of my sight for more than a few minutes this morning, and I had slept on the couch in the same room as them last night. But somehow, he got his hands on that box.

"Aunt Germani, I didn't put it in. It was already in there. I didn't want to watch *Ratatouille*. I already saw that movie at home. I wanted to watch something different." He batted his eyes innocently.

I slid the disc from the player and stared at the cover. The front of the disc read *Latina Caliente* and had to be new. I didn't recognize the title from the collection I had stored.

Scott must have recently bought and watched it. How irresponsible of him. He knew Elijah liked to watch his movies in the family room. The least Scott could have done was watch his sex flicks in our bedroom if it was that serious for him. After all, he acted like he was going to quit watching the stuff. I couldn't believe him.

Scott wasn't at home. He had gone to the pharmacy to pick up a prescription of Codeine for his niece. Beverly had called early this morning because Alexis was up all night crying in pain and there was little else they could do until the pharmacy opened at eight. I would have to address his obsession with pornography yet again, and after he told me that things would be better. Foolish me. Now I had to go tell Mishelle and Nicole how their children accidentally got a hold of a sex movie while they were supposed to be watching a cartoon. I didn't like being put in that position to explain at all.

I looked up to see all four children staring at me. I snapped the disc in two.

"What you saw was a very, very bad movie. You are to never watch anything like that again. We are all going to get dressed so I can take you home. Camry," I pointed to the bathroom around the corner, "you go first. Lexus, I'll take you upstairs with me. Josiah and Elijah, when Camry comes out of the bathroom, you two go brush your teeth. I will help you get washed up and dressed in a little bit."

As I drove the children home I rehearsed different ways to tell Mishelle and Nicole about their kids' accidental exposure to Scott's sex flicks. In one scenario, I could explain how remorseful I was about my husband's lack of discretion and they could be assured that it would never happen again. In another scenario, I could play down the incident as if they flipped past national geographic and saw some bushmen running through African fields instead of the kinky lust triangle. I knew my conscience wouldn't let me go with the second scenario, but it sounded easier to explain.

Mekhi's children lived closer to me than Nicole, whose home was going toward South Charlotte, but I dropped off Josiah first anyway. After I told Nicole about the movie being left in the video player, she hugged me and said I couldn't be held responsible for my husband's actions. She knew I was upset about it and prayed with me over the issue. I felt a little better when I left her house, but the nagging guilt lingered.

Mishelle's new residence sat in the middle of a new development off Oak Drive. When I first picked up Camry and Lexus from the brick front two-story home, I wondered if she gave up her Section 8 or had it transferred, but it wasn't my business so I didn't ask her about it.

I rationalized that maybe Mishelle wouldn't be bothered by her children watching a little nudity. She was a round-the-way kind of female. Considering that she let Camry cuss like a sailor in front of her and laughingly remarked, "Kids say the darnedest things;" or when she had Lexus hump the floor to the music video *Laffy Taffy* so her girlfriend could see her baby's dance moves. I doubted that she took offense all that easily.

After I pulled up to her house, I got out to unstrap all the children. My Cougar was loaded down with car and booster seats. I wondered how people managed more than three small children without a minivan.

"Take you and your sister's bag up to the house," I told Camry who had the small luggage on rollers between his legs in the backseat.

Camry was at the steps by the time the other kids' feet hit the pavement. In my haste to bring them home, I forgot to call and let Mishelle know that I was bringing them back early. When she opened the door in silk pajamas, she looked surprised to see us.

"Good morning," she said with a raised eyebrow, standing to the side as Camry rolled the bag inside.

Lexus trailed in on Camry's heel. Elijah stood by my side.

"Lexus, get your thumb out your mouth," Mishelle told her daughter, who was sucking away, before closing the door behind us.

"Mind if I talk with you for a moment?" I requested, still not knowing how Mishelle would respond. So often when I was around her, she was going off on Mekhi.

Mishelle looked down at Elijah. "You can go play with Camry," she told him.

He followed Camry and Lexus up the stairs.

We walked down to her living room which was adjoined to an eating area where her boyfriend, Cyrus, was drinking from a mug while he read a newspaper on a barstool.

"Uh-oh, what did Camry do?" Mishelle sat on the couch placed diagonal to the kitchen opening.

I stood by the overstuffed chair explaining what happened. "Actually, Camry wasn't the one who did something wrong. It was my husband. Scott left a little flick of his inside the DVD player and I didn't know it. The kids were supposed to watch *Ratatouille* while I cleaned up after breakfast, but it turned out that they ended up seeing something they didn't need to see."

"So my kids saw a dirty movie?" Mishelle's posture shifted. She wasn't going to make this easy.

"They only saw a little bit. As I said before, I thought a cartoon was in the player and I encourage Elijah to be independent, so I didn't think anything about it when he asked to watch his movie, because it's his favorite and we usually leave it in the DVD for him. Believe me, I feel awful about this and I don't know what Scott was thinking. Well okay, I knew what he was thinking, but it was still inappropriate. You have my deepest apologies. I guarantee that it won't happen again."

The whole time I talked, Cyrus, whom, I didn't know from a can of Dutch Boy house paint, shook his head between slurping his coffee. I only saw him in passing the other day, but up close, his features were defined. He appeared to be at least fifteen years her senior, his mustache slightly graying, forehead wrinkled; not a man I pictured with her. Mishelle's demeanor remained reserved, almost too pleasant. Nothing like I was used to with her. I could not have felt more awkward.

Mishelle looked over at Cyrus again from her position on the couch. I was certain that he gave a nod before she said, "My kids won't be going back over to your house."

When she saw how stunned I was she decided to elaborate. "Listen, Germani, I don't think you are a bad person over all, but I'm trying to make some changes in my life. Doing things for the better. And to be real honest, I thought you and your husband had different morals than that. No, let me rephrase that. I know you go to church and it seems like a contradiction."

I pulled out a chair and sat down. Even though Scott had a lapse in good judgment, I didn't expect for her to take it the way she did. It wasn't like her kids hadn't been to my house many times over without incident, and Camry could be outrageous in his behavior, but I hadn't banned him from my house. We were family.

Mishelle continued on. "No offense to you, but I'm tired of church people faking. Talking it ain't the same as walking it. You go to church just because it's the thing to do, but then you look down on people who aren't interested in being phony. I'm not raising hypocrites, and I don't want them around perpetrators confusing them about life."

I thought it was big of me to admit that my husband was at fault. Her personal assault on my religion was unnecessary. "I don't know what's up with the church bashing. I came over here to talk to you mother to mother because I didn't want you getting the wrong information if Camry or Lexus mentioned seeing naked people over at my house. I didn't want any confusion."

Cyrus set his newspaper down while he gave complete attention to our conversation.

"It's nothing new that I don't go to some uniform fellowship, but I do watch the news. I see priests molesting little boys." Mishelle started jabbing the counter with her fingers. "Then you have those mega church pastors soliciting their members to fund their personal planes and multi-million dollar mansions. Explain to me how a church leader can afford thousand dollar suits, but most of his members are living raggedy. We were just talking about that last night. What did you call it?" she asked Cyrus.

Cyrus answered, "Hyped up emotionalism. The feel good services."

So Mishelle finally found somebody that thought like her.

"Yeah, that's it . . . playing off people's troubles," she stated.

He got off the barstool, placed his mug in the sink and walked past us saying, "I'm going to Home Depot before it gets too crowded." He seemed to want to leave rather quickly and probably didn't want to be a part of our conversation.

She waved at him before finishing her talk with me. "Case in point, Mekhi came over here talking about he was going to enroll in the Minister-in-Training program at your mom's church. Like I was supposed to be impressed. I don't know who he thinks he's fooling with the way he used to smack me upside my head." She threw back her head and laughed like his efforts to get his life right was the best joke she ever heard. She wiped a tear from her eye, her chest heaved as if she was trying to keep from cackling again. "The only reason he's trying to be all holy is so that he can pimp the church. Mekhi hasn't had a job since Lexus was born. He doesn't want to work. I'm so glad we're through."

She made him sound terrible, like she wasn't dishing out slaps, kicks and punches, as much as she was taking it. There were plenty of times that Mishelle was the one going upside Mekhi's head too. Couldn't neither one of them call themselves a victim. I had no idea that Mekhi was thinking about joining a ministry, but I thought it was a great idea.

I needed to get out of her house before I said something I regretted. "I'm happy you broke up too. If you don't want your kids at my house, then that's your business. I know I've taken good care of Camry and Lexus. I guess I will have to see them when their father has them."

"Oh, they won't be seeing him either. Even if I have to take out another restraining order to keep him from here. Cyrus and I are going to get married and I plan on petitioning the courts to have Mekhi's paternal rights terminated. He's not bringing anything to the table to be calling himself Daddy. Cyrus wants to take care of me. My man will adopt Camry and Lexus. Give them his last name. He would make a great father to them," Mishelle said boisterously.

They barely knew enough about each other to be taking the relationship seriously, yet Mishelle was talking about marriage. I wondered if Cyrus knew about all her plans.

Instead of saying anything else, I walked back toward the stairs and called out to Elijah that it was time to go.

"I don't want you to take this decision personal. I have to look out for my family and get rid of bad influences." Mishelle crossed her arms over her chest.

Elijah must not have heard me calling him. I went upstairs to get my child, blocking out the rest of her conversation before she ticked me off.

Of all the things Mishelle had said, only one stuck out in my mind as I put Elijah back into his car seat. *"Talking it ain't walking it."* My Christianity meant something special, and if Scott and I wanted to eliminate some of the temptation and frustration in our lives, we would have to spend more time walking in our blessing. I would need to do everything necessary to get Scott to understand.

CHAPTER EIGHTEEN

SCOTT

Germani hit me in the chest with a Bible as I entered the living room.

"What's this for?" I asked, holding the leather bound book in my hand.

"I think we need to do more Bible study and there's no better time than the present."

"For what? I just walked in the house. And since when did we start needing Bible study at home? That's what Wednesday night service is for." I might not make it there every week like her because of my work schedule, but I did go. She didn't used to be so argumentative or demanding. It was a new thing. A new thing I didn't like and didn't know if I would get used to. "What is going on with you lately? You keep changing things around here without discussing them with me first."

I didn't want to read my Bible, I wanted to sit down and chill for a little while. Alexis had cried the entire time I was over at Beverly's house. It took two hours for the Codeine to take effect and put her to sleep. She wouldn't let me leave her side and I was worried about her having another seizure. Her mother couldn't handle her when that disease was at its worst.

"Have a seat. Let's talk," Germani said, patting the cushion next to her. A pink leather bound Bible rested in her lap. "You already know that I have been reading a scripture a day for life application and I think I'm getting better in my Christian walk, but some stuff got me to thinking maybe this should be a family affair."

Elijah sat at a little blue table set we had in the family room. Even his thick children's Bible was open as it leaned against his ten-piece robot collection.

I eased onto the couch, wondering what had caused the new revelation.

"You know, Scott, I'm teaching Elijah that if he buries God in his heart at an early age, then maybe he won't have many battles with trials and tribulations as an adult. In order for that to happen, he must understand the difference between light and darkness. Tell Daddy what verse you read," Germani instructed Elijah.

"E-feet-some five." He grinned showing all his front baby teeth.

"Good job, Elijah," she said as she picked up her Bible and opened it to a marked page. "Ephesians, chapter five, verses eight through thirteen. *For you were once darkness, but now you are light in the Lord. Walk as children of light, for the fruit of the Spirit is in all goodness, righteousness and truth. Finding out what is acceptable to the Lord.*" She paused, turning the page. "And this is the most important part of this passage. *Have no fellowship with the unfruitful works of darkness, but rather expose them. For it is shameful even to speak of those things which are done by them in secret.*" She closed the Bible, stood up and stared at Elijah. "Scott, once something is exposed, a manifestation occurs. What is hidden becomes magnified by light. Dirt can't bury itself in the sun."

She went from staring at Elijah to watching me. Her mouth clinched into an angered perch.

I wanted her to get to the point. "Are you mad at me about something?"

Germani folded her arms and continued staring at me with a blank face. "Mad wouldn't be the word to describe me right now."

"You want to tell me what's going on?" I unlaced my shoes so I could get comfortable.

Germani dropped a broken CD on the couch next to me. "You left your movie in the DVD player and the kids got a hold of it. They watched a nice portion of it too."

I had forgotten all about that movie. "*Latina Caliente*. Who broke my movie?"

She groaned before shaking her head. "You don't care about nothing I just said, do you? The kids watched your movie."

Elijah stared at us with wide eyes as he clashed two robotic toys together.

"Little man, go to your room for a minute. I want to talk with your momma," I told my son. I waited for him to gather his robots and leave the room before I said anything else. If there was going to be a scene, Elijah wasn't going to be a part of it.

"Of course, I care. I didn't purposely leave the flick in there." I picked up the two jaded pieces of my movie. "I'm human. I made a mistake."

"I thought you said that we wouldn't be doing the porn thing anymore. You're not living up to your part of the deal. You haven't given up porn at all. How are we going to get better if you keep doing the same ole thing? Do you know that Camry and Lexus can't come over anymore behind you watching a sick flick? Mishelle thinks we are bad influences on her children. She said that we are church faking and she didn't want her children confused by mixed messages of phony people. Scott, we are supposed to set the standard. If people can't see God through us, then we aren't living right."

Since when did she begin listening to Mishelle? Mishelle couldn't talk about nobody and I wouldn't waste my time talking about her. But it wasn't Mishelle's jabber that stuck out, the first part of what Germani said caught me. "Sick flick! You're talking like I was watching men having sex with animals or child pornography. They weren't sick flicks when you were watching them with me. You didn't used to complain. And in regard to Mishelle . . . all I have to say is consider the source. Don't start spewing Bible verses at me because I have a weakness." I bent down and took off my shoes.

She squinted at me before standing up. Germani reached around the side of the couch and shoved a box up next to me. "They are movies. What's so hard about giving up movies? Especially when it's affecting our marriage, our child and other people's children too."

I got up and looked inside the box. She had broken all my movies, even the VHS tapes. She was messing with me. "What did my movies do to you? You are taking it over the top now."

"Just movies. You didn't answer the question. Why can't you give them up?" Germani had her arms folded like she was trying to make me choose between her and my weakness, but she didn't understand that choosing wasn't that simple.

She didn't realize how hard it was for me to give up those movies. How I felt pulled by a strong desire and nothing else seemed to satisfy my need for gratification. It drove me crazy that I made a promise to her that I couldn't bring myself to keep. I had been frustrated that I couldn't rise to the occasion when we did try to be intimate without the video foreplay. Every time I sat at the computer desk and logged on, I wanted to stop myself. Every time I pushed a movie into the player, I told myself that it would be the last time I watched a porn flick without my wife.

There weren't words to explain it to her. "I don't know why? There's no science to it. It's a habit that I have a hard time breaking. Do you need me to call Mishelle and apologize for my evil ways?" I joked as I tried to cut some of the tension thickening in the air.

"See, now you're trying to be funny." Germani had such disappointment in her eyes that I couldn't help but feel remorseful that I left the video in the DVD player.

I stood up, pulled her toward me and wrapped my arms around her waist. "No, I just don't think it's as big a deal as you are making it into. Besides, when I watch those movies I'm thinking of you. Wishing we were doing some of those things."

She removed my hands from around her waist and hissed. "*Latina Caliente* . . . Don't insult my intelligence. I'm not Mexican and I don't do threesomes. You could not be thinking about me. Guess you married into the wrong ethnic group."

I had enough with the dramatizing. "If I wanted a Mexican wife, I would have married a Mexican woman. *Latina Caliente* is a movie."

"Scott, I'm trying real hard to be a supportive spouse, but you aren't making this easy." Germani took the broken disk still sitting on the couch and tossed it in the box. "All I'm saying is we need to do better for ourselves and our son. He shouldn't even know what porn is."

"I got what you're saying. I promise you it won't happen again. Now, let it go."

"Fine. I'll let it go."

She said it, but I didn't believe her.

CHAPTER NINETEEN

GERMANI

"Has anybody seen the pre-registration sheets?" I shouted out as I searched the community room where eight volunteers went setting up the space for food distribution. Our church was a new host site and was assigned to Angel Food Ministries duty for the first time, in which we gave out boxes of pre-packed meals that were ordered and paid for by families within the community. The organization was national and offered economical prices, especially for those on low or fixed incomes.

Scott and I bought the meals ourselves because of the inexpensive cost and had already placed the box in the trunk of his car.

"I saw the list taped to the top of a box in the storage room," the church coordinator, Harmony, said as she and some of the other members of Deliverance Temple organized the area.

Taylor, Cliff and Doug pulled rectangular tables from the wall and set them up side by side.

I walked toward the refrigerated storage room to grab the sheet. We were opening the doors in less than an hour, and I didn't want to be unprepared. Nobody could get their food until I verified what they had ordered.

Scott and Jose walked past me in the church hallway. Jose was a short Mexican with brown skin and straight short black hair. They were carrying two boxes each and I stopped them momentarily.

While holding a door open for them, I looked on top of the box Scott held. "You guys don't have a sheet of paper on either of your boxes, do you?"

"No. What are you looking for?" Scott asked, shifting the weight of the box as he locked his fingers underneath it.

"Pre-registration sheet with the list of names on it," I responded as I walked around them.

"I thought I saw a paper on one of the boxes I already set in the community room," Jose said as he paused in the doorway.

"That might have been the shipping order. I saw that in there. Don't worry about it. I will find it." I checked my watch and hurried on.

I shivered as I stepped into the cold freezer area. Seven boxes were stacked in the middle of the room. I placed each one on the floor until I got to the fifth box. Ripping the tape off, I removed the sheets. I could hear footsteps approaching.

"Scott, when are you going to let me take you down on the court? Doug asked my husband as they came into the freezer to retrieve the last boxes.

"Yeah, Scott, we never see you outside these church walls. What's up with that?" Jose asked as he picked up the box I had ripped the tag off of and stacked it on top of another box to carry.

Scott's eyes fell on me. "Well, you know . . . me and the wife have family obligations."

I interjected as I shook my head while again holding the door open for the men before leaving the cold room. "Oh no, don't put me into that. I am not a ball and chain type of wife. You are free to hang out with these fellas anytime you choose."

In fact, I would be overjoyed if Scott spent more time with other Christians. Maybe a change in associations would improve our relationship. Scott sometimes acted like befriending someone new would be a betrayal to Damon.

"See. You can't use your wife as an excuse," Doug said as they all walked in front of me back to the community room.

"Yeah, man, stop acting like we stink or something," Jose remarked jokingly. "We get together and have a lot of fun."

Scott said, "I'll see what I can do. Do you have a game planned soon?"

Ahmad piped in, "I'm having a fellowship barbecue at my house next Saturday if you want to come by. We try to do something once or twice a month. It's always something different. Bowling, fishing or whatever."

"These brothas keep me in line, because I was acting a fool before I got connected. Ain't that right, Taylor?" Doug pulled on the hem of his wife's blue T-shirt.

"Yeah, it was pretty bad. We were at divorce's door and I was ready to kick it down. I had already separated our bank accounts and paid down my credit cards. If he hadn't stopped 'acting a fool,' like he said, I was prepared to get out of the marriage with minimal combined debt." Taylor pushed back a chair to sit in.

I glanced at Taylor in her candid description of her plan to leave Doug. As bad as things were getting between Scott and me, I hoped I never got to the point I'd have to secretly plot to leave the relationship.

Jose said, "You didn't tell us about all that, but I could feel the tension rolling off of you when you started coming to men's fellowship. Things must have been real bad in your home if Taylor was about to divorce you."

Doug shrugged as he leaned against a table. "She was well within her rights. I wanted to be married and single at the same time. I straddled the fence. I needed to change my focus."

"Being married is hard enough, but being a married Christian is seriously extra hard work. People assume we have fewer problems because we're saved," Ahmad stated. He and his wife were veterans of the group, being married for twenty-three years.

"I wouldn't even have y'all in my business if it wasn't a testimony to how good my God is. He brought these men into our lives right on time."

Jose spoke as he sat facing the back end of a chair. "I may not be married, but I still look forward to the stress relief of good male fun. Working for airport security will make anybody go crazy if they don't have a grounding source. This man was going to fight me because I told him to take his shoes off and put them on the conveyor belt. I was sure he was cursing me out in French, literally. He was screaming *'L'idiot viole mes droits.'* The only thing I understood was the word idiot. That word is universal. After we took him back for a strip search because he refused to remove those shoes, we had to call a translator over before I took his insults personally."

"What was up with that? Everybody has to be prepared to take off their shoes for airport security," Scott balked as he came and stood next to me.

"Evidently not over there in Marseille. Foreign airports must be letting anybody on a plane. That man thought we were trying to keep his shoes. Why would we want to keep his shoes? People are mental," Jose said as he frowned.

"What does *l'idiot viole mes droits* mean?" Taylor asked. She mouthed the words to herself as if she were trying to memorize them while she waited for Jose's response.

"The idiot violates my rights," Jose said as if the entire incident was beyond his understanding.

"The idiot violates my rights," I said. "They were just shoes. You would think he was asked to strip down naked."

Taylor, Doug, Ahmad and Scott all nodded their heads in agreement.

"Different culture means different value system," Ahmad stated.

Ahmad's son, Quinn, a tall lanky young man, cocoa brown with acne spots covering his face, came into the community room. "We should probably open the doors. It's starting to rain out there and I saw a lot of people standing by the door waiting to get in here."

"And they say black people don't know how to be on time for anything," Doug remarked as we all began to stand in preparation for the crowd to filter the community room.

For the next several hours, we stayed busy in spurts. I kept track of who needed what. There seemed to be either a line full of people, or no one at all waiting to get their box of goods or school supplies as they prepared for the new semester, two weeks away, at the end of August. We talked amongst ourselves during the lag time and tried to keep busy to make time go quicker.

By two-thirty in the afternoon, only a few names remained on the pre-registration list for the Angel food boxes. We still had several containers full of donated back packs, pencils, notebooks and pens. I took items from an almost empty bin and tossed them into a full container.

Scott came and sat next to me after taking several boxes of food and school supplies to a family of seven. The mother had a set of twins that were five years old and four other children younger than the twins. They were four, three, two and eight months of age. The mother looked tired even though the children were well behaved. The children walked together, handin-hand, wearing matching blue jean Osh Gosh short sets as she pushed a stroller.

I had to exhale on her behalf at the thought of that responsibility. Elijah was enough work; multiply his need times six and you have me sitting in the city psych ward waiting for my daily medication.

"Baby, if I ever ask for more kids, you have my permission to slap me dead in my mouth." Scott huffed as if he had just run track in the Olympics.

"Wow, dead in the mouth, huh? I don't think I've ever heard you talk like that, Mr. Wilson." I put my fingers to my lips in fake shock.

"Probably because you haven't, Mrs. Wilson." He leaned back in the chair and stretched his legs. His expression was one of horror. "I don't never, ever, ever want my own self-made baseball, basketball or hockey team. That's more responsibility than I can handle."

"Oh, come on. You want a few more children." I poked at his side.

"No, can't say that I do. One is plenty." He poked me back in the ribs as I playfully pushed his hands away.

"Mommy. Mommy, that's Mr. Scott from over at our house," a little voice squealed.

I turned to see a beautiful little girl with long French braids standing at our table. Hazel eyes stared at me. Right between her was an adult version of herself and next to the little girl stood a toddler. His 49er's basketball cap swallowed his small head. I didn't recognize any of them. I was surprised that they knew Scott. I wondered when he had been at their house, and more importantly, why.

"Hey, Cheyenne." Scott leaned forward in his chair and grinned.

Curiosity had my interest piqued. A look crossed his face of glee mixed with familiarity and I didn't like it. I didn't like it in the least.

"What are you doing here?" he asked the child's mother as his voice seemed to change octaves, soften slightly.

"I came to pick up school supplies for Cheyenne. She's going to the second grade at Shamrock Gardens Elementary. That's a magnet school. You know this is her first year there since we moved from Yonkers." The mother had a tinge of rouge as white even teeth appeared. She was blushing at my husband.

I waited for an introduction, be it formal, informal, or even respectably polite. Their eyes stayed fixated on each other as they made conversation. It didn't feel like casual acquaintances struck by happenstance.

I waited . . . and waited . . . and . . . waited.

"Excuse me," I exclaimed in irritation by Scott's rudeness. "I'm Germani, Scott's wife, and you are?"

She took my hand and I wasn't sure if it was an attempt at maintenance of pleasantries or a nemesis challenge, as if she were saying "I know your husband just as well as you do, now what?"

"Oh, I'm sorry. I didn't mean to be rude. My name is Lisa. Lisa Guarillo."

Scott finally decided to acknowledge my presence. "Lisa, uh, this is my wife, Germani. The one I told you about."

I believe she heard me say I was his wife. It was unnecessary for him to repeat my words. The fumbling from his mouth bothered me just as much as knowing he was in some strange woman's home recently and he didn't tell me.

"Are you set up for Angel Food Ministries?" he asked Lisa as he rolled his fingers down the pre-registration list in search for her name.

Lisa frowned with confusion as she scrunched her eyebrows. "Never heard of Angel Food Ministries. What is it exactly?" She glanced at the sheet he had his hand on.

"Well, it's too late to order anything for August and we don't have any flyers left to explain the dates or menu selection for September, but for twenty-five dollars you get a huge box of food that should last awhile. For example, this month we had four pounds of leg quarters, a pound of ground beef, a pound of ground turkey, a bag of chicken tenders, some pork chops, smoked sausage, seasoned potatoes, green beans, baby carrots . . . Ummm, what am I forgetting?" Scott looked at me for answers.

I was too miffed to speak, so I just looked back at him like I didn't know what he was talking about.

"Of yeah, rice, pinto beans, onions, waffles and some dessert stuff." He was pleased with his memory.

I listened to Scott sounding like a salesman at a discount food store and wondered what other information he was holding out on me. How come certain knowledge escaped me; bypassed my view like a broke down minivan on Hwy 601.

Maybe he found somebody to do the things I no longer chose to do. Perhaps he decided my spiritual renewal was an insult to his sexual libido; one in which my role as wife wasn't nearly as valuable as I presumed. Husbands cheat for far less. I read somewhere that more than half the men who attend church creep out on their wives. Although statistics aren't always reliable, those numbers were still staggering.

It didn't say much for the sanctity of marital vows or family union. God's plan for His people gone awry. Skeletons in closets wearing gold crosses. Dirty business kept on the hush.

My thoughts must have distracted me for a while because Ms. Lisa and her two children had walked away. They were headed toward the exit doors when I snapped back into reality.

Scott was no longer sitting at my side. I looked around to see him breaking a table down with Ahmad.

I wondered if it would be crass for me to chase after her and ask what the nature of her relationship with my husband was, whether currently or previously.

The Holy Spirit had to hold me in my seat as the desire for answers gained strength. Momentum rushed through me like a surge of adrenalin during a fifty-yard dash. I wanted to say something so bad to Lisa that it felt as though my emotions were jumping in anticipation.

I prayed for a calm to come over me and take the ugly feeling away. I couldn't question that woman about her sex life in front of her children. That would take tacky behavior up a notch to straight ghetto. Yet, the battle was raging in me to do exactly what I shouldn't and say what I shouldn't.

I stood, and my feet moved in the direction they walked.

"Hey, Germani, can you help me take some of these supplies back to the teen center? I'm thinking that some of what's left can be given out after service," Taylor asked.

"We have a lot of kids, but I don't think we have that many." I allowed my mind to step back into a positive place.

"My sister works at Shady Oaks Elementary. I know she wouldn't mind taking some supplies off our hands. Schools can never have enough pens and paper."

"That is a good idea. I think we should do that."

We completed the task at hand and I tried to keep my mind busy, but Scott had some answers to give and they better be good.

CHAPTER TWENTY

SCOTT

Bellowing clouds dusted the sky as heavy raindrops pelted the car while we made our way down Davidson Street in the No Da District. A man with a paper bag atop his head tried to battle the elements as he waited for the light to turn green on the corner of Tirty-sixth. His teal shirt darkened in color as it absorbed water.

I paused in spite of traffic to let him run across. His hand went up as a gesture of thanks while the wilted paper bag came down. The makeshift umbrella was useless against the raging storm.

I nodded my head to acknowledge his gratitude as I began to tap the gas pedal and roll by him.

The day was purposeful. I felt like I accomplished plenty in the hours spent for community outreach. There was a sense of gratification from the event that I didn't receive selling car parts.

Which reminded me that I needed to stop by the store after I dropped Germani and Elijah off at home. I left Craig in charge, but I held the responsibility for anything that went wrong.

The previous Thursday, I called my entire staff into the store to discuss the missing inventory. They all acted baffled, perplexed or dumbfounded. The optimism of one of them admitting to the removal of parts for personal reasons or discounted from our inventory for friends or family quickly died as I surveyed their faces. Although the cash amount wasn't very large, charges could still be pursued.

It added unwanted stress to my life, not that anybody ever desired to be stressed. I had my job and integrity on the line. As a manager, I had a certain expectation for my employees; trusted their ability to do the job accurately and honestly. The coldhanded slap was that one of my staff disrespected that expectation and put all our jobs in jeopardy.

"Are you sleeping with her?"

Germani's blunt question caught me off guard, causing me to swerve onto the median, in an effort to avoid smacking the left side of a blue Dodge Neon, while I merged into traffic.

"What?" I said, agitated as the owner of the car moved into the passing lane and laid his hand on the horn.

"You heard every word that came from my mouth." Germani's attitude expanded to astronomical proportions as if she were oblivious to the accident we almost caused.

"Say what?" I didn't know why her words didn't make sense as they penetrated my brain. The implication wouldn't logically click in my head.

"You . . . her . . . intimate." Her eyes drilled into me like she was searching for some kind of admission.

"Say what?" I repeated. "No . . . better yet, who are you talking about me sleeping with besides you?" I knew the only sheets I had laid beneath in the past five years were ours. Who she thought I was sleeping with was a whole other matter.

"That woman at the church, you know, the one in the community room. I believe her name was Lisa. I also believe that you were at her house and I know that *you* didn't tell me nothing about her or being at her house before this afternoon when I met her myself. So stop acting clueless and tell me whether she's your lover, or ex-girlfriend or whatever."

"You are trippin'. Since when did you stop trusting me?" I asked Germani as I soaked in her disposition. I glanced back at a sleeping Elijah. His head was bent to the side, mouth wide open.

His little body secured by a booster seat. I was glad he couldn't hear the conversation.

"Since when did you give me reason to not trust you?" Germani countered.

"I am not nor have I ever slept with Lisa. I don't know her like that at all," I stated as calmly as I could. Germani was acting emotional. The gestures, remarks and attitude challenged my ability to react reasonably.

"So you don't know her well?"

"No."

"What were you doing at her house?"

"Putting together her daughter's chifferobe."

Germani spoke in a condescending voice as she squinted at me. "How sweet of you, offering a helping hand to put furniture together for a stranger; mind you, a beautiful woman, but a stranger nonetheless."

"Don't patronize me, Germani. I almost ran one of her kids over while I was picking up Torrance. They were outside by themselves and I just wanted to make sure they got home safely. We talked and I realized the reason she wasn't out with the children was because she was trying to assemble the chifferobe by herself. I offered to help. That's it." Justification shouldn't have been necessary.

"Oh, really?" Germani's eyes became oval slivers.

"Yes, really. If you don't believe me, then that's on you, but I can assure you that I have never nor will I ever sleep with Lisa," I replied.

I made my way down Tryon past a Compare Foods store. A man with tousled black hair and wrinkled clothes carrying a 'Will Work for Food' sign limped up and down the sidewalk. The rain had ceased and left a wet sheen on the ground. Not too far from him, a cappuccino-colored woman stood pensively against a transit bus pole.

I caught a glimpse of her face as I drove past.

Her short yellow flowered sundress made her look twenty years younger than her actual age; up close, small wrinkles formulated on direct areas of her face, around her lips, and at her eyelids. Fine elegant lines that disguised the hard life she lived.

"That's Ms. Ilene, Damon's mom," I said as I made the block to turn around.

Germani turned to look in the direction I was referring to. The distraction seemed to end the uncomfortable conversation about Lisa. "Damon's mom, are you sure?"

"Positive. I'll see if she needs a ride." I pulled into the Compare Foods parking lot and looped around toward the street.

"Going somewhere?" I asked as I pressed the automatic power button on my window and spoke outside as the glass went down.

Ms. Ilene squinted at me. "Hamhock, is that you?" she called me by a childhood nickname I long ago stopped answering to.

"Yes, ma'am."

She edged a little closer to the car.

"Boy, well, aren't you a sight for these eyes. It is wet out here. Can you drop me off on the east side near the big university?"

I got out of the car and opened the back door. "Which one, UNCC or Johnson C. Smith?"

"Johnson." She looked to Germani. "Hey suga, you must be Hamhock's girlfriend," she said as she slid on the tan leather seats.

I shut her door and got back behind the wheel.

"Wife, I'm Hamhock's . . . Scott's wife." Germani corrected herself as she turned to briefly talk with the new car passenger.

I noticed Germani trying to keep her attitude at bay as she spoke.

The man with the sign came up to my window as I closed my door. "Can I get a couple dollars? I haven't eaten all day. All I need is five, no two dollars."

I thought about giving him something out of the Angel Food box, but I didn't want the man pawing through our personal food. I reached into my back pocket for my wallet and stopped at Ms. Ilene's abrupt shrill.

"Uh-uh. Don't give him no money. He's a crackhead. Only thing he's going to feed is his habit. He ain't slick. Tried to get me for some money too. Get on out of here begging. Get, get, get." Ms. Ilene leaned toward my headrest and shooed the man away with her hand.

The man looked offended as he began to stutter, "I . . . I . . . Imna . . . I'm no crackhead."

"Stop lying. Go get a job and get away from this car. You can't wait to smoke up somebody else's hard earned money. Like I said, get gone. Hamhock, roll your window up," Ms. Ilene demanded.

I obliged.

The man frowned, but turned on his worn heels and limped back to the sidewalk.

I felt a slap on the back of my neck as Ms. Ilene popped me. "Boy, you too old to be acting naive. Don't be pulling your wallet out like that unless you want it stolen. You got to be more careful," she scolded me.

Germani looked fascinated. She was probably getting a kick out of seeing me disciplined like a child.

Ms. Ilene continued to talk. "I thought I was going to die in this summer heat. I can't stand waiting for the bus when it's humid. My son, Devon, normally would have picked me up, but he was in a car accident and totaled out his girlfriend's car. His license was already suspended, so he ended going to jail and the car had to be junked. My kids and I are going to combine money and buy a newer car when income tax time comes."

Ms. Ilene scooted back in her seat next to a woken Elijah and buckled her seatbelt. I looked in the rearview mirror and watched her pinch Elijah's cheek. My son cocked his head to the side and stared at the stranger touching his face.

"I didn't know you were married and with the cutest little boy too," Ms. Ilene stated. "He has got some long eyelashes. He almost looks like a girl, he so pretty. Um, um, um. Time sure does fly. I remember when you were a small boy. I didn't know you at his age, but you were young. It's been some years. Um, um, um." Ms. Ilene dozed into a temporary reminiscent gaze.

"Where to, Ms. Ilene?" I glanced in the rear view mirror one more time as I waited for traffic to thin.

"542 Bacon Avenue, off of Trade Street. Suga, what's your name?" Ms. Ilene asked my wife.

"Germani," she responded pleasantly.

"Like that country with Hitler?"

Germani seemed a little surprised to hear her name merged with a reference to a Nazi. She furrowed her eyebrows and jerked her head slightly. "Uh. Well. It's spelled with an 'i' instead of a 'y,' but same country."

"Chile, why on God's green earth would your momma name you after that crazy killing fool? I could never figure out why people would follow such a nut job. Murdered millions of Jewish families, and for what? To stroke his crazy ego. You know he killed women and children too. I watched a documentary on the Holocaust and saw this room with nothing but shoes in it. Big shoes, little shoes and baby shoes. Imagine that. Baby shoes. The babies hadn't done a thing to be murdered like that. I had to change the channel because it was making me mad." Ms. Ilene rambled on with her criticism.

Germani turned to look at Ms. Ilene explaining, "My father was stationed at the Ramstein military base in Germany when

I was born. Both my parents named me after our home. I also spent the majority of my childhood there. Germany isn't a bad country. It had bad people in a position of power that caused great harm to a multitude of people. Just like ours does now. Bush does what he does because we let him do it, and just like some people hold all of Germany accountable for what Hitler did, other countries outside of the United States hold us accountable for what Bush does," Germani made subtle references to the Iraq war. Although she was raised in the military, she didn't have a fondness for the current government and would quickly comment on the subject any given chance.

"Oh, my, you sound like an intelligent young lady. Scott, I think you got yourself a good one. You better treat her right."

Germani grew silent.

"He is treating you right?" Ms. Ilene inquired.

"Why are you talking about me like I'm not sitting here? Of course I'm treating my wife well. That's my responsibility," I chuckled nervously as I stole glances at Germani.

"You were always a good guy, would give some-body the shirt off your back."

Germani smirked.

Ms. Ilene asked, "Why don't I see you any-more? You know I still live at the same address. Just because my son don't come around doesn't mean you need to be a stranger."

"You're right, Ms. Ilene." I couldn't argue with her. Damon's resentment toward his mother had no relevance to me. He kicked her to the curb like she was a butt ugly ex-girlfriend. I couldn't dismiss my mother the way he had. Some ties deserved to be severed, but mom is mom no matter how imperfect.

I didn't want to delve into an unpleasant subject, so I decided not to even remark on anything about Damon.

"Do you still make those chicken and dumplings?" I asked Ms. Ilene, smiling. "Germani, Ms. Ilene could create a mean chicken and dumplings. Have your tongue kissing the bottom of the bowl." I tapped Germani's arm to get her attention as she stared out the passenger window.

She didn't look at me as she nodded her head. Germani was showing me no love. If it wasn't apparent that we were having problems before, it had become blaringly obvious. I was embarrassed at how she was acting in front of Ms. Ilene. I decided I better leave Germani alone and just drive.

I turned off Trade onto Bacon Avenue, stopping in front of a chipped white house with green awning. The porch appeared to be tilted to the right where a crumbling foundation of bricks protruded from the exterior. Two men sat on the top steps, drinking forty ounces covered by paper bags; one looked to be in his early twenties while the other could have been a father or uncle. They watched as I got out of my car to open the door for Ms. Ilene. The younger one with a black and gray urban wear hoodie atop some black jeans threw his head up at me as I glanced their way.

I did the same.

Ms. Ilene got out of the car and kissed me on the cheek. She embraced me in a tight hug. "My phone number is still the same too. Call me sometime and I will make that chicken and dumplings. Bring the family with you."

She leaned down, waving her hand at Germani and Elijah. Germani waved back, while Elijah just looked. He didn't respond very well when he was sleepy.

Ms. Ilene stood back erect and clutched her purse under her arm. "Tell my son I still love him." Sadness clouded her eyes. It didn't match the broad smile she dressed up to appear happy.

"I'll let him know," I responded as I shut the back door.

Her yellow sundress swished against her wide hips as she ascended the porch steps. She stopped to say something to the older man before they both went into the house.

I got back in my vehicle. "Ms. Ilene invited us to dinner. She didn't give a specific date, but I didn't know how you would feel about going over to her house."

Germani shrugged. "Is that what you want to do, Hamhock? Ham . . . hock." The corners of her mouth twitched like she wanted to laugh.

"Ha-ha. I used to sneak and eat all the hamhocks out of the pot of mustard and turnip greens. I got a many whuppins' over it. Now you know my childhood shame. Laugh it up if you want to."

A rumble burst from her mouth as she did exactly that. "How could you be ashamed of such an endearing name like Hamhock?"

I embraced her relaxed mood and smiled as we got back onto Trade Street and headed home.

CHAPTER TWENTY-ONE

GERMANI

As I ventured through cyberspace on my office break, I found women just like me. Wives married to men obsessed with porn. There was a sense of camaraderie amongst that newly found distinction: Wives of Porn Addicts.

As I read each story, I felt sympathy for the women placing their frustrations on the Internet for the world to see. Sade knew her husband watched dirty movies, but she didn't realize how bad his addiction was until after a gynecological exam that confirmed that she had the sexually transmitted disease, Human Papillomavirus, otherwise known as HPV. He admitted to picking up random women for the duration of their marriage. Joy accidentally found an animal bondage tape while trying to sneak a love note into her husband's briefcase. Katrina investigated a money transfer on a joint charge account and discovered the funds were going to a massage spa for extra services. Just like in Sade's situation, her husband confessed after getting caught in something else. Watching porn for those men seemed to not be enough to fulfill their fantasies. They had to up the thrill by sleeping with strangers.

I continued reading real life depictions of deception, denial, rejection and regret, well past my lunch break.

Story after story broke my heart just a little more; touched my soul just a little deeper. Many of the couples had some kind of church affiliation and attended service regularly. They weren't that much different than Scott and me. Nothing I read made my family exempt. I thought about Scott's need to go to a strip club after almost five years of marriage in which he never mentioned that desire. Maybe there was more to his actions.

Later that night, I found myself scrolling through Scott's recent calls on his cell phone; searched through forty-six outgoing and fifty incoming. I didn't find any incriminating evidence that he was cheating on me, but the thoughts still lingered that something was up, or rather not on the up and up. Let Scott tell it, I had no reason to be suspicious. He lived to love me. If that were true, I wouldn't be competing with high definition, extended version sex movies.

It wasn't that I planned to be snooping through the pants pocket of his Levi jeans. My intention was to get Elijah up and to the bathroom. My son had several accidents, and it's much easier to program myself to wake in the middle of the night instead of spending my mornings spraying my four year old's toddler mattress down with my concoction of hydrogen peroxide and baking soda.

"Wakey, wakey up my tired, little man. You got to get up," I said as I shook the mattress of his engine red toddler bed.

Elijah grunted, but didn't budge an inch.

"Elijah, you need to go to the bathroom."

He yawned and stretched with his eyes squeezed shut. "Mommy, I'm *sheeping*," Elijah complained in a little voice.

"Well, you can go back to *sheeping* after you go to the bathroom. Come on, you know the drill." I lifted him by his arms out of the bed, placed his bare feet on the ground and patted his behind gently. "Scootch."

He slipped into his Spiderman slippers and shuffled to the bathroom. I waited outside the door until I heard the toilet flush. It was a new habit I was forming to give him some independence.

The knob to the bathroom door turned and I stated loudly, "Wash those hands." I saw the knob released and immediately heard the faucet water running.

Elijah came out and I followed him to his room where I tucked him into bed and kissed his forehead. My little man was an angel.

The beep of a low battery drew me in after I put Elijah back to bed. At first I didn't distinguish the sound. I stood in our darkened bedroom fine-tuning my hearing. I kept holding my breath like the hiss of air through my lungs would impede my ability to listen. Each beep brought me closer to the pile of clothes thrown haphazardly on the closet floor. Once I shifted through each garment, I found the phone in Scott's back pocket. I planned to turn it off and set it on the dresser, but the screen was flashing two missed calls.

I couldn't very well be expected to ignore that. I investigated like a regular wife holding her husband's phone. Some women trust blindly and probably would have shut off the phone with no hesitation. I didn't fit into that category of women. Four days ago, after our discussion about Scott's friend-butnot-really, Lisa, I became a little more conscious of where he was, what he was doing and with whom. And once I read the stories about what other women in my situation go through, I realized that I needed to be concerned. So searching through his phone was just a precaution.

I must admit to a sense of disappointment mingled with relief at not finding an unusual number or questionable text messages, especially considering that I took his phone back into the bathroom with me and turned on the shower full blast to muffle the pressing of digits. Then the guilt came. The guilt of mistrust. The guilt of letting my thoughts assume my husband was a trifling, two-timing ho. The guilt of wasting shower water to play Detective Wifey.

Right there on the tile floor I got on my knees and prayed. Well, I started to pray, but my knees were hurting on the cold Formica. I grabbed the baby pink thick cotton bath towel off the towel rack and folded it three times into a nice rectangle against the tub and placed my knees centered in cushion. Then I prayed.

"Lord, I need to hear a word from you to know whether I am tripping and jumping to unnecessary conclusions. I'm having a hard time dealing with the porn thing and I don't know if I could take it if Scott cheated on me. You probably already know that because of how I'm acting. My flesh won't let me rest on the subject. You said to flee from sexual immorality and I have done that. It's my husband that doesn't want to follow your will."

I paused, thinking about my frustration with the whole situation of my husband not wanting only me. My heart overflowed with sorrow, so I poured it out to a higher power.

"Lord, I need you in a mighty, mighty way. Help my husband get through his wicked ways. If you could cleanse his mind and purify his heart, I would be forever grateful. If I must be blunt, Lord, I'm asking you to fix him. Demonic forces are trying to devour my home and I know you don't want that. I stand in prayer on behalf of my husband's soul. Give him strength to conquer the lust demon. The devil can't have what's mine and he dang sure can't have what's yours. Bind those unholy spirits that taint his mind. Govern his walk in you that it may be righteous."

Whenever I prayed, I took a minute to absorb His presence. Nobody could put me in check like God could. Hopefully, the same move would reign in Scott.

As I turned off the shower head, water splashed on my bare arm. It dripped from my wrist to my elbow. An idea culminated in my mind.

Scott needed to be blessed.

I wiped my arm off with the towel I had prayed on. I put it back on the rack and opened the cabinet door under the sink. Inside a white metal medicine kit was a vile of Abramelin anointing oil I had saved when we first bought the house. I got it from my old church and intended to bless the house, but never got around to it.

It seemed like an appropriate, safe place for storage, next to Ace band-aids, packets of Ibuprofen, hydrocortisone cream and other methods of healing wounds.

I palmed the clear vile and turned the oblong sphere upside down, watching the liquids move from one end to the next. I wondered how long blessing oil stayed good. Could it spoil like raw Angus beef, or rather, did it get better with age like Pinot Gris wine? I didn't know, but I prayed for the latter as I shut the medicine kit and carried the cell phone and the vile down the hall to my bedroom.

I crept to the chest where I laid Scott's cell phone next to the jewelry box, tiptoed to my side of the bed and slid in softly. As I lowered my body to the mattress, I placed the vile in my other hand.

Scott was sound asleep facing me. I kept expecting his eyelids to pop open, but just like Elijah, Scott was hard to awaken. He could sleep restfully through a tornado, hurricane or tsunami.

I watched my husband with peace on his face. I guessed demons needed rest too. I lay on my side and twisted the cap off the vile. Dousing my fingers with the Abramelin anointing oil, the liquid felt like silk. Moistened fingers pressed against Scott's forehead, I silently whispered the only thing that made sense after my earlier long conversation with God.

"In the name of the Father, Son, and Holy Ghost, I bless you. Let God's will be done."

CHAPTER TWENTY-TWO

SCOTT

"He will be here," Beverly said optimistically, as we sat in the pre-op room before Alexis' scheduled surgery.

They had taken her down an hour earlier to see how her blood was reacting to a conditioning regimen of chemotherapy that was supposed to destroy some of the diseased cells and suppress immune reactions prior to the bone marrow transplant.

The entire family was waiting for Alex to show up.

"What time was his flight supposed to get in?" Momma asked Beverly.

"I'm not sure. When I called him this morning he was leaving for the airport. If he took a connecting flight, then he may be stuck in a layover. I'll go call him again and see what's taking him so long. He also said that they were having a hailstorm in Minnesota. Maybe his flight was delayed." Beverly got up with her cell phone in hand and left to go make her call outside the hospital lobby.

"That Negro is lying. He ain't coming here," Daddy said as soon as Beverly stepped out of the room. He knew it was a sensitive subject for Beverly, but Daddy had no faith in Alex following through on anything that pertained to Alexis.

"We don't know that yet. Alex might just have a conscience and decide to go ahead and do the right thing. Beverly said he bought his ticket a week ago," Sharon explained as she let Elijah get out of her lap and go to my mom who had a box of animal crackers.

"Didn't he have tests done there to make sure his bone marrow matched?" Corbin, Sharon's husband, asked as he leaned against the wall behind Sharon.

"Yeah. They shipped his test results here. That had to be done before a surgery could be scheduled," I explained.

Germani shook her head as she sat in a chair next to me, but she didn't share her thoughts.

From what Beverly had told me, Alex had been calling regularly to check up on Alexis. He even told Alexis that next summer he would see about sending for her so that she could spend some time with her younger brothers. He seemed to have made a complete 360-degree turn in attitude.

Daddy replied, "Well let's just hope Alex is on the up and up this time around. Took him long enough to become a real man."

"Better late than never. Some people have to grow at their own pace to become responsible," Mom said, taking a handful of cookies out of the box and handing them to Elijah.

Beverly came back into the room with a long face. "His flight was canceled."

"Yeah, right," responded Daddy, unconvinced.

"He said they got a heavy hailstorm. All flights leaving out were canceled and the incoming flights were delayed."

Momma tried to be optimistic. "Stuff happens. At least he's coming. Alexis is still in pre-op. You need to find out when the doctor can reschedule the surgery. Maybe they can do it tomorrow."

"It wouldn't matter when they could do the surgery. He's not coming at all," Beverly told us, disappointed.

"What? Why not?" I was pissed.

"Alex said that he spoke with his wife and has some concerns that the transplantation might be too dangerous for him. He apologized for Alexis being sick, but said he has to think about his sons too. They need their father around."

"There is no more risk to him than if he were going to the dentist for a root canal. If anything, Alexis has to worry about the risk, because she's already fragile. What is he talking about?" Sharon asked as she angrily tapped her foot on the tile floor.

Beverly sat down in a chair like she had the weight of the world on her shoulders. "I tried to explain the percentage of successful transplants, but he had a rebuttal for my every word. He had been on the Internet reading about how a man went into cardiac arrest while giving bone marrow to his sister, and during the process, he died on the table. And I don't know. He kept talking."

Beverly was too emotional to finish.

I was even more pissed after hearing that. Alex had been playing with Beverly's emotions for too many years.

"That's a cop-out. He never wanted to help Alexis in the first place," remarked Daddy as he put the magazine back on an office table. He said exactly what I was thinking.

Momma put her hand over her heart. "Alexis needs that transplant. He must not realize how serious this is for her."

"Alex told me that the flight cancellation was confirmation by God that he had to look at the bigger picture. Alexis isn't the only person he's responsible for."

"Confirmation by God? The God I know doesn't confirm stupid. That Negro is ignorant and his family is ignorant for not putting him in check. If he were responsible like he's claiming to be, we wouldn't be having this conversation. Alexis has been sick all of her life, and only recently, has he acted like he cared. God should strike his lying tail down. Give him some real confirmation." Daddy wagged his finger at Beverly like he did when we were little and got caught in something dumb.

"There's a torture chamber in hell for people like him." Germani folded her arms.

Sharon suggested, "You should go ahead and take him to child support court. At least sue him for half the doctor bills you've had to pay. If he can't be a man about this, then take it out of his pockets."

"I don't want to go through all that trouble. If he doesn't want to act like her father, I can't make him. I'd rather leave well enough alone. Besides, he might change his mind about the surgery later on and I don't want to make him upset." Beverly waved her hand like inconveniencing Alex wasn't an option.

"Don't none of us care about Alex getting upset. Stop letting him run over you," Daddy drilled into Beverly. "I don't know what kind of backward bayou voodoo magic that fool has done on you, but you better wake up. I didn't raise you to be a doormat."

Beverly put her hands over her eyes. She shook her head, looking ashamed and defeated. "I don't know how I'm going to explain this to Alexis."

My heart sank for Alexis. She deserved a better father. If Alex was in front of me at that moment, I would have beaten him within an inch of his life and then watched him cry for mercy.

Alex obviously cared about his two sons' well being, but not Alexis. I remember when she was born how disappointed he was that she wasn't a boy. There was nothing on this earth that would allow me to let my child, regardless of her sex, get near death and not do something about it.

I wanted Alex to feel his air composed to the point he couldn't breathe or have his body paralyzed by pain. I wanted him to feel a little of what Alexis felt on a regular basis.

I asked, "Beverly, how much does it cost for a plane ticket to St. Paul? If he won't come on his own, then I will go get him and bring him back for you."

Beverly shook her head. "Stop talking crazy. You don't need to go get Alex. What goes around comes around. He will get his due. If not here on earth, than in the afterlife."

Germani agreed. "Beverly's right. We need to pray for Alex and every man like him."

Words coming from the same woman that hacked up my DVD's because my son got a thirty-second viewing. Germani wouldn't allow me to disregard our son the way Alex was disregarding Alexis. They could talk about divine intervention if they wanted to. Alex needed a rude awakening about how he treated my sister and niece. I didn't want to wait for an afterlife for him to give them the respect they deserved. "Pray for him? I think we are past praying for Alex."

"At this point, we need to stick with the treatments she has been getting. Maybe take Alexis out to the Mayo Clinic for testing there." Beverly tried to think of alternative solutions.

I looked over at Germani and thought to myself, I would never take our family for granted. Not on purpose. Not after seeing what my sister had to go through. As a man, I planned to always do right by my family.

I didn't realize that soon enough, my obligation would be put to the test.

CHAPTER TWENTY-THREE

GERMANI

I pulled the zipper up on the straight angle, sequined, silver, floor length dress. I stuck my leg out to check the view of my right calf in the slit rising above my knee. Turning in the three way mirror one more time, I took a deep breath before exiting the Group USA dressing room.

Kira was engrossed in text messaging as she sat on a cushioned chair.

I stood in front of her waiting for her to notice the dress.

"It looks very nice on you," said an older man sitting a couple seats down with a purse in his lap. He was probably waiting for his wife or girlfriend. I gave him a slight smile.

I had no idea who Kira was vigorously typing to, but I coughed to get her attention.

Kira glanced up. "Turn around." She twirled her finger.

I slowly shuffled in a circle.

"I don't like it." Kira began typing on her cell phone again.

I had already tried on four dresses and none of them seemed right.

"I know. It definitely looks better on the hanger. I was hoping to find something that would . . . I don't know," I sighed.

"I think you should go with the first one. It fit you nice without looking sleazy."

"Yeah." I wasn't totally convinced, but I was tired of trying dresses on. "Who are you texting like that?"

Kira looked up at me and grinned like a smitten teenager. "My husband."

"Oh." Jayat had been Kira's second skin since we all went to their wedding in his homeland on Huahine Island three years ago. He seemed to be with her even when he wasn't physically present. I hadn't felt that kind of love with a man in a long time.

"He has tickets to the Actor's Theatre and he's hinting at some other special plans he has for the evening."

Kira stared at her phone and kept smiling. Kira had been my best friend since transferring as a foreign exchange student from Barcelona to South Mecklenburg High School in the tenth grade. She tutored me in Spanish and soon, we were going to all the cultural events held at the school together, soaking in as much international information as we possibly could.

She and Autumn had come with me to pick out a dress for an event that Scott had me going to with Damon and Cherish. I initially declined, but he said it was a research fundraiser, so I figured it couldn't be too bad. Boring, but not seedy. I enlisted their help because I was getting more and more self-conscious about Scott's lack of attraction to me.

"Where is Autumn?" I asked.

"She went to get a cinnabon. She said you were taking too long trying to make up your mind."

The man who complimented me got up and left with a girl from the dressing room.

"I haven't been that bad. You act like we've been here all day long."

"No, we're acting like we've been here over two hours, watching you be indecisive no matter what we say. You didn't like the ones we did. Not the wildfire red Charmeuse that I picked out nor the peach satin dress with the shawl that Autumn picked. Stop making this so hard."

I saw Autumn coming our way as she squeezed between racks with both hands in the air. A piece of gooey icing dipped bread in one hand and the cinnabon container in the other. She took quick nibbles as she made her way over to the dressing room.

"Ain't that right, Autumn?" Kira tried to get a co-sign on her comment.

"It's just a matter of what I'm agreeing to. Did you see the sale down at Perfumania? I found a small bottle of Feminine by Dolce and Gabbana for thirty-eight dollars. See . . . smell." Autumn waved her wrist in front of Kira.

"That smells good," Kira agreed. "You have to be careful about buying perfume on sale for too cheap, because you don't know how long they've had it sitting on the shelf."

Autumn smelled her own wrist again. "True, but I just dabbed a little on and it's pretty strong. I think it will last for awhile."

I placed a hand on my hip. "Excuse me, but is this a keeper or not? If you were Scott, would you love me in this?"

"I already told you what I think. That dress you have on right now doesn't flatter your figure. Go with the eggplant colored dress you first tried on," Kira responded.

"And I definitely don't think like Scott to even answer that question." Autumn gave me an if-you-know-what-I-mean look.

Kira caught the non-verbal exchange between me and Autumn. "Uh-uh, hon-nee. Spill it."

Kira wasn't the most religious person I knew. I generally shied away from her relationship advice. Loved her to death, but she would give me an entire avaricious response. It wasn't that her advice was bad, but sometimes it turned out that way.

"I'm going to get out of this dress and pay for the other gown before I change my mind again." It was safe to say that Autumn wouldn't say anything while I put my clothes back on.

When I came back out of the dressing room, both Autumn and Kira were already standing near checkout. I got my purchase and draped the long plastic dress bag over one arm.

As we left the store, I explained in a low voice to Kira what was going on in my marriage. "I had told Autumn that Scott and I were having sex problems."

"I assume you are still having the same problems." Autumn took the last bite of her cinnabon.

It had been over two months since I told Autumn about the strip club fiasco. I hadn't told her about Scott's new friend, Lisa, who I met last week. Things were looking bad enough already.

"Things had been going good, but certain aspects still aren't right. We're still having issues. No more strip clubs, but he's on this porn kick. He wants to watch and I don't." Neither Kira nor Autumn knew, until recently, that we had been watching porn movies for years. I was too embarrassed to mention my part.

"Okay, I agree with that. Jayat and I aren't into watching other people do it for our own personal pleasure. There are too many ways to satisfy each other without needing porn. How about toys? You and Scott should go to Kinky Ways and get you some spice for your life."

"I don't think that Kinky Ways is my solution."

Autumn shook her head in complete disagreement with Kira. "Nowhere in the Bible does it say sex toys are allowable."

Kira rolled her eyes. "Where in the Bible does it say they aren't allowed? As long as you aren't idolizing, it shouldn't be a problem."

I silently listened as we passed Victoria's Secret where a salesperson was holding a sample bottle of Very Sexy II right outside the entrance way. She was a short, perky blonde with a bright smile trying her best to persuade evening shoppers.

We politely declined the test spray.

"What it does say is 'Be not conformed to the ways of the world, but transformed by the renewal of your mind'. Worldliness can lead to destruction," Autumn said as she threw the empty cinnabon container in the trash bin.

"If that is the case, then you shouldn't have bought that cinnabon or perfume because they come from this world too. Autumn, you bought what you wanted because it felt good to get it. It is human nature, whether you are holy or not, to want to feel good," Kira stated.

Autumn responded, "Dolce and Gabbana doesn't lead me to sin like a vibrator would."

"No, but if your body's a temple, you wouldn't be putting cinnabon's with all those 840 calories of sugar and fat in your system." Kira pointed back at the trash bin. She then playfully shoved Autumn. "And you aren't married, so this isn't your subject."

"I don't have to be married to have an opinion." Autumn gave Kira a sour glance.

"Ssshh," I said as we walked into a crowd of teenagers. Kira had parked outside of TJ Maxx at the mall and I didn't need a group of kids listening to my life story.

"Where did we park?" Kira asked as we entered the dry tepid night air.

"Two rows over. That orange Geek Squad Beetle is still sitting there." I pointed in that direction.

"Oh, I see it. As I was saying, we all like to feel good, and a man's libido is universal regardless of race, creed or religion. For me and Jayat, sex toys enhance our relationship and keep us close. And I'm not talking about vibrators. There are a slew of tasteful things to keep lovemaking interesting between married couples, such as motion lotions, rings and massagers.

If you want, we can stop at Kinky Ways before I drop you off. I can show you some of the things that Jayat and I use."

It felt like Kira had parked a mile away. Autumn stopped one car before we got to her Passat, like she wasn't with us. "Oh, no. Drop me off first. I don't want to know what you and Jayat do behind closed doors."

"Don't worry. We won't be going to a sex shop," I said as I got into the car. We were all close, but we weren't that kind of close.

Kira looked at us and rolled her eyes again. "Oh, my goodness. We don't have to go together, but I seriously suggest that you and Scott find the time to go. I'm telling you, it can be a marriage saver."

"Listening to you is how I ended up married in the first place," I replied.

"How are you blaming me for that decision?" Kira asked as she started the car.

"You told me to get with Scott to take my mind off of Tre."

"No, no, no, honnee. *Get with* and *marry* are not the same thing." Kira's straight black hair swayed on her shoulders as she objected.

Those months after Tre left were dark times. I was vulnerable to any advice that would stop the heartache. Autumn came to my defense. "You were determined to keep her from moping. I remember that too."

"What! I am not taking credit for that. I didn't make you marry Scott. I told you he would be an easy distraction. We all knew how much he wanted to be with you. Now, you decided to do the rest and make him your husband. Scott was the rebound guy. Nobody marries the rebound guy. You weren't even over Tre when you went down that aisle. Autumn and I both told you that."

I wasn't receptive to their words during that time. Scott's attentiveness made my life brighter and I clamped on to him like a giant lobster. "Yeah, well, I did and now I have to deal with my repercussions."

Autumn must have noticed my downcast expression. "Scott isn't a bad guy. Prayer changes things. You know that. It's not always about how something starts, it's more important about how it ends. God can make the wrongs of the past right for the future. Plus, the blessed oil can ward off those demonic forces he got on him."

Kira interjected. "You don't need any blessed oil. There is nothing wrong with Scott that the right loving won't cure. Karma Sutra is your answer."

I didn't admit that I had already tried the blessing oil and it hadn't worked yet; instead, I listened to all their advice as they discussed how to fix my marriage. My thoughts drifted like hay in a Nevada desert storm. God couldn't want this for me. He just couldn't.

CHAPTER TWENTY-FOUR

SCOTT

Phony airs combined with pretentious dialogue; a personal pet peeve of mine.

I observed the round table discussion and remained aloof. Chatter just to be heard never impressed me. Sometimes observation beat out the relevance of shallow conversation. At least, it did for me.

Eight people sat in that particular dining area. Damon invited us to the fundraiser after garnishing extra tickets from a physician friend of his. I accepted because it was free and I wanted to take Germani somewhere nice. We hadn't been anywhere as a couple since my birthday turned into a fiasco. Damon also said there would be research information to help with Alexis' sickle cell anemia.

One of the four other people seated with us was Roland Hill, a biological scientist from a research company in Raleigh. He spoke briefly of having a patent on a hormone supplement. His wife, Carmen, accompanied him. The third was Omar Jennings, a dermatologist with two practices, one in Matthews and the satellite office in Ballantyne. Then there was a very vocal Sophie Duran, heiress to the *Her Naturals* hair care dynasty. She wore obnoxious vibes like a chinchilla wore its fur.

Her conversation sounded like gloating. "My husband just purchased a fifty-foot yacht for our Lake Norman property. I must admit that I was a little miffed at first. It is nearing fall, for goodness sake. I didn't think we would get to enjoy the yacht like we should at this late time of year. Last year, the waters were choppy from the brisk winds. But nonetheless, I am throwing a Harvest Soiree. Roland, I know you and Carmen aren't from the area, but you should consider coming down to enjoy the event. Damon and Cherish can attest to the efforts I put forth in the extravaganza. They were at my Luau in July Soiree held at the Country Club for the Fourth of July last year." She looked to her left for confirmation.

Damon responded, making eye contact with all the occupants of the table. "I loved the pomegranate ice sculpture in the shape of a volcano. It was an extremely unique idea. The successions of fireworks off the middle of the golf course were also a treat."

Cherish listened, but she was unusually quiet and distant. Almost like she was there in body, but not mind.

Damon's arm rested on the back of Cherish's chair as he spoke. "My personal favorite was the hula dancers. Their routine personified upbeat, fun and sexy. I'm telling you that you haven't partied until you attend a Duran Soiree. I've never seen anything like it."

"It sounds fascinating," Carmen said. "What date will that be?"

"Oh, I apologize. How could I forget that tidbit of information?" Sophie's coy smile seemed artificial, or maybe it was the cost of marriage to a plastic surgeon. Too much Botox. "October thirteenth. The soirée will be on the second weekend in the month. Leave me your address and I will have an invitation mailed to you. I'm sort of old fashioned when it comes to that.

E-mail invitations are so impersonal and rushed. I like to take a personal touch on anything that will represent the Duran name."

A waiter came around to fill the wine glasses.

Roland took a sip of Cabernet Sauvignon before saying, "We look forward to it. I'm always amazed at the connections created by attending these functions."

"It used to be the only money was old money. Now I find that people are quite creative in the pursuit of wealth. Do you not agree?" Sophie geared her question to no one in particular.

Damon answered. Always eager to impress. "Technology opened the doors for greater wealth. Capitalism is the capstone of American culture. The larger the desire for materialism, the greater there is the opportunity to advance. Plus, knowing the right people always helps."

His hand wrapped around a glass like he was making a toast to Sophie. I could imagine the imprint of his face on her behind from all the kissing up he was doing.

"But of course." Sophie lifted her glass to him before taking a sip herself.

Maybe it was because I was seated next to Damon that unwanted attention was drawn my way.

"Scott, you're so quiet. I never did ask. What do you do for a living?" Sophie intently watched me.

I wasn't surprised by the question. That's what people ask at functions such as this.

"Sell car parts," I replied dryly.

"Oh." Her interest in me waned as she turned her head to adjust the pendant on her right shoulder.

Damon spoke up like I needed defending. "My friend here is modest. He's been in management for years."

There was no need to hype my position. I couldn't care less about Sophie's opinion of my mediocre status quo.

"I just sell car parts." I rubbed the crevice behind my ear where a nagging pulse developed.

Applause vibrated throughout the room as the mistress of ceremony, Paulette, a petite ebony female in a blue and silver evening gown, introduced Dr. Javir Cavella, the renowned neurosurgeon from Brazil. I'd seen pictures of him from browsing through his *Gene Relations* book on a shelf at Damon's place.

A distinguished aura followed the guest speaker as he approached the podium. Dr. Cavella nodded his head as he exchanged places with Paulette. She stepped out of the spotlight and became a shadow in the background.

He lifted the microphone to accommodate his size. "Good evening, Charlotte family." He smiled into the crowd. "It is my honor to stand before you today." Dr. Cavella took a sip of water from a bottle placed on the podium. "There have been miraculous advances in medicine within the last century. Medical professionals pioneered research that was unheard of. For example, Dr. Christaan Bernard performed the first open heart transplant back in 1967. His perseverance enabled thousands with cardiac problems to now have a new lease on life. By the same token, Dr. Charles Drew discovered that plasma could be separated from red blood cells, thereby allowing blood to be stored for transfusions."

"Many lives are saved because blood donations are available. Due to studies by researchers at Kyoto University, stem cell cloning has developed a new meaning. The ethical controversy behind human embryonic stem cell use will be no more with a new technique the Kyoto team used. They used skin cells to insert essential genes into viruses that infect the cell and become active as the virus replicated. The skin cell's own copies of the gene were repressed due to their interference with functioning. Quite remarkably, those four genes were sufficient to reprogram skin cells."

I listened to Dr. Cavella break down the stem cell process and wondered if some of what he was talking about was foreign to anybody else besides me. I got the gist of his presentation, but the information seemed drawn out and over analytical. During times such as this, I found my mind wandering. The subject didn't captivate me. I surveyed the table where everyone else seemed to be listening intently.

Dr. Cavella continued his speech. "Funding has been limited. A bill for more research that went to the House of Representatives in June was approved, although it is expected to be vetoed by the president."

Damon leaned over to me and whispered, "Hey, come on. I want to show you something."

I knew it must have been what his persuasion in inviting me was about.

"Germani, I'll be back shortly," I said as I removed the cloth napkin from my lap and set it on the table before excusing myself.

She gave me an inquisitive glance, but then turned her head back to the speaker.

I followed Damon out of the conference room and to the elevator. He spoke as we passed several hotel guests that appeared to be checking in. Damon seemed to be exceptionally giddy, a rarity I'd seen. There were only two other times that Damon shared overweening delight. The first time was when we saw the *Del Rio* video. On the second occasion, Damon received a generous gift from an Economics professor at A&T that paid for his entire academic program, plus an electric blue T-top Thunderbird to flash around campus. The dream of all cars made real. I remember the way Ms. Ilene boasted about her son's jazzy automobile more than she did about his academic career.

"Man, I forgot to tell you that I saw your mom last Saturday," I stated.

I had no intention on souring his mood, but any sign of a smile disappeared from his face. He looked at me like I had socked him in the mouth.

"So?" Damon said with disdain in his voice.

"She wanted me to give you a message." I paused as we stepped off the elevator and took a right down the hall. "She asked me to tell you that she loves you."

"The mother I knew died when Brandon took a bullet. Garbage needs to stay in the ghetto." The acid in his voice only got thicker.

His youngest brother, Brandon, had passed away five years ago, right before I met Germani. Stray bullets pelted his body as he went up for a jump shot on the basketball court at a park near their home.

Before it happened, Damon had begged his mother to move from the high crime West Corridor area she lived in. He was even willing to pay her rent at a nice place near him in Ballantyne. Ms. Ilene was loyal to her hood. She refused to accept his offer to become 'uppity black folks' as she called it. Damon blamed Ms. Ilene for Brandon's death. Brandon was the only one of his siblings doing anything productive with his life. A multi-gifted honor student, the boy had planned to start college at Howard University that fall where a full academic scholarship awaited him.

Damon had stopped talking to all his siblings, but Brandon, after some of his prescription samples went missing during a party he had at his first house. He accused his brother, Devon, of stealing his stuff and his sisters verbally jumped on him for making the accusation. That was when he banned all of them, but Brandon and his mother. When Brandon died, Ms. Ilene got kicked to the curb too.

It seemed trivial to me that five years later, Damon would still be mad at his mother about something she didn't directly do. "You should let the past go. Mend the relationship between you and your mom," I advised. "How would you feel if she died and you were still holding a grudge?"

He responded with no emotion as he pushed the door open. "Relieved."

I paused for a minute. Damon couldn't be that cold blooded. He was just bitter. I didn't have anything else to say about it.

As we stepped into the lavish aqua and chocolate decorum, I wondered why. I didn't know where I thought we were going, but I didn't expect it to be a room.

"Damon, what's with the hotel suite," I asked as he tucked the key card back into his wallet.

"This isn't my room. It's a business associate's, Dr. Cavella, the presenter of the night rented this room. I have something I need to show you." He gestured toward a table in the sitting area.

On a mahogany and marble oval coffee table there was a tier of champagne glasses next to a bowl of ice with a bottle of cognac. I moved over a chocolate throw pillow and sat next to an engrossed Damon. His mind twirled. I could see from the way he shifted the glass of liquid how the gears of his brain were churning.

"So what is it?" I asked.

"I got something I know you'll enjoy."

All I saw was a remote control that Damon picked up. He pressed a button and music began playing. It sounded like Charlie Wilson from the Gap Band.

"Man, what are you doing?" I asked.

Damon glanced over at me. "Sit back and watch."

A door from an adjoining room slid open and a woman in a black lace short top that stopped at her belly button with a matching thong slowly moved forward. Her hips swayed to the beat of the song.

She had her eyes on me as she bit her bottom lip and performed a seductive dance.

Damon sipped on his drink with a devilish smile.

"My wife is downstairs," I told Damon, quickly becoming uncomfortable with the heat rising in me.

"Yes, she is, and she's not giving you any. I know you're frustrated and your wife is causing you way too much grief. *Pleasure* here is willing to give you a little excitement. If you don't remember, I paid her that night we were at the club and she was nice enough to let me get a rain check. She will be here all night long for some other activities we got going on later this evening, but I wanted you to get a taste of how it's supposed to feel." Damon pointed to the woman who had her top unbuttoned as she shrugged the material off and threw it on me.

I didn't know when strippers started giving rain checks, but I didn't want to get caught up in the thunder storm.

CHAPTER TWENTY-FIVE

GERMANI

I couldn't believe they left us sitting at that table for half an hour. I expected them to be gone five or ten minutes. Fifteen tops.

Cherish had gone to the bathroom to powder her nose. Carmen and her scientist husband had relocated to a table across the room with some business associates they knew. And the very sophisticated Sophie had cut loose on the dance floor. Her hips thrust in awkward gyrations. The partnerless moves didn't match the music, but she lip-synced the beat of "Brick House" while her head swayed.

I was left alone with Omar who looked even more bored than I felt. A sigh escaped as he drummed his fingers against the tabletop. A few times, our eyes met as they roamed around the European designed Pomodoro banquet room set for four hundred guests with its crystal chandeliers, cream table clothes, black tie wrapped chairs and exquisite yellow orchid flower arrangements throughout. We'd shared polite smiles, but no words.

If my boss, Peter, were here, he'd reprimand me for not taking the opportunity to network. *"There's never an inappropriate time to market Job Track. You can meet an employer in the grocery store, your doctor's office or at the utility company."* I could hear his hyper, full-blooded Irishman voice as if he were sitting in a chair next to me.

"What are you doing sitting there like a wart on a witch? Get up and mingle. Show that outstanding and friendly personality we brought on staff. Always be prepared to talk about the great people we have for hire through Job Track. Even when you're not in the office, you are still working; and you're sitting in a room full of medical professionals. It doesn't matter if their business is small or large. If they have a business, then they may be hiring. It's perfect timing for one of our recruiters to make a connection. They aren't going to contact you if you haven't shown yourself worth the call. Or worse yet, you didn't let anyone know what you have to offer."

It was boredom, more than Peter's voice, playing in my head that made me decide to engage

Omar in a conversation. Time would keep dragging if I didn't smooze.

"Omar, you said you operate two practices. How many people do you staff at each location?" I asked the dermatologist who looked startled that I was speaking to him, as he turned toward my upbeat voice. He probably was surprised that the boredom had left my face as I sipped from a glass of lemon water and waited for him to tell me all about his company.

"Our Matthews office houses seventeen staff members," he answered, "including myself and two other dermatologists. There are two registered nurses, five medical assistants, three receptionists, one of which is part time, two medical transcriptionists, an insurance biller and our office manager. The satellite location in University City is much smaller due to that office only being open two days a week and one weekend per month."

"Do you find a great need for adequate ethnic sensitive laser treatment and skincare products?" I knew Charlotte was an ever growing diverse city that demanded services to fit the needs of people with various hues of color.

"Actually, we are finding ways to expand our operations as we speak because of the rapid interest in repair and preventative treatment.

I think we will need a couple more doctors to make that happen. Myself and the partners are in the interviewing stages for associates who've applied to us through Carolina Medical."

I knew we weren't in the business of finding doctors; physicians didn't need help with placement. The office staff was a definite possibility though. "Sounds like a wise choice for your practice. The firm I work for may be an asset to your operations. We specialize in high quality staffing. Job Track confers with our employers to discover what path to take for your specific need. Our applicants go through rigorous skill testing, as well as an extensive background and criminal check. The business journal cited us as a top placement agency with one of the highest success rates in the city."

I wanted to sound confident, not boisterous. I paid close attention to his body language, which would tell me his level of interest in a possible business relationship. Much could be communicated by physical response. His chair was at a side angle, but his leg faced inward. One under the table and one not. That alone would give me the impression that he was apprehensive, but his consistent nods told me that he was, at least, listening.

"I usually leave staffing for the office up to our Human Resources Manager, Sheila. She's pretty good at picking people that fit into our work environment," Omar responded almost apologetic.

"I completely understand. How about you give Sheila my business card? I would love to hear what she's doing to keep the office operation afloat." I smiled brightly as I reached into my satchel and pulled out a card. "You wouldn't mind that, would you?"

He took the card and placed it in the inner pocket of his suit. "Not at all."

I logged Sheila's name in my memory. If I didn't hear from her in a week, I would call to set up a meeting. As I closed the clutch of my bag I noticed the time on my watch read 10:30 P.M. Another half hour had passed with both Scott and Damon absent. I slid my satchel off the table and straightened the hem of my teal floor-length silk evening gown as I stood.

I walked down several halls of the Omni Charlotte Hotel. I got to the exit where the outdoor pool lay before I decided to go back to the banquet and wait.

I rounded the corner near the front desk, and down a hallway near the elevators I saw Cherish's back. I recognized her coral, backless, designer Vera Wang as she spoke with Dr. Cavella. Her body language was off. The stiff posture seemed defensive like she didn't want to be near him. He stroked her folded arms which she allowed, but the act seemed obtrusive. He stood too close. Invaded personal space. It looked like she needed to be rescued from unwanted company.

As I approached, I could only hear the tail end of their verbiage.

"Your hesitation concerns me. I'm willing to give you luxuries beyond this if you'd allow me." His gray eyes bore seductively into Cherish. Dr. Cavella was easy on the eyes with black, tapered hair and smooth olive skin. He had an athletic build, but not super muscular.

The doctor's lips pursed as he saw me. Cherish turned her head to see what drew his attention. Surprise, then what I thought was relief, crossed her face.

"Cherish, I came out here to find our husbands. Is everything all right?" I emphasized her marital status to a man who seemed to have less than honorable intentions.

Cherish blinked rapidly before responding, "Yes, everything is fine. We were just talking." It certainly didn't sound as innocent as she made it to be, but maybe I was reading more into it than I should. It wouldn't be the first time I was wrong. I had accused Scott of cheating on me and still hadn't found evidence to back it up.

Dr. Cavella extended his hand. "I don't think I've had the pleasure."

"I don't think you have," I responded, taking his greeting for a quick handshake. He put my hand to his lips and kissed the back of it gently before I abruptly pulled it from his grasp.

All that overly affectionate touching might have been a Brazilian thing, but I wasn't from Brazil.

"Were you going back to the conference room?" I asked Cherish as I pointed down the hall.

"Yes, we can go back," Cherish said as she began walking away from the elevators.

Although his attempt at charm didn't persuade me, I did find his speech to be interesting and wanted more details.

I complimented Dr. Cavella as we all headed back toward the conference room. "Your speech was fascinating. I didn't realize all the benefits to stem cell research or that there was an alternative method to performing tests that might counteract the controversy behind embryonic destruction and human cloning."

Dr. Cavella nodded his head. "Many people don't. Not until it directly affects them, like someone in their family becoming ill. I'm trying to spread the word of its usefulness. That is the only way to get the global private funding that we need."

"What brought about your interest in this particular study?"

We walked back into the Pomodoro room to a jazz rendition of "Endless Love." The banquet floor was filled with slow dancers, swaying to the Diana Ross and Lionel Richie classic love song.

Dr. Cavella stood in the door entrance to allow us in first. "I see long-term illnesses and genetic disorders killing people for no other reason than political fear and public ignorance. For the amount of money used to treat chronic diseases, stem cell research could be paid for one hundred times over." He paused as the mistress of ceremony gestured for him toward a small group she was talking with. "I'm being summoned. Cherish, I'll talk to you later." He stroked her arm before going off to join the mistress of ceremony.

Dr. Cavella had no qualms about showing feelings for Cherish, and as much as I didn't like Damon, a family divided didn't sit well with me.

"Cherish, are you sure everything is okay?" I asked with serious concern. Close up, her skin appeared ashen under artful make-up and false eyelashes.

She didn't respond.

We weren't close enough for her to tell me her problems. That was mostly my fault due to my ill feelings toward her husband. She'd asked me to go shopping or out to lunch and I'd made up an excuse every time. I didn't like the way Damon treated her; as if she were for beautiful display only, with no feelings of her own. An extension meant entirely for his personal use and pleasure. I thought she was a doormat and I could never respect people who allowed themselves to be walked all over.

I felt bad for my judgment. There was no telling what she was dealing with while I was acting like I was better than her. Like I was incapable of having drama in my marriage. God had a funny way of showing me who I really was by the way I dealt with others. Once again, I was convicted on my ego.

Cherish and I sat down at the now completely empty table we'd left. I rested my hands on the cream cloth and turned toward Cherish, who sat on my left-hand side. "Listen. I know me and your husband bump heads on a regular basis, but that doesn't mean we can't be friends. If you need to get some stuff off your chest, please know that I will keep the conversation in the strictest of confidence." I spoke from the heart with as much sincerity as I could muster. Even with our husbands being best friends, there were some boundaries that need not be blurred.

"Thank you, Germani." Before her eyes dropped down I was sure I saw the glint of a tear.

I was being pushy, but I couldn't help it. "If you don't want to talk now, I understand. The door is open for you to call me at anytime. You have my house and cell numbers."

Cherish nodded her head as she wiped the outer corners of her eyes.

The uneasiness that tapped at my soul like a fleet of African dancers told me there were some skeletons wreaking havoc in the Spears' home, ones about to come out. Considering my past judgments, I hoped I was ready to be the kind of friend Cherish needed.

CHAPTER TWENTY-SIX

SCOTT

Sara was on one register and Torrance on the other. Craig had come on for the evening shift and was scheduled to relieve Torrance.

Craig stopped me as I passed him while he stocked a shelf. "There are two boxes of hubcaps that won't fit on the shelf, and since you rearranged everything back there due to inventory, I'm not sure where you want me to put the extras."

"It's all still arranged by manufacturer. You just have to look on the labels to see what goes where," I explained to Craig before turning my attention to Torrance.

"Torrance, I need to speak with you." I pulled him from the register. Craig and Sara exchanged glances as we walked to the back room. The space was used for an office.

I wanted to keep the conversation light, play it by ear as I pushed the door closed.

"I'm straight." Torrance tugged at his sagging black pants. The waist was three inches lower than it should have been.

"Maybe that belt you're wearing needs to be tightened." I stood against the desk with my arms folded against my chest in business mode.

Torrance grimaced as he looked up at the ceiling, but tucked his dangling green button-down shirt with the black Car Care logo into his pants. He stretched the belt into another hole and lapped it around his waist. His hands slapped against his waist.

I pulled the ledger off the desk and handed it to him. "I ran some reports for inventory, and although your drawer was never short, per se, it appears that our accounts don't match the inventory. Corporate office requested an audit. I probably wouldn't have noticed for another few months otherwise."

I didn't want to automatically assume he was running game on me. Misuse of my kindness. The numbers didn't lie.

"That's all your cashier transactions. For the past month and a half, you've been giving fifty percent off for things that shouldn't have discounts."

Torrance gave me a look of sheer confusion. "I thought you told me I could do fifty percent off for my friends and family?"

"No, I'm pretty sure I said fifteen for a select few and not to make it a habit." Torrance played with the inside of his pants pocket as I tapped a pen against the ledger. "You also took back three items without bothering to get a receipt for the initial purchase. Do you recognize this?" I put the pen and ledger down, reached behind the desk and picked up a large metallic red object. It landed on top of the desk with a thug sound.

"Cam Shaft Rocker Stud for a Dodge Intrepid made in 1997," Torrance responded with scrunched eyebrows.

I was certain of one thing. The boy knew his car parts and had a great memory. "Exactly. And you notice anything else?" I inquired.

Torrance examined the cam shaft; walked around it like a student studying a class project.

I twirled the part around so he could see the serial number. "It's not ours."

"It's not our product?" he asked with bulging eyes like he didn't believe me.

"Oh, I'm sure. The question is why didn't you get a receipt before you gave that person their money back, or at the very least, run the serial numbers in our system? That's almost a five hundred dollar lost for one item." I held up my index finger as irritation bounced from my voice. For as long as I'd worked at Car Care, I hadn't been responsible for that kind of loss. I had let my supervising duties slip.

Any explanation Torrance gave wouldn't be acceptable, no excuse sufficient for corporate office. Once Sid Matthews, our District Manager, got wind of what happened, it would be grounds for Torrance's automatic dismissal.

I had to be honest and let Torrance know the implication behind his actions. "You might need to start seeking other employment. Maybe retail isn't the place for you."

"Scott, man, don't let me go," Torrance pleaded with a pitiful look on his face. "I need to help my moms with the bills. It's not like I stole parts and sold them on the street. I misunderstood policy while trying to look out for the peeps I'm cool with. You know our people can't afford some of these outrageous prices. Made in Korea for ten cents, sold in America for a hundred dollars. Sh . . . I mean, shoot. Now you know, you know, you know."

Torrance came at me like we were boys representing the hood instead of a boss and his employee discussing irresponsibility and negligence. I had to take the credit for minimizing my role as his superior. When I hired Torrance, he had just moved from New York, where he was a street vendor who sold name brand tennis shoes in Brooklyn; a kid with a filthy mouth, but a good work ethic. He had a habit of cussing whenever he got frustrated. As he got acclimated to the job, he learned to keep his language under his breath where nobody else could hear him. It was my encouragement that got him to change some of his bad habits. Maybe I crossed the line of professionalism when I started giving him advice on how to treat women and picking Torrance up for work during the whole month he didn't have transportation to get back and forth.

I had to nip his 'we boyz' attitude in the bud.

"Torrance, what I know is we are not buddies. You work here. Furthermore, Car Care has lost too much money since you came on board. That's a serious problem for the big bosses and a serious problem for me. I don't think you understand that when the heat comes down through the ranks . . ." I jabbed my finger in my chest. The lines of my forehead stretched long and wide as I vented my own frustration. "I'm the one that gets burned. I look bad and so does this store. Corporate office already has this location at a different standard because it's in a high crime area. I can't afford for my store to take any more criticism. If it comes between you keeping your job and me keeping mine, we already know how it's going down."

Torrance stood there and blinked at me. Several long seconds ticked by before he responded. "Why you coming at me like that? I know I messed up, but you don't have to treat me like I'm a flunkie. If you didn't want me here any more, all you had to say was, 'Torrance you messed up big and we can't keep you any longer.' I can comprehend being fired. Instead, you're talking to me like I got one testicle. You supposed to be big on respect and righteousness, but when push comes to shove, I can't tell you know jack about those words." Torrance began to walk backward as he eyed me with contempt. "It's all good. We ain't got to be cool."

I wielded my power hard, thinking he needed to recognize me as an authority figure. I didn't mean for it to come out the way it did.

"Torrance, we are cool, but you are my employee first. I can't cut you anymore slack than the rest of the staff. I would give this same lecture to Craig, Sara or anybody else working for me."

Torrance threw his hand up in a waving gesture, like he wasn't trying to hear me. "Man, Scott, man. You keep your lectures. I don't need them if you gonna fire me. A lecture is for somebody that's staying in a position. No, I'm good on that. As a matter of fact, I'm glad you and corporate office are letting me go. That way, I can collect my unemployment. Peace out!" Torrance threw up two fingers and rammed the door against the wall as he exited the tiny office space.

My nerves had remained on edge since Torrance stormed out of the building. Sometimes we get this sense that things are about to go wrong, but we ignore the feeling. I didn't think things could get any worse.

"Car Care," I quickly answered the phone in the backroom after Craig had hollered that it was for me.

"Scott, we have a shut off notice from Duke Power." Germani paused, and when I didn't say anything quick enough, she continued talking. "What's going on that you didn't pay the light bill?"

"I did pay the bill. I think I paid the lights." My speech slowed as I tried to remember which bills I had paid at the beginning of the month. I knew there was one of them that I said I would pay later because it wasn't due yet.

"No, the light bill didn't get paid because I am staring at the notice right now." I could hear Germani rustling the paper through her connection.

"Oh, that's right. I forgot all about paying that," I admitted.

"How could you forget to pay the light bill? We pay all the same bills at the same time of the month? We haven't been getting shut off notices before today. What are we going to do?" Germani was breathing hard into the phone piece. There was panic in her voice.

My thoughts were still on the blow-up with Torrance and the heat from the corporate office. Even with Torrance being let go, I still was accountable for the things he did while under my watch. When I called James, our District Manager, to tell him about Torrance's actions and his firing, James explained that there may be an investigation into my store operations.

"I've got stuff on my mind. Don't stress. I'll take care of it,"

I said calmly as I walked over to the office chair and sat down. I shoved sheets of paper off the middle of my desk and propped my elbows up on the wooden desktop. It was decided when we were married that I would handle the finances. Germani said, at the time, that she knew I would take care of us and that she trusted me. I majored in business management in college and felt well equipped to budget for our household.

"You've been awfully forgetful lately, Scott. What's going on that has your memory all twisted up that you can't remember to pay our bills?" Germani's irritation came through the phone line like thunder and lightning.

All I could do was sigh as I swiveled back and forth in the chair. My memory wasn't that bad. Her only other example of my so called forgetfulness was when I didn't tell her about being at Lisa's house and that was over a month ago.

I had already told her that I'd take care of it. I would be getting paid on Friday; I would just pay it then.

As if reading my mind she said, "You don't get your check deposited into our account until Friday. The disconnection is on or before Thursday. This Thursday."

"Well, I guess I will make a payment arrangement or something." It wasn't like we were the first family to ever be behind on our bills.

"Are there any other bills that haven't gotten paid?"

"No. Everything else is taken care of. I paid the water, telephone and cable bill on the first."

"So you paid the cable bill before you paid for the lights to stay on?" I hoped she was hormonal because that would only last a few days. If we were back to not trusting me again, then we had real problems.

I had to sigh again to keep from getting mad.

"You put the cable before our utilities. Omigosh. I can't believe this. Since when did the cable become so important to you, Scott?" Her words sounded judgmental as if I fell off as a responsible person. My wife questioned me about how to handle things, just like corporate office.

It got under my skin that I had to defend my management ability. I could hear Damon's words rigging my ears. *"Get your manhood out of your wife's purse."*

I'd had enough. "I'm a grown man, Germani. Don't call my place of employment nagging me. I said I would take care of it and I will. Furthermore, what I watch on television is my business as long as I pay the bills. If you don't like what I do or how I do it, then you need to get over it."

"But—"

I didn't let her finish. "I don't want to hear anything else from you. I am hanging up before you get on my last nerve. Bye." I slammed the phone down.

She picked the wrong day to trip out on me.

CHAPTER TWENTY-SEVEN

GERMANI

I couldn't believe his nerve. He hung up on me. Now, he was the one in the wrong, but I got hung up on. He had some nerve.

To say I was furious would be putting it lightly. My anger smoldered like a Girl Scout camp fire; beneath the smoke lay a whole lot of hot flames. When I got pissed—and I do mean really pissed—one of two things occurred. I either prayed or I paced. The latter fit the bill for my mood.

I started talking to the flat screen television as I walked back and forth across the floor with the light bill still in my hand. "Just when I try to be civilized and call my husband to discuss an unpaid bill, instead of degrading his manhood by paying the stupid bill myself, I get graced with a dial tone. How does that make sense?"

My day had been going fine before that. I'd met with Omar's Human Resources Manager.

He came through and gave me the contract for their new employees. Plus, when I got to the office, another company called me because they were so pleased with the twenty temps we sent them that they wanted to bring on thirty-five more for seasonal contract jobs. I spent the entire afternoon scheduling interviews for those positions. It was a lot of work, but well worth it. My boss told me that I would be getting a bonus check from the additional revenue I'd brought to the company that month.

For me to have my joy dashed at the sight of a shut off notice was like a camel in the midst of a haystack filled with straw. My hope in calling Scott was for him to say there must have been some mistake at the light company; that they'd lost the payment and he had a confirmation number in his wallet to verify he had paid the bill. Or, at the very least, I expected him to say the ordeal would be handled by morning. I honestly didn't expect him to basically tell me to mind my business, like the bills weren't supposed to be my concern. I also didn't expect him to pay all the other bills but that one. All that said to me was that the water, telephone and cable were more important than the lights. The lights could wait for another payday. Who cares if they get cut off? That's what candles are sold for. Who needs a working hot water heater when you can boil water on the stove to take a shower or bath? Oh, wait . . . we need power for the electric stove too. Go figure.

I couldn't help but feel sarcastic and condescending about his actions.

I searched through the drawer where we kept bills and grabbed an outdated cable invoice from June. The cable cost half as much as the electric bill and should have been the last thing paid if something had to go. It didn't add up.

From Scott's response to me, I felt he might have lied to me about where our money was going.

I picked up the phone fully acknowledging that I was about to make myself even more upset than I already was. I traipsed across Berber carpeting, waiting for customer service at Dish Network. After waiting for too many prompts and pressing too many buttons, a guy named Colby answered the call.

"How can I be of assistance?" he asked.

"I can't seem to find my current cable bill. Would you be able to tell me my outstanding balance?"

"Sure, I should be able to help you with that. Do you have your account number?"

"I do." I repeated numbers from the shut-off notice I held.

"Please give me the last four digits of your social."

"It's in my husband's name. His last four digits are 4133."

"And the address on this account is at 621 Harris Oak Avenue for Scott Wilson. Is that correct?"

"Yes." I tilted my head side to side, trying to control my mood. *Was all that necessary to get a bill balance?* I had to force myself to be pleasant.

Colby finally said, "The bill was paid in full on October 1st."

I knew that already. "Okay and what was the amount paid." I hoped that Colby couldn't detect my irritation.

"Three hundred and forty-eight dollars and fifty-two cents."

Anger and disbelief didn't work well together. I had to repeat what I heard. "Three hundred and forty-eight dollars and fifty-two cents? No, you must be mistaken. Our bill couldn't possibly be that high," I spoke with confidence. Our monthly bill only averaged about seventy-five dollars."

"Well, Ms. Wilson, the bill *was* paid in full."
I guess I was supposed to feel better about that,
but Colby didn't know what I knew.

"My husband paid that bill and I'm not sure
he realized that much would be taken out of our
checking account."

"The payment was called in. We don't have
your account set up for automatic pay," Colby
hesitated. "Although that is an option if you'd
like."

I specifically remember having the conversation about the convenience of our bill pay-
ments being automatically deducted from our
joint checking account. We were putting the bill
dates on a calendar to merge both our incomes.
Originally, I paid the lights, water, my car insurance and half the rent, and Scott paid the other
half of the rent, cable, telephone and his car insurance. When Elijah was born, which added an
enormous debt for daycare and we decided to
buy a house, it just seemed logical to merge our
finances and pay the bills from one pot.

"Mrs. Wilson, are you still there?"

"Yes, I am. I don't want to change our service
at this time. Could you give me a break down
of where that amount came from?" My voice
sounded hollow, kind of similar to how my heart
felt. My feet took me from the living room to

the kitchen back to the living room. Non-stop motion. Rapidly going nowhere, but my legs couldn't rest and my sense of deceit wouldn't cease.

"Two hundred seventy-three dollars and forty-nine cents is for pay-per-view movies."

That halted my pace. "Pay-per-view movies don't cost that much. Your systems most have a computer glitch."

"No, Ms. Wilson, that was the amount for pay-per-view at your address."

"Give me dates, times, titles and individual cost for each movie." I pulled a date book and pen from my purse and waited to write on a tasks-to-do page. If any of the movies were during our work hours, Dish Network was giving us a refund.

"*Wet Dreams 4 U* was ordered on August tenth at 1:45 A.M., *Sex Sandwich Sluts* on August sixteenth at 11:30 P.M., *Ghetto Girls Get Nasty* on August sixteenth at 2:50 A.M.," Colby continued down the list and my disbelief deepened.

Embarrassment warmed my face. I couldn't handle it anymore. "You know what, Colby; I think I've had enough . . . um . . . information. Thanks for the help."

"Sorry for the confusion, Ms. Wilson. I hope you have a nice night."

The night was going to be anything but nice.

"You do the same, Colby," I said pleasantly. It wasn't his fault that my husband's brain cells had slipped from his head down to other parts of his anatomy. No. That was Scott's fault.

That call ended and I wanted to hurt my husband so bad I could taste my bitter rage. I could understand the reason Mekhi slapped the stank out of Mishelle for her blatant disrespect. Sometimes, the anger became an unstoppable catalyst and a person snapped.

All the love I had to give physically, mentally and intimately was cast aside by Scott's compulsion, and for what? A fantasy I'd never be able to compete with.

I was back to being that camel in a haystack of straw. And I had to do something . . . to get my mind in a different place.

CHAPTER TWENTY-EIGHT

SCOTT

"Time to close shop," I said wearily to myself as I stacked bundles of ones, fives, tens, twenties, fifties and the three hundred dollar bills on top of each other in the office. I had to go home to that woman I hung up on.

The day had been unusually slow with customers trickling through in small numbers. It made my job easier since I had all those boxes to put back into the storage room after the inventory audit.

At the end of the evening, there were only Sara and myself left to cash out. I shut down one register at nine after Craig cashed out, and it only took forty minutes to tally Sara's register. I usually could expect to be at the store until midnight, and occasionally, one or two A.M., but it was nearing eleven and everything that needed to be done had been taken care of.

I placed the bundles inside a deposit bag, zipping it up and setting it on the counter as I prepared to go make a drop at the bank.

"Sara, if you're ready to go, I will walk you to your car."

Sara pulled the ponytail holder from her shoulder length strawberry blond hair; the bone straight mane fell to the collar of her Car Care uniform. "I'm ready," she said, pulling keys from the book bag she seemed to always carry. "I was even able to get some homework done during our down time."

"Yeah, I saw you drop that book under the counter whenever the door opened. What exactly are you studying?"

"Engine Fundamentals. Boring material, but it's part of the curriculum. I have to do it, though. I'll admit that I'm more into the hands-on stuff." Sara put her book bag on her shoulder.

"I've probably said this before, but you're the only girl I know in a mechanic program." Sara was average height for a young woman, but had a thin build. I couldn't visualize her underneath a car changing brake pads or dismantling a transmission.

"Yes, Scott, you say it all the time." She laughed at me as I held the entrance door open. "I couldn't believe how dead it was tonight."

I locked the door and said, "It has been fairly slow, but I'm not complaining because I need to go home and take care of some things," however unpleasant they were going to be.

"Yeah, and I have more studying to do. Two more semesters and I am done with this program."

Sara's classic midnight blue Cadillac Eldorado Coupe with a V8 engine that was rebuilt by her uncle sat near the front entrance of the Car Care building. Her tires touched the lines of a handicapped parking space. I waited for her to get in and start the car.

"Have a nice night, Scott," she waved. The car purred to life with a quiet hum as she talked to me with the door open.

"Thanks, you do the same and drive safe," I said as I closed her door.

Sara lived in Myers Park, on the South side of the city, an area that was recently on the news for having laws that prohibited ownership of homes by black people. The publicity made Myers Park sound like a completely divided part of Charlotte. Supposedly, the laws dated post-slavery and were never revised to reflect current times. There were a couple residents on the news expressing their outrage that on the books, blatant discrimination still existed. One man dismissed the law and allegations of discrimination as past occurrences, and suggested people needed to stop playing the race card.

I waved at Sara as she exited the parking lot. I could hear "Just Fine," a new song by Mary J. Blige, from the Power 98 radio station blasting from her stereo system. I put the money pouch under my arm as I fished out my keys from my front pocket and pressed the keyless entry.

Because Germani didn't call back, I could imagine her sitting in the recliner of the living room waiting for me with her arms crossed and her foot tapping.

As I put the car in reverse and rolled backward, I felt the tire on the passenger side wobble. I placed the car back in park as I got out and went around to see what the problem was. After leaning down, I noticed that the front passenger side tire was so flat that the rim almost touched the ground.

"Ain't this a trip," I said to myself as I stood up and put my hand on top of the hood of the car. The light at the street was broken and the one further down didn't give off enough.

An indescribable twitch tugged at my spine as I could have sworn I heard footfalls nearby. My head jerked to the left of a vacant parking lot, vacant with the exception of a 1979 Chevy Caprice that had littered my company's property for the past three days. I kept telling myself to call the city and have it towed away, but as I've said before, distractions make you forgetful.

I glanced to the right where Farm Pond Lane sat amongst deserted cement, although I could hear traffic driving down Albemarle.

The tire needed to be changed. I went back to the driver's side and popped the trunk then fished around in the unlit area for the dummy tire and jack. As I searched, I realized that there was no flashlight.

My emergency kit was in Germani's Cougar. I had given it to her for the trip to the annual women's retreat over the past summer. She'd driven to Atlanta with Taylor and Stephanie, her church friends. They didn't want to be confined to a bus for long hours.

The store had a storm lamp in the back office. I decided to go grab that and thought it might be wise to get a can of fix-a-flat while I was in there.

It didn't take long for me to change my tire. When I got back in the car, the cell phone I had left on my seat was flashing with missed calls. All of them were from Germani. I hoped she wasn't trying to start something else about the power bill before I got home. As I decided whether to call home, the phone rang again.

Germani spoke in rushed choppy words, and at once, our earlier argument was replaced by somebody else's problems.

CHAPTER TWENTY-NINE

GERMANI

Scott wasn't going to work my nerves.

That's all I was thinking as I pulled the take-out container from its bag and placed the contents on a thick Dixie paper plate.

I had dropped Elijah off at Momma's house before I went on a feed-my-soul mission. My emotions were all over the place after the argument with Scott. I was prepared for an ugly, heated conversation when my husband made it home, and if I felt like hollering my aggravation from the rooftop, I didn't want Elijah caught in the middle.

On the way back home, I stopped at Board-walk Billy's. They had a hot wing special. Ten for five dollars. I thought about getting the ribs, but my appetite craved mozzarella sticks. Ribs just didn't go with fried cheese.

Once my plate was in hand, I angled a glass bottle of Sobe Tsunami between my thumb and forefinger, dangling my dinner on the way to the living room couch for an episode of *Grey's Anatomy*. Just like my momma to Howie Mandel in *Deal or No Deal*, I rearranged my schedule around Isaiah Washington in *Grey's Anatomy*. I admired his easy swagger as he gravitated to emergency victims. The man was a complex cardiothoracic surgeon with an obvious dominant presence. Although always competent, his role choices had evolved since I first saw him playing in the movie *Crooklyn* thirteen years ago. Since they fired him, the show wasn't quite the same, but I continued watching anyway and lived for the re-runs where I would get to see Dr. Burke.

I took a swig of my peach mango beverage, savoring the *me* time more than the drink itself. I placed the food on our end table and curled my feet under my bottom as I cozied up in the nook of the couch. I emptied my thoughts as I tried to focus on my favorite show. My thoughts kept bouncing to the growing tension between Scott and myself, then I would focus harder on television. By the end of the episode, I couldn't remember half of what the show was about.

The shrill sound of our house phone jolted me from my self-conflicted mental zone. Cherish's phone number came across the television screen caller ID.

"Hello." I tried not to smear buffalo wing sauce on the phone console as I answered.

The hollowness of her voice almost made it inaudible. "Germani, can I talk with you?"

I had called Cherish at least five or six times since the charity in hopes of building a friendship, but she never returned my calls. I was glad that we were finally connecting.

"Sure," I said, pressing the phone against my ear with the palm of my hand. Something seemed strange in Cherish's voice.

"Why have you been calling me so much lately? I know you don't like me," she whispered.

I straightened my back as a chill went down my spine. "Uh . . ." I didn't know what else to say. Maybe I was pushing for a friendship that wasn't meant to be.

"Germani, I know it shouldn't matter, but I was wondering why all of a sudden you want to call me." She paused.

I explained, "When we were at the banquet you seemed to be going through some things and I felt bad for not being the type of person you felt you could confide in. Basically, you looked like you needed a friend and I haven't been good in that area. I used my feeling toward your husband against you and I was wrong for that. I wasn't trying to be nosy about your marriage. I truly was worried about you."

"Yeah, my marriage." Cherish paused again. I could hear her breathing. I thought she was on the verge of tears, yet her voice remained placid and detached.

"Are you okay?" I asked.

"I've been living all wrong, Germani. Damon's not the man I thought he was. Arrogantly selfish, that's my Damon." I could hear Cherish crunch on something. "The problem is . . . I was raised to please my man. That's how things were done in my home. My mom always told me that if I wanted to be happily married, then I had to make my husband's priorities my own. A wise woman lets her man do what he wants as long as he's taking care of home."

Cherish gulped. "My father always had other women and my mother always knew about them. She used to say that she had no reason to be jealous, because she was his wife, not his whore. A wife is priority, while a whore is temporary. I respected both my parents, but I wanted something different. I didn't want my husband to feel like he needed mistresses or like I needed to ignore what he might be doing when he wasn't with me. The chemistry I had with Damon was intoxicating. I knew that I would never feel that kind of electric intensity with another man. Completely uninhibited love."

I could hear that crunching again, like she was eating peanuts or hard candy. But with her words, I was beginning to understand Cherish in a different way. She wasn't that different than me, when I was experimenting with porn to please Scott and keep him interested in our marriage.

"I feel like I lost myself somewhere along the line," she continued. "Started doing things I didn't want to do. Believed that he could be my everything. Believed I could be his everything and all the people around us would be enhancements to our lives. Damon had me convinced that the more we pursued heightening the excitement in our lives, the happier we would be."

Cherish inhaled sharply before confessing, "I've been stealing drugs from his work supply, trying to numb myself for the past couple of years. Damon thought someone in his family was taking samples, but it was me. I feel terrible about it. I never meant for him to disown his mother and siblings, but I couldn't tell him what I was doing either. It all started when Damon and I became part of this swinger's club. We've been having sex with other partners and couples every weekend since before we got married. I mean . . . anything kinky and risqué, we've probably tried it."

I stopped her, because I didn't want to hear sordid details of their sex life.

"It's not necessary for you to share everything with me. I don't need to know details." To put it tactfully, I was saying TMI, Too Much Information.

"No, I have to get this off my mind. I've held it in for too long. Justified . . . too long. So, please, listen to what I'm saying. We were interacting with physicians of all kinds from cosmetic surgeons to orthodontists and family doctors. Damon met them through his job." I could hear a gulp like she was drinking. "We didn't take precautions, didn't think protection was necessary. The people we dealt with were highly respected, exceptionally intelligent, medical professionals for God's sake. How asinine." Cherish suddenly cackled.

I stayed quiet. The conversation had me off kilter.

"Somehow things went wrong. I love Damon and would do anything to please him, but he wasn't the type of man I could trust unconditionally. He was blinded by his ambition; began letting too many people into our swinger's circle. Damon refused to admit how out of control things were after I found out that I was AIDS infected. He refused to get tested himself and didn't want me to warn the people we were sleeping with. He wanted to act like things were normal."

My mouth dropped open and the phone slipped from my palm. I smeared red grease on the arm rest as I scrambled for the phone, which fell under the couch. I got on my knees to get it.

When I picked up the phone Cherish was still talking. "I can't go on with the guilt. I just can't."

Oh, Lord. I was stumped, baffled and seriously shocked. All I wanted was to enjoy my buffalo wings in peace. This confession took me into a whole other realm.

"Um . . . um . . . well," I couldn't think. This wasn't a conversation I felt prepared to handle. I silently prayed for God to help me to help her.

Before I could say anything, Cherish spat, "You're judging me, aren't you? That's why you're so quiet. Probably thinking how pathetic and despicable I am."

"That's not what's on my mind," I said truthfully as I tried to keep her calm.

"My, my, my, what a pretty little mess Cherish has gotten herself in," she said in a strange sing-song voice.

It felt like Cherish was edging off an emotional cliff, close to losing any rationale. I measured my options. My next words could make all the difference.

"No, Cherish, I think you're wounded. Life choices have severely wounded you. Often times, when I'm feeling like the world is weighing on my shoulders, I pray for guidance and I use my Bible for encouragement. I can't say that I do the right thing every time I go through some kind of suffering, but I know that prayer works and God listens. Look, let me get my Bible and I'll be right back."

I waited for her to say something, but besides light breathing, the line was silent.

I knew what person in the Bible I wanted Cherish to relate to. Rahab stuck out to me. I searched my study Bible to make sure I wasn't giving her the wrong interpretation of the Word. In the Book of Joshua, in order to save her family, Rahab helped Joshua and his men in their defeat of Jericho. My pastor taught us that Jesus was a descendant of Rahab, a former prostitute who later married and became a virtuous woman. A woman who used her body to please many men extended to the greatest man in the Bible. She and Jesus shared the same bloodline. I wanted Cherish to know whatever faults she had now, any mistakes she previously cultivated didn't have to dictate her future. Damon had Cherish's mind all twisted up.

I put markers in the books of Joshua and Matthew to confirm the lineage and then made my way back to the phone. She was gone when I got there.

I quickly dialed her back with trembling fingers. I didn't want her to think that she was alone or that I was condemning her. If she called me with a conversation as personal as that one, then she must have felt like I was her best option in her time of need. I was more scared than I'd ever been in my life. Petrified for Cherish. The voice mail clicked on. My nerves were on edge. Instead of calling her again, I dialed Scott.

I said breathlessly, "I need you to meet me right now. Right . . . now."

"What's wrong?"

My thoughts were moving too fast. "I can't talk, I need to get over to Cherish's house. In fact, don't come home. Something is very, very wrong. Can you meet me over there?"

"Whoa. Tell me what's going on."

"I can't. We've got to get over there." My voice kept rising as I jammed my feet into a pair of Sperry loafers and headed to the door.

"I'm on the way." Scott's voice exemplified the worry I felt as I headed to Cherish's home, unaware of what I was walking into.

CHAPTER THIRTY

SCOTT

Germani's Cougar was in the driveway when I made it to Damon and Cherish's house on Pemswood. There were no other cars parked outside, but that wasn't unusual. With the rash of recent break-ins throughout the city, it was understandable that Damon and Cherish would have their vehicles parked in their garage.

I stepped into the warm, dry night air and looked down the quiet tree-lined street. Strolling up the walkway, I checked my phone screen, hoping that Damon would get back to me. I had left him a message after hanging up with Germani. I knew he wouldn't be home, because Thursday nights he usually frequented the Gentleman's Lounge for an after hours nightcap. When I spoke to him earlier, he told me that he had a busy schedule and would be meeting up with a couple of new sales reps at his favorite stripper's spot.

I walked up to the front door. I could see the shadow of a light streaming through the stained glass window. The doorbell chimed loudly inside the home.

Germani was nowhere in sight. I assumed she and Cherish were having some woman talk. I even thought maybe my wife had over-reacted when she called me. Lately, she seemed easily riled and moody.

I waited several seconds for Cherish to answer, but nobody came to the door. I turned the knob, but the door was locked. I checked the time on my cell phone. After waiting three long minutes I dialed their house number. Germani should be expecting me.

"Where are they?" I murmured to myself as I stepped back and looked up to see if any other lights were on in the house.

Germani rounded the side of the house by the garage, squeezing between the garage door and the front end of her car. "Nobody's answering."

This was a declaration of what I already knew.

She made a circle with her finger. "I also checked all around the house and I don't see any movement. The back patio door was slightly open, but I was afraid to go in."

Still being a skeptic, I asked, "What made you think something was wrong enough for both of us to come over?"

"I don't know how else to describe my conversation with Cherish, but she told me a lot of personal information, and toward the end of our talk she sounded a little crazy." Germani whispered the word *crazy*. "Like she might be suicidal."

I frowned. "Cherish?" It just didn't sound believable. Damon's wife was a happy person. The kind of woman that kept a smile on her face; had a warm disposition. In fact, she was probably the most easy-going female I knew.

"Did you try calling Damon? Were you able to reach him?"

I shook my head. "I left him a message before I got here, but he hasn't called me back yet."

"Cherish isn't answering her phone either. You can't tell me that doesn't sound bizarre to you. "

"There have been plenty of times Damon hasn't answered my calls. We don't know what he could be doing. Sometimes people are too busy to get to their phones"

"Umph," Germani replied.

"What's that suppose to mean?"

"Look, we can't just be standing here . . . we need to do something quick." Germani flayed her arms in panic.

"Come on," I said as I took the trek around the house that I had seen Germani come from. I headed to the patio near a Koi pond with my wife on my heels. I stepped into the floor-to-ceiling glassed in sunroom and instantly felt chilled. The air had to be on full blast. "You know this is invasion of privacy, right?" I told Germani as we moved from the sunroom through their kitchen.

I turned on lights in each room I went through. If Damon was home, I hoped he had a sense of humor about the intrusion. He wasn't big on un-invited company.

Germani nodded as she linked her arm with mine in the darkened area. "It's the risk we have to take. Believe me, if you had heard her talking, you would understand why I'm here. Scott, I got a really bad feeling about all this."

She shuddered and I didn't know if it was from the cold or fear.

"Maybe they're sleeping," I said to Germani as I noticed a set of car keys on an accent table. "Anybody home?" I called out as we entered the lit hall entry.

"Cherish can't be sleep that quick. I just got off the phone with her less than an hour ago."

It was obvious that no one was in the down-stairs area. I strained my eyes and could hear vague rhythmic thumping from above my head.

The sound was so obscure that I had to strain to hear it, almost like music was playing, but I couldn't be positive.

"Do you hear that sound?" I asked Germani as she picked up the keys off the table.

She nodded her head with a deep scowl. "Uh-huh." Germani examined the set. "Aren't these Damon's?"

In the palm of her hand lay a wired ring with a miniature VIP access card, his Lexus keyless entry button, a baby blue Charlotte Panther's emblem and eight keys.

"Yep." I was starting to feel that Cherish's panic had some merit. I turned on the hall light that led to the second floor and bounced up the stairs two steps at a time.

I went directly to Damon and Cherish's bedroom and what I saw made me stop dead in my tracks.

Both of them were in bed under a sheet covered in blood. Even from the dim light shining from the hallway I could see the circular smears across Damon's upper torso.

I don't know what made me think I could revive him. I guess natural response, instinct. Who knew, but I rushed over to his body and pressed my hand to the ooze of a gaping hole right below his sternum.

Germani let out a high-pitched scream as she remained in the doorway. She inhaled sharply and screamed again. Her entire body shook like she was convulsing.

With my hand pressed to Damon's chest, I searched the room for something I could use to stop the flow of blood.

When I was barely out of high school I wanted to be a paramedic. Thought that would be the coolest job without having to endure years of college courses with completion in eighteen months. I took CPR courses in the Adult Education program at the community college. When I discovered that I would be required to complete Advance Biology and Chemistry classes, I dropped the EMT program. Regardless, there were some things I still remembered.

It was too dark in the room for me to see clearly.

"Turn the light on," I told a hysterical Germani.

Her screams ceased. She slowly shook her head as though the rest of her body was paralyzed.

I reached up with my free hand to check for a pulse. I thought I felt a faint, slow vibration against my fingers, although his body was growing cold. Probably from the freezing central air.

I let out a small sigh of relief as I looked over at Germani again. "Call an ambulance. I think he's still alive," I requested,

scared to move my hand from his wound.

She still wouldn't budge.

I hollered with pained frustration, "Dang it, Germani, snap out of it and help me. Get the telephone."

She jolted from her trance and began shifting her feet. "Okay . . . okay. Where's the phone?"

"Downstairs, I think." Damon didn't keep one in the room for his own personal reasons. He said the last place he wanted to be disturbed was when he was in bed.

Germani left the room and I could hear her running down the stairs.

I also heard a gurgled groan over the music playing from the other side of the bed.

"Cherish, everything's going to be okay. An ambulance will be here very soon," I said.

She mumbled something.

I leaned over Damon to listen.

I could only understand one word. "Bad."

I didn't know what else to say, so I simply replied, "Everything is going to be fine. Just hold on, everything is going to be fine."

Germani ran back into the room. "I called 911 dispatch. Help is on the way. They said an ambulance should be here in less than ten minutes."

"Good. Cherish was just talking. Can you see how bad her injuries are?"

Germani walked over to Cherish's side of the bed, then paused as I stared at the blood soaked sheet.

"I can't touch that sheet, Scott. I think we should wait for the paramedics."

"All I need you to do is see where her wounds are and how bad."

Germani frowned and shook her head again. "I'm not comfortable doing that. Cherish told me she has AIDS."

I snapped my head up and looked straight into Germani's eyes. "What?"

"AIDS. She said she has AIDS." Germani spoke slowly, accentuating each word.

I recoiled at the thought and almost removed my already red hand from the wound site, not knowing if he had the deadly virus as well.

"Did she say whether Damon had it too?"

"No. No, she didn't."

I tried to think of things I should do next and couldn't. I shifted the weight on my legs as I stayed bent down. My knee crackled. This was the worst night of my life.

I finally said, "Germani, go downstairs and wait for the paramedics to get here. The front door is still locked."

After she left the room for the second time, I checked Damon's pulse again. I didn't feel a vibration except from the slight trembling of my hand. I convinced myself that it didn't mean anything. I prayed that the paramedics would hurry up. I prayed harder than I had in my whole life that God would spare Damon and Cherish's lives.

CHAPTER THIRTY-ONE

GERMANI

Damon Spears was pronounced dead at 12:14 A.M. after arrival at Carolinas Medical Center.

Scott seemed to become numb from the news. The police hadn't allowed us to follow as gurneys were lifted into an ambulance and sped away from their house. We answered questions about what little we knew. I was hysterical. My words jumbled together like a wrinkled cassette in a tape player. Scott spoke for me, repeating things I had told him when we first arrived. He said I called Cherish crazy, but I couldn't remember what I told him. There had been blood . . . so much blood that I would be seeing red for the rest of my life.

It didn't help that the police thought that it was supposed to be the makings of a murder-suicide. They had suspicion that Cherish was the one who stabbed Damon. She didn't have any visible wounds and they bagged a wood carving knife under the bed. My sense of understanding was pillaged under layers of disbelief and guilt. I should have been able to talk her out of it.

Scott walked away from the attending physician, Dr. Ellison, and collapsed in a cushioned chair. A look of disbelief covered his face. I stood with the doctor as he explained the extent of Damon's injury.

His tricuspid valve was severely punctured. He bled out before the ambulance made it to the scene. There was no way they could have saved him.

Dr. Ellison looked as worn as I felt. His eyes had poofy bags under them as if he'd worked too many shifts without sleep.

"I believe Mrs. Spears is going to be okay. The medical team pumped out the contents of her stomach and they're working on stabilizing her vitals," he said. Dr. Ellison adjusted the face mask hanging from his neck. "I assure you that she is in the best care North Carolina has to offer. We don't know how long ago she ingested whatever she took. We still have to run labs to see what kind of drugs are in her system, so I can't honestly tell you how much damage was done."

I rubbed my forehead. My temples throbbed and exhaustion had me nearly dead on my feet. Things were going from bad to worse.

"I'm going to try and stick around for a while to see how she's doing. I'll be sitting right over there if anything changes." I pointed to the row of chairs by Scott. I had placed my purse in the seat next to him. The waiting room was full of people. Death, sickness and injury surrounded us.

After Dr. Ellison went back through the double doors, I sauntered over to Scott. His elbows rested on his knees, while stretched hands connected against the back of his bent head.

"You want some coffee?" I asked him.

He looked up and I felt like his gaze went straight through me. His expression was blank. I turned to see if maybe he was staring at something behind me, but besides a few people walking across the floor, I didn't see anything.

"Scott," I said with concern.

My husband blinked twice before his gaze met my eyes.

"Coffee?"

"No. I'm tired and ready to go home." He abruptly stood and stretched.

"They're still working on Cherish. I was planning to stay until I found out how she was doing."

Scott's face frowned up. "For what? She's a murderer. She killed my best friend. Why do we need to know how she's doing? If she's alive, she is already doing a whole lot better than Damon. We wouldn't even be in a hospital if it wasn't for Cherish being jacked up in the head."

He was snapping at me. I wasn't used to him snapping at me. I stepped back a few steps. It wasn't appropriate for us to have this discussion in the hospital waiting room, but I was the one that Cherish had confided in. I felt I had to rally in her defense.

"Do you have any idea what she was going through?"

"Whatever she was going through didn't justify her taking Damon's life."

"Damon wasn't blemish free. Cherish was tortured by her life with him. I couldn't believe some of the things she told me. They were going to sex parties and having orgies with doctors that Damon sold prescription samples to. And it gets worse. Even though she had AIDS, Damon didn't want her to tell anybody." I spoke quietly but there were still a few people nearby tuned in to our conversation. One woman who sat next to a pale sickly man in a wheelchair covered her little boy's ears. We walked over by a water cooler, out of earshot of the general public.

"He was putting all kinds of people at risk unnecessarily," I whispered.

Scott threw up his hand like he wasn't hearing me. "Nah, you don't know if that's true. That is just her version of what happened. Damon didn't have her doing nothing she didn't want to do. It wasn't like he was controlling her or something. They have been doing that swingers' thing for years."

"You knew?" I questioned Scott as my eyebrows raised. Truth was a reflection of itself, and at that moment, I saw it as an ugly devouring beast. I saw my husband in much the same way. Mirror images. "Of course, you knew."

Scott ignored my statement. Automatically made me wonder what else he knew that I didn't. True enough, couples had secrets. Nobody told their partner everything, but it was the big secrets that could destroy a relationship, annihilate a marriage.

"Now you can stay if that would make you feel better, but I don't have a whole lot of sympathy for Cherish right now." There was acid in his voice. Scott began walking toward the glass doors with the exit sign.

I stood for a moment thinking, *What if I did stay, how would I get home?* My car was still parked in the driveway at Cherish's house. Right along with the purse I left in the front seat. In such a rush to get to the hospital, I didn't think I would need my car or my purse. They were blocked in by a fire truck, ambulance and two police cars when we left the scene. Even thinking 'scene' made me cringe. Death wasn't supposed to be so close. I could smell it lingering in my nose hairs.

I knew Scott had to be grieving. His best friend was gone . . . dead. The anger wasn't meant to be directed at me. I shouldn't take it personal.

As I watched his infuriated steps stomp from the building, I felt disjointed. Somehow, during tragedy, when Scott and I should have been closest, there seemed to be an evolving wedge. He was walking away and I was standing still. How much worse could things get between us?

CHAPTER THIRTY-TWO

SCOTT

If you don't respect where you came from, then you won't appreciate where you're going. Those were the words I would say to Damon when he complained about his momma, but he wasn't even remotely receptive. He resented being raised poor and was obsessed with having more than he was raised with. He constantly complained that his mother never stayed at one decent job. Her main income came from hustling. Ms. Ilene taught them to survive, but not to succeed. Ironically, he hated Ilene for being a hustler, yet he used those very skills she taught him to get paid as a sales rep. Wasn't much difference between a sales representative and a hustler. Both had to perfect the game of persuasion.

The brick ranch-style house in Hidden Valley was nondescript except for the row of cars parked down the street in front of it. The inside of the house was also full. There was a card game going on. Three men and Ms. Ilene were playing spades with money on the square glass table. A group stood around watching. Nay-Nay, Damon's older sister, was the one that led me through the maze of people. She looked almost exactly like Ms. Ilene, except she was about one hundred and fifty pounds bigger, with a raspy voice. Her eyes were half closed and she swayed when she walked. When we were kids, she used to follow me around, getting on my nerves. On that night, her gift for gab seemed to be locked away.

Ms. Ilene was addressing the other players of the game. A hill of dollars lay on the table.

"Ma, Scott came through and he wants to talk to you," Nay-Nay said before turning her attention to one of the card game on-lookers, holding a joint. She removed it from his hand and took a draw.

"Hamhock." Ms. Ilene looked up and smiled as she shuffled the deck of cards. "What a surprise. You came through to see me. Get comfortable and enjoy yourself. There's all kinds of liquor in the kitchen if you want a drink," she said to me.

I watched her flick cards around the table; one . . . two . . . three . . . back to herself and then around again.

Ms. Ilene trashtalked while she finished dealing out the deck. "Me and my partner ain't moving from this table. Y'all have sat down with the wrong ones. We about to send you home broke and disgusted. You might as well call yourself De La Hoya. In fact, if you want to just hand over the money and get up with your pride intact, I won't be mad at you."

I couldn't deliver the kind of news I had in that room full of strangers. I had hoped my solemn expression and unannounced visit would be warning that I had something bad to say, but she was too involved in her game and Nay-Nay was too high to care.

I walked over to her side of the table. "Ms. Ilene, can I talk with you alone for a moment? It's about Damon."

"Baby, I just sat down to play this game. Ain't no pausing in Spades. Speak your mind. I'm listening." Ms. Ilene had her set of cards fanned in front of her as she counted the three high clubs and two hearts. Her set was mostly black. I knew enough about the game to realize that she had a good hand.

"We got six. How many you bidding?" asked a chunky, dark-skinned man to her right.

Ms. Ilene looked at the man across from her. "Howel, I can pull six by myself. What you working with?"

I recognized Howel from the house I had dropped Ms. Ilene off at. He shook his head. "My hand is kinda ugly. I can pull out one for sure and maybe even two."

"Put us down for eight. Somebody about to bump heads," she said confidently.

I bent down close to her head. "This is important. I don't think you want to hear it like this."

Ace of diamond went on the center of the table, followed by a three of club and a five.

"Is he dead?" she asked bluntly.

It felt like the whole room shifted their eyes to me.

"Yes," I hissed through my teeth like I was in pain. And in a way, I was.

"Okay." She dropped a two of spades on top of the others and pulled the stack toward her. "Guess we got to plan a funeral."

I didn't expect the response I got from Ms. Ilene. I waited for it to sink in, but she kept playing the game like I hadn't said a thing. All I could figure was that she must be numb. Ms. Ilene wasn't the type to be cold over her children. Shoot, I was numb when I first heard. I had just talked to my best friend this morning. We laughed about our crazy schedules and how we didn't hang out like we used to before we got married. In less than twelve hours, he had been taken from this world. I couldn't figure it out. What could have happened at Cherish and Damon's house to make her snap so unexpectedly?

We left the hospital before we learned any more about Cherish and her condition. Germani was mad at me, but I didn't care. I dropped her off before I came to Ms. Ilene's place. She kept defending Cherish and talking about how depressed the girl had been lately. I was about ready to go off, so I felt it was in both of our best interests if I took her home. Damon was dead; my boy was gone. That knowledge diminished any level of good feelings I could have had about Cherish.

Ms. Ilene thumped out a cigarette from a Virginia Slim pack in her lap. "Nay-Nay, hand me your lighter."

Nay-Nay took one from her pocket and slid it across the table.

Ms. Ilene lit her cigarette. After taking a long draw, she blew cigarette smoke in the air from the side of her mouth and said, "I have a friend, Flossie, that works at Phillip Morris. They'll be closing down that plant over in Concord, and Flossie's thinking about moving to Richmond with them. She only has four years to retire. Might as well get her due. Anyway, Phillip Morris makes Virginia Slim. Flossie brought me a carton last Tuesday, I believe, and since they was free, I didn't turn it down, but I still prefer my Newport 100s."

"So, he's dead. You know he had no love for us," Nay-Nay said as she leaned one arm on the back of Howel's chair. I guess that part of the conversation was finally registering through her marijuana fog. "He didn't even act like we existed, why should we act like he did?" Even with her eyes half closed, I could see the contempt in them.

She used to adore her big brother. When we were about eleven, Nay-Nay was five years old and the baby girl in the family. She had this pumpkin patch doll she took everywhere with her. She used to strap the stringy-haired doll to the pink bucket on the front of her bicycle and ride behind us. If she saw us leaving the house, she ran to get on her bike and follow us. Usually, Damon and I were going to the corner store to get candy and chips, or we would go to the elementary school up the street to play basketball. Without fail, Nay-Nay was on our trail. She was the only one. Ke-Ke and Mario had their own friends to play with and wasn't thinking about us. Brandon was still a baby, so he wasn't leaving the house anyway.

Damon used to turn her bike back toward the house and tell her to mind her business. She would turn the bike back around, then pedal up to us like we were in a clique. If Damon yelled at her, she'd run inside to tell Ms. Ilene, then we would get cursed out and were forced to baby-sit Nay-Nay. I'd bribe her to leave with a bag of red hot potato chips and some Boston Baked Beans. I knew that would get her to leave us alone the majority of times. Things sure had changed over the years.

Nay-Nay had passed the joint to a female with a bright orange waterfall-looking weave pony-tail. The woman was light brown, but had black-heads all over her face. She stared at me with a buck toothed smile.

Nay-Nay was waiting for a response.

I kept a blank face, like I was playing poker. I didn't know none of them people staring at me and I wasn't going to put Damon's business out there.

When I didn't say anything, Nay-Nay lifted a beer bottle of Old English by its neck. She took a swig.

"Nay-Nay, come take over my hand." Ms. Ilene waved her daughter over to that side of the table.

Ms. Ilene took me to one of the rooms at the back of the house. It was packed with boxes, but I guess that was the only quiet place.

"What happened to my son?" Her attitude had softened.

"He was stabbed to death . . . murdered by his wife. I guess it was supposed to be a murder-suicide. At least, that's what the police think happened. Germani and I found their bodies. Cherish tried to kill herself with some pills."

Ms. Ilene puffed hard on that cigarette as she nodded her head. "I assume that we will be the ones to get his things together. Do you think he had an insurance policy to cover some of his expenses? I know I have a small one, about five thousand to help in the funeral costs, but we need to go through his things and see what all can be taken care of."

"You don't want to see the body and say good-bye?" That seemed like the first thing a mother would want to do.

"No. I want to remember him in the living. If you say he's dead, then I have no reason not to trust the truth of that and do what is necessary to provide a proper burial."

I sat against an old washer that was placed in the corner, and tried to absorb the reality of my friend's death.

Ms. Ilene took a long drag from her cigarette. Her hands slightly shook. "You know, Scott, I'm not sure how I'm supposed to feel about Damon being dead. When I lost Brandon I was devastated. He was my baby boy. My pride and joy. Damon had so much hatred in his heart for me, for his sisters and Devon, and for the hood. For everything he came from. I've been waiting for his heart to soften up, for him to make amends with his family, and now, that will never happen. And to think his last memory of us was that one of his family stole prescription drugs from him. I may not have always done right by my kids, but I didn't raise thieves. To know that he thought so little of us . . . I don't know how I'm supposed to feel."

Ms. Ilene was a strong woman, but I could hear the pain in her voice.

This was another reason for me to be pissed off at Cherish. While we were at Damon's house being questioned by the police, Germani told the officers that Cherish had been stealing samples from Damon's briefcase. She believed Cherish took some drugs before calling her.

"Cherish told my wife that she was the one stealing from Damon. She was supposedly doped up when she killed him. She's probably been doing it for years."

That cigarette halted two inches from Ms. Ilene's her mouth. Her face frowned up. "You mean to tell me that Damon's wife was the reason he kicked us to the curb?"

"Yes, ma'am."

She cursed under her breath. "I should have known. I should have known that, but I thought Damon was looking for an excuse not to be around. That his nose was too far up in the air. Kay-Kay didn't like that girl from the first time we met her. She was too quiet . . . devious. Soaking in everything we said and did, so she could use it to her benefit. And he thought we were the messed up ones. Ain't that nothing. You say she's in the hospital right now?" Ms. Ilene resumed her smoking as she looked at me. Her numbness changed to anger.

"Yes, ma'am."

"Okay." She paused. "Okay."

Her anger trumped mine.

She took one last puff before extinguishing the cigarette on the washing machine behind me. Ms. Ilene tossed the cigarette into a metal garbage can.

I didn't know what Ms. Ilene planned to do about Cherish, but I hoped I didn't become a part of another crime.

CHAPTER THIRTY-THREE

GERMANI

I burned all of Scott's clothes that he wore that night. Set aflame everything down to his socks and Hanes briefs. After putting on a pair of industrial use rubber cleaning gloves, I took that heap he left on the bedroom floor, tossed it in a black garbage bag and dropped the bag on the barbecue grill in the back of the house, then lit a match.

It wasn't that I was an AIDS-phobic, but if something was hazardous and contagious, then I didn't want it openly displayed in my house, on my floor, near my bed. It was enough going on that I didn't need the added discomfort. The smell of his blood-soaked garments made me nauseous. It was so bad that I put rubbing alcohol on a makeup sponge and crammed it up my nasal passage, trying to get some relief.

Scott had long left to go talk with Damon's mother. He refused to take me back over to the house so I could get my car. I hadn't wanted to go back either, but I needed my vehicle and I wanted my purse. The entire trip home, he drove with his gaze set on the road and his eyebrows furrowed. Every word I spoke seemed to be rapidly dismissed with a *"Not now"* and tense silence. I might as well have been talking to myself. By the time we made it home, I was done saying anything to him. When he came out of the shower and changed clothes, he finally acknowledged my existence. Told me that he needed to inform Damon's family of what was going on. He didn't ask if I wanted to go, and from his foul mood, I didn't offer. What I did do was try to give him a hug, show him some love in the midst of his loss, but he said those words again, *Not now*. I was offended and felt abandoned. He brushed past me, knocking my shoulder with his. I could feel the grief and pain in his shove.

I gathered his soiled clothing and had a bonfire. Smoke circled the calm air as I sat in a lawn chair, watching the flames. The smell of melting plastic was repulsive, but it was a world better than the aroma of death.

The neighbor's dog two doors down, whimpered. I could hear him rattle against the small box cage like he wanted to be free. Ms. Maverick kept her German Shepherd, Warner, on a leash in that cage every night. I usually ignored the sounds, but a few other people had called the Home Owners Association on Ms. Maverick for not keeping Warner quiet.

Her son, Lucas, bought the dog as house protection, but she obvious didn't want a pet in her home. She was the epitome of old with a short silvery mane, frail limbs, wrinkled skin and a humped back. I had once heard them arguing outside about Lucas thinking she needed to go live in a nursing home where people could take care of her. Ms. Maverick told him that he just wanted to get rid of her and she wasn't going to no place that mistreated the elderly for profit. I rarely saw Ms. Maverick except when she answered the door for Meals on Wheels. Once in a while, Lucas would pass me while walking Warner as I strolled Elijah around the neighborhood. Didn't know much about him or Ms. Maverick. The houses in my neighborhood were close enough for me to learn vague information about my neighbors, but what do we really know about the people living next to us?

As black smoke took over the sky in my yard, I decided to contact Autumn. I needed to go get my car. Her house was twenty minutes away. I thought about calling Mekhi, but Momma lived too far away for me to wake him up and to come across town in the middle of the night. He would do it, but Scott would probably be back before Mekhi made it to my house and I was already antsy about my car still being at a crime scene.

Autumn sounded like she had been wide awake. Surprisingly, her voice was alert, "What's wrong?"

It was dang near three in the morning. Only people in crisis called their friends at that hour.

"Something bad has happened." I instantly felt déjà vu, by using Cherish's words when she had called me. "You will never believe my night. It is unbelievable. Do you remember Scott's friend that I'm always talking about?"

"Yeah, Damon. The friend you said Scott should hurry up and get rid of."

I winced. "Yeah, him."

Considering the circumstances, my previous comments about the man sounded kinda of disgraceful. Almost like I was heartless, which was the furthest thing from the truth. I didn't want Damon around, but I also hadn't wished ill upon him.

"Damon's dead. His wife is in the hospital. Autumn, they think she did it and Scott left to go tell Damon's mom."

"Back it up. Come again."

I knew it sounded bizarre, probably like some episode from *Snapped* on the Oxygen channel. People we knew weren't supposed to be involved in murders. That kind of stuff happened to other people.

The events of the night destroyed any peaceful thought I could have. I felt the hairs on my arms stand up like it was freezing outside, but the warm breeze, plus the heat from the barbecue grill touching my skin said different.

"Dead. Damon is dead." I paused, lifting my eyes to the sky.

"Supposedly, Cherish stabbed him to death. And that wasn't the worst of it. She called me earlier tonight. I knew something was wrong. I just didn't say the right thing . . . do the right thing. She hung up on me because she was trying to confide in me and I made her feel like I was judging her. And maybe I was. I hadn't exactly been treating her with kindness. Anyway, she told me that her and Damon were doing those swinger parties. You know what I'm talking about, right?"

"Yeah, orgies."

"Well, now she has AIDS. I think she took finding out pretty hard, but then Damon had her keeping it a secret, while they continued to have unprotected sex with other people. I think all that combined was more than she could handle."

Autumn replied, "I bet it was. It goes back to what I was telling you at the nail salon. If you keep sacrificing for the wrong people and wrong purpose, eventually, you will have nothing good left for yourself. It is awful that such a tragedy happened though. How did you get the news?"

"Scott and I were the ones that found them."

The fire had smoldered down to blackened ashes. Light ambers peeked from the bottom of the grill.

I stood up and took the lawn chair to the garage.

Autumn hummed into the phone, "Um . . . um . . . um, the devil is busy."

"Yes, he is. I can't even explain to you how messed up I am by all of this. But right now, I don't even want to talk about this anymore. I can't. I called you because I need to go get my car. It's still parked over in their driveway."

"Give me a few minutes to throw some clothes on and I will be right there."

"I'll be waiting."

I was so used to being the one to rescue Mekhi during his multiple dilemmas that I never imagined that I would be the one in crisis.

Fear was riding my back. Cherish had placed Damon on a gold encrusted pedestal. Idolized him like he was God, but man could never replace Him. I feared for Cherish because the consequences of her choice were devastating whether she lived or died. If she lived she would have to face criminal charges and the guilt of knowing she killed her husband. And if she died, her soul may be damned. I only hoped God wouldn't punish her eternally when she was already living on earth in torment.

As I sat by the front door and waited for Autumn, an old song recorded by Fred Hammond came to mind. I sang part of the verse to "I Will Find A Way" to comfort myself and apologize to God for my own bad decisions.

"And though my life is broken I'll find a way to give you praise."

Thoughts of me and Scott, growing farther apart, scared me. I couldn't fault Cherish. I was out of order myself for some of the decisions I made to keep Scott happy. I had placed Scott above God and saw the result. I didn't know if I could handle a marriage with a man acting unsaved. Or his trying to get me to straddle the fence with him. Knowing that the company he kept was a reflection of him only made our relationship seem doomed. I couldn't sacrifice my sanity or soul the way Cherish had for Damon. The cost was too great.

CHAPTER THIRTY-FOUR

SCOTT

Exactly two weeks after Damon's funeral, I watched porn at work.

I had been stretched so thin that I couldn't see straight. My nerves were shot from the stress of it all. Men weren't allowed to grieve. We were supposed to stand like solid rocks through any and all crises, but even mountains crumble when too much weight wears them down.

Cherish had fallen into a coma after Germani and I left the hospital that night. I think because Cherish lived, Ms. Ilene was on a war path. It started with the planning of a family gathering after the wake service. Ms. Ilene wanted it held at Damon's home—the same house he died in. She and my Uncle Gabe, her ex-boyfriend, got into a heated argument at the wake service. He told her she was trying to turn the family gathering into a spectator sport.

I was the one with Damon's house keys. Ms.
Ilene knew I had the keys and although I refused
to give them to her, the family gathering ended
up being held at Damon's place to squash the
drama. The very next day, Damon's family was
trying to move some of his things out of the
house he shared with

Cherish. Ms. Ilene said that she wanted items
to honor his memory. For all I know, they could
have grabbed some stuff during the family gathering. I suggested that they wait and get legal
advice because Cherish had ownership of the
home. Ms. Ilene had me call a lawyer to see what
rights she had. I became her middle man when
dealing with the legalities. I didn't want any part
of it, but felt obligated.

On top of that, Germani had been constantly
making little comments about the lifestyle of
sinners and how she needed to get better in her
Christian walk. Damon's death made mortality
more real to her. She even kept a Bible on the
nightstand and made reference to certain verses
whenever we were in the bedroom together.
She talked in general statements about people
needing more intimacy with Christ and how they
were missing an opportunity to get their lives in
order; like I really wanted to hear that after I lost
my best friend. And to make matters worse, we

still weren't having sex. I wanted to feel her close to me. I needed some kind of physical connection with my wife. She was too busy standing by her asinine convictions.

It was easy to access porn sites from the back room at Car Care. As manager, I made up excuses to retreat to my office in the back room for an hour or two at a time. That first time was a Wednesday. I had Sara take over my register, because I wanted to go online and make price comparisons of some products for an upcoming sales promotion. After I got the information I needed, the temptation to peek at other things overwhelmed me. I convinced myself that I wasn't harming anything by getting a quick viewing. I stayed on for less than ten minutes. I felt guilty and knew it was wrong, but the temporary release became my 'high.' It wasn't enough to just watch porn at home after Germani went to sleep. My actions on my work computer became bolder as I increased my viewing time to twenty-minute increments a few times throughout the day. I realized I needed to be a little more careful.

It had been a slow night, so I sent Sara home two hours early. There was a new employee, Antonio, who replaced Torrance, scheduled to close with me. Antonio had worked a few years at an auto dealership as a technician before three of his fingers got mangled in a motorcycle accident. Left him with a pinkie and thumb on one hand. The auto dealership let him go because he could no longer do the job. He had been on my staff for about eight days, but had enough knowledge that I felt I could leave him unattended for a little while.

I made up a quick lie to have to go to the back once Sara walked out of the building. "Hey, Antonio, I need to call this manufacturer for some parts we have on back order. Think you can handle the front for a few minutes?"

"Sure thing," Antonio responded as he handed change back to a customer for their purchase.

I anxiously headed to the back room. I knew exactly which site I wanted to go to. After shutting the office door, I quickly clicked into the one that had longer free viewing time.

I felt something telling me to stop, but I didn't listen. Instead, I glanced up at the closed door as the video began playing on the screen. Told myself not to worry. I had everything under control. Before long, I was completely engrossed in my computer fantasy. Thoughts about my wife, about Damon's death and about anything that caused me stress, vanished.

I turned up the volume on my speakers slightly.

Got lost in the feeling.

Until . . .

"Scott, we have a problem," Antonio explained with a frown protruding from his brow as he stood right in front of the desk.

I nearly jumped out of my skin when I realized he was standing there.

I quickly clicked off the porn page, heart beating fast, thumped against my ribcage like an Amtrak train en route to Texas.

Maybe Antonio didn't hear the noises coming from my computer. I hoped he didn't. I could lose my job if he told headquarters that I was watching porn on the clock.

I tried to act oblivious to what I'd just been doing. "Wha . . . What's wrong?" I stuttered.

"Guy out here needs a diagnostic test and the code won't clear on our machine. I was wondering if you could reset it." Antonio was still frowning at me.

I bet he knew.

I glance at the cleared computer screen, pushed myself up from the desk and walked alongside him to go help out.

If he didn't mention seeing anything, I sure wasn't.

Fear had me in a vice grip. I needed to stop watching porn at work. I needed to stop right away.

CHAPTER THIRTY-FIVE

GERMANI

Two cops stood outside my door.

"Are you Germani Wilson?" the one in a short black winter jacket, asked from outside my screen door. He had a serious scowl. One of his hands was tucked in a coat pocket. Next to him, stood another cop with a gray overcoat. Short black guy with a bald fade. He was close to my height, maybe an inch taller.

"Yes, that's me. How may I help you?" I answered.

He pulled out a CMPD badge and flashed it quickly. "My name is Detective Hart and this is Detective Brooks. We're with the Charlotte-Mecklenburg investigation division. May I come in?"

I looked behind him at the police car sitting in my driveway. "What's this about?"

"I have a few questions regarding a homicide investigation that you and your husband were listed as witnesses to. We need to verify details from the incident." He saw me frown up as I held the screen door fastened. Him on one side of the glass with me on the other, hesitant to let him in.

I truly couldn't remember what I told them to fabricate a story. Damon had been buried for three weeks. Cherish had awaken out of her coma only a couple days ago. I'm sure they'd spoken with her by now and wondered if Cherish had anything to do with them being at my house.

The wind whisked by, shifting the strands of his short ash blond hair. It was bone chilling cold out. Barely eight o'clock. I could feel the raw early morning chill touch my feet from beneath the metal screen.

"It will only be a minute, ma'am." I saw what I took to be a slight annoyance as Detective Hart put the badge back in his coat pocket.

I opened the door and escorted them to the living room. "My husband is upstairs. I hope you don't mind standing here for a moment while I go get him."

They nodded their heads.

I rushed up the few stairs and checked on Elijah who was playing in his room with an electric train set. I then went into our bedroom where

Scott was still in bed. He hadn't gotten into bed until three this morning. I had felt the bed dip when he got in. Always knew when he was coming to bed after watching his porn. The computer got far more action from my husband than I did. Our intimacy had been reduced to pecks of kisses every now and then. The fire that used to burn between us was extinguished months ago.

I gently nudged him. Had to poke Scott three times before his eyes would open.

I put my face close to his. "There are two detectives downstairs that want to talk to us."

"Huh . . . for what?" he asked, slowly lifting his body to a sitting position.

"Something about the case with Cherish and Damon. I really don't know yet. I came to get you. They are downstairs waiting."

He slid out of bed, threw on a pair of jeans over his boxers and walked back down with me.

"Morning. How may we help you?" Scott asked as we met them in our living room.

I felt like we were being impolite. "Please have a seat," I said, pointing at both the couch and loveseat.

Scott was prone where the hall meets the living room, with arms folded.

"If you don't mind," said the short cop.

"No, not at all. I'm just curious about what would bring you out here on a Saturday morning." Scott came by the couch, but wouldn't sit down.

"We are here to discuss your statements made on October 11, 2007, regarding the subsequent death of Damon L. Spears," said Detective Hart.

Scott scratched his nose before folding his arms again. "Okay . . . and?"

Detective Hart pulled out a small yellow pad from an inner pocket. He leafed through scattered notes.

"From what it says here, when you got to the house on Pemswood Street, the front door was locked and you went through a patio door to gain access. Is that correct, Mr. Wilson?"

"Yes," Scott replied.

"It also says that you and Mr. Spears were best friends."

Scott nodded his head.

"Can you remember seeing anything unusual or out of place while you were there?"

"My best friend was laying in a puddle of his own blood next to the woman who murdered him. Everything about that night was unusual."

The detective ignored Scott's hostility. "What about you, Ms. Wilson? Did you see anything unusual besides the murder scene in itself, at any point after you entered the home?"

"I'm not sure what you mean, Detective Hart, but I hadn't been in their house enough to notice that something would be out of the ordinary," I cautiously explained with measured words, confused by the range of questioning.

"Do you know why Cherish Spears would have had reason to murder her husband?" Detective Brooks asked as the other detective jotted down more notes. His voice had bass, a tone I didn't expect from his size."

"No," Scott said quickly.

At the same time I said, "Yes."

I gave Scott a puzzled look. Didn't understand why he was acting defensive. He made it seem like we had something to hide.

"Ms. Wilson?" All eyes were on me.

"They were having problems," I stated. I didn't know what I should or shouldn't say. I was worried that they would think we had something to do with the crime.

Detective Hart asked, "What kind of problems?"

"You know . . . marital troubles. Same as anyone else, I suppose." I was starting to feel nervous, interrogated. I didn't mention the swingers parties. Thought it might place Cherish in prison for a longer period of time. Courts wouldn't have mercy on her due to her lifestyle.

"On the night in question you told the police that Mrs. Spears called you and you rushed over because you thought something might be wrong. That she was crazy."

Did I say that? I couldn't remember saying that. "I don't recall saying that about Cherish. Everything was crazy. The whole night was crazy."

"How about a Dell computer? Did either of you have access to the computer in the Spears' home? Or do you know of someone with access?"

"No and no," Scott responded.

I shook my head, biting the inside of my cheek.

Scott sat on the armrest next to me. "You already have your suspect. What's with all the questions?"

"There has been new evidence surrounding the case that we need to check into. Do the names Omar Jennings, Sophie Duran, Jackson Parker or Martin Scalli mean anything to you."

Once again, Scott was abrupt in his answer. "No. Why? Are they suppose to be familiar to us?"

Scott should have recognized some of those names. We met Sophie and Omar at the stem-cell fundraiser.

Even if he didn't remember, I wasn't going to sit there and lie. "I know Dr. Jennings from a fundraiser we attended with Cherish and Damon. Dr. Jennings became my contact for hiring we do at the employment agency where I work. My knowledge of him is based purely on a professional level."

"And the others?"

"I also met Sophie Duran once at the same fundraiser, but I haven't had contact with her outside of the one introduction."

Scott stood back up. "Once again I ask, what's with all the questions?"

"For the last week or so, there has been a video circulating the Internet with the four people I named. It was a very explicit video of them in compromising positions. It was posted on I-Tube from the Spears' home computer on the same night that you found Mr. and Mrs. Spears. There were others in the video, but the four I mentioned are prominent figures in this community."

The story had been on the news. I remember watching the story on the news, but they didn't say names. That part was kept private.

"So, basically, you are here about an I-Tube video, not about Damon's death." Scott's eyebrows furrowed together.

"We're trying to find the link between the video and Mr. Spears' death."

Scott began walking toward the front door. "Well, I think we are done answering questions. You should really go talk to Cherish Spears about all that." He opened the door and stood there.

Detective Brooks and Detective Hart got up from the couch. Brooks pulled a card from his pants pocket. He handed it to me. "If you have any more information to help us with this case, it would be greatly appreciated.

After they left, I said to Scott as he walked upstairs, "Scott, you were rude to those detectives."

He walked into the bathroom. "I wasn't rude; I just didn't want them feeling overly welcome."

"What's going on, Scott? You know something you're not telling me?"

He pulled out his toothbrush and smeared toothpaste on the bristles.

"I know the police don't care about Damon or how he died. I don't need to entertain their questions. And they told on themselves when they mentioned those *prominent figures* of the community put on I-Tube. They're more concerned about some naked rich folks exposed on video rather than Damon getting stabbed in the chest. They wanted us to say Cherish posted the video or Damon did before she killed him, or better yet, they were looking for a confession from us. Ridiculous." Scott put the toothbrush in his mouth.

I rolled my neck. I felt a tension headache coming on. "Even if that is true, we looked suspicious by giving them conflicting answers about what we know. Me saying *yes* and you saying *no*. If I were those detectives, I would be thinking we were hiding something."

Scott looked at me from the corner of his eye while he brushed his teeth.

"What did you know about their swingers lifestyle? I'm sure Damon shared all the sordid details with you. Were you tempted to do the same thing?"

Scott spit into the sink and swished with a Dixie cup of water, before spitting again.

"Just because I respected Damon's right to choose how he lived, doesn't mean I wanted to be like him. Now, if you will excuse me, I'm going to go get dressed for work."

The only thing playing in my mind were birds of a feather flock together.

I moved to the side and let him pass. He was hiding something; and as God as my witness, I was going to find out what.

CHAPTER THIRTY-SIX

SCOTT

I found Alex's number on a calendar attached to a refrigerator magnet at Beverly's house. As soon as I saw that number, there was no question that I needed to dial those digits. Beverly needed a break, so I offered to stay with Alexis while she went to IMAJ Salon. That singing bird, Fantasia, owned the place and paid for Beverly to pamper herself. Alexis' illness had her stressed out. Her hair was falling out in clumps. She had a bald spot at the top of her head that she was trying to hide, but the comb over wasn't working for her. She was looking like Donald Trump and it was disturbing me.

Germani acted like she didn't trust or believe in me anymore, but both Alexis and Beverly relied on me. Family was supposed to believe in each other. Family was supposed to have one another's backs through thick and thin. If Germani didn't appreciate me, I was glad somebody in my family did.

Alexis and Elijah were in the living room watching *Animal Planet,* while sharing a carton of Cold Stone Creamery's Founder's Favorite ice cream. We had stopped at the creamery's West Mallard Creek Church Road location an hour ago. I checked in on them before I tried to handle that other business. They sat together in an overstuffed recliner. Alexis held onto the red carton while Elijah used a plastic spoon to dig into it.

"You good?" I asked Alexis.

"Uh-huh." She was completely engrossed in the show she was watching.

"*Animal Detective.* They rescue tortured and abandoned animals in New York." She pointed to the television with her free hand. "Some guy was evicted from his apartment and left his guard dog chained to a fence in the courtyard. Look at him; he's starving. People are cruel."

She was looking and feeling better for now.

I needed to know where Alex's head was. Even though Beverly kept insisting that Alex refused to help Alexis and there was no convincing him, I had a hard time believing her. He did go through some tests and he had planned to come previously. He might have needed some male encouragement to actually do what he was supposed to do.

It took a minute for Alex to pick up the phone after I dialed his number, and when he did, it wasn't a kind greeting.

His first words were, "Beverly, I told you to stop calling my house so much. My wife is starting to get upset about this situation."

I had to check myself. My first instinct was to tell Alex a few things about dissing my sister like he did, but I decided against it.

"This isn't Bev. It's Scott." We hadn't spoken in eleven years; not since he skipped town on Beverly.

Still no warm greeting. "How did you get my number? Did Bev tell you to call me? Because if she did, I'm going to tell you the same thing I told her. I'm not risking my life and I don't have any money. Other than those two things, I'm willing to help anyway I can," Alex sputtered those words like I was calling to blackmail him.

"I'm calling for Alexis. You had planned to come to town and donate your bone marrow to help your daughter. Help me understand why you backed . . . decided not to show up. Alexis's condition is dire. She needed that transplant and you are the main one that can make the surgery happen."

"I don't mean to sound disrespectful toward Beverly, but I don't think Alexis is as bad off as Beverly makes it seem."

"You think Bev's lying about Alexis having sickle cell anemia? You both have the trait. There was no getting around Alexis contracting the disease. What are you talking about?"

"I know she has the disease, but I've been talking to some of my friends. I also have family members with sickle cell anemia and they've all been telling me that sickle cell anemia doesn't kill. Some of them get sick on occasion, but not to the point that they require constant hospital care or transplants. None of them believe Alexis is that bad off. And I'm inclined to agree with them."

"Do any of your friends or relatives have a medical degree?"

"Yeah, Garnett is a medical assistant. She has been working at a doctor's office for a couple years now."

All I heard was ignorance. "I'm not talking about medical assisting. I would bet money that none of the people talking to you have an advanced medical degree that they spent eight or more years to get."

"No, but they are living just fine with sickle cell anemia. Don't get me wrong, I want to be there for my daughter, but I can't let Bev over exaggerate to keep contact with me. I can tell she still has feelings for me."

"Alex, you give yourself way too much credit. Beverly isn't into you that hardcore. What she does feel is guilt about putting herself in a situation where she has to ask for your help and it's not looking too good for her to get Alexis well any other way. If you did some research, you would find out that sickle cell anemia doesn't respond the same in everybody. There are some people whose bodies can't handle the disease. Have you even talked to her doctor?"

"I don't need a diagnosis or prognosis from her doctor. For all I know, Beverly could have that doctor telling me anything. He gets paid more money for each extra test he administers. As a matter of fact, you all should be careful what you believe."

"There has been more than one physician working on Alexis and they all say the same thing. She's in bad shape. Why don't you admit that you don't care what happens to your daughter. It's not like you have a close relationship with her. Call it like it is. You accidentally knocked up her mother and want both of them to stay out of your life."

Alex sputtered some more. "I've already explained to you the same thing I told Beverly. I don't have anything to give Alexis. If you insist on harassing me about her, then I will be forced to change my number and cut off all of you, including Alexis."

If that was the way he talked to Beverly, I didn't know how she put up with him. Alex was going to remain close-minded because he could. If I kept talking to him, I was about to get pissed off.

"I'm done with it. If you believe nothing is wrong with Alexis, then you have it twisted, but you better hope Alexis doesn't lose her life."

"Tell Beverly to stop calling me so much. Alexis can call, but Bev needs to stop."

We both hung up.

Talking to Alex was a waste of my time. Some men shouldn't be allowed to procreate. I was more of a father to Alexis than that imbecile would ever be. Yet, a sense of helplessness for my family fell over me and I couldn't shake it off.

CHAPTER THIRTY-SEVEN

GERMANI

I went to see Cherish after church, right after I left Momma's house. Mom had been upset because Mekhi got himself arrested again, and she asked me for help with bail money. Evidently, Mishelle's new man hit Camry and left marks. Mekhi confronted him about the bruises on Camry's legs and they got to fighting. The police were called and Mekhi was booked on another set of assault charges.

I explained to Momma that I didn't have access to any money on a Sunday. His bail would have to wait until the next business day.

I moved a blue curtain as I entered the hospital room.

They had Cherish's right wrist handcuffed to the bedrail.

It was the first time I'd visited her since it happened; had felt awkward at the thought of making casual conversation with a murderer. But I couldn't avoid the inevitable. She brought me into her drama and I had to deal with it.

I sat in the chair across from her bed. Her hazel eyes were sad, like she regretted the hospital staff had kept her alive. She looked as if she would try to kill herself again, given the chance.

"Surprised to see you here," Cherish said with a chalky voice.

I shrugged. I wasn't going to act like we were best buddies. "The police came to my house asking all kinds of questions about you." I pointed to the handcuffs dangling between her and the railing. "Um . . . you officially been arrested?"

"They came and read me my Miranda rights the day after I woke from the coma." Cherish picked up a foam cup and sipped from a straw.

"Have you seen a Detective Hart or Brooks? Those were the policemen at my house yesterday morning."

"They weren't the ones that arrested me, but I was questioned by Detective Hart on Friday."

"About the video posted on I-Tube?"

"Yeah, I-Tube. I also sent a list of the people we slept with in the Swingers Network. I planned on dying, but wanted the people involved with us to get tested. I wanted somebody to warn them. It was the coward's way out."

"The video sounds malicious, like you had an ax to grind."

"I did . . . with Sophie. She's a nasty, aging hag who filled Damon's head with ideas of grandeur. He ate her advice about getting to the top like lobster on a buffet table. He didn't become pompous until we met her." Cherish held on to her anger.

"She didn't make you kill Damon?"

"No . . . I take full responsibility for that. I lost my mind. I was coaxing him into giving up the lifestyle we'd been living. But then he called me stupid . . . said I needed to get with the program. I heard him degrading me and I snapped. I just snapped. Everything from then on happened so fast. I—" She stopped talking, covered her mouth and closed her eyes.

I felt her remorse. Decisions made in spontaneity.

I reached for Cherish's hand and did the one thing I thought I should have done when I was looking up Bible passages on the night she called me. I had tried to find the right words when the words were already inside me.

"Lord, I come to you on behalf of Cherish, seeking peace for a troubled soul. Through your grace and mercy, I know all things are possible."

I heard Cherish breathing heavy as she whispered, "Yes, Lord, yes."

"You guide us with a tender, but steady hand. You continue to love us in spite of ourselves and the things we do to bring you sorrow. When we are sad, you open your arms and hold us close to you. When no one else understands us, you do, because you knew us first and made us in your image. We delight in your creation. When no one forgives us for our transgressions, you say your grace is sufficient. When we fall prey to the wrong hands, you say come back home anyway. I ask that you show Cherish the mighty, omnipotent Father that I know you to be. Bless her, Lord, during a dark hour. She needs you now more than ever. Amen."

Cherish's eyes watered. "Thank you."

"We all do it at some point . . . allow our outer to influence our inner."

"Yeah, that sounds about right."

She smiled at me. I smiled back. It was the start of a new friendship.

"When are they transporting you?"

"In a few days, I believe. Paperwork needs to be done. My doctor has to verify that I'm well enough physically to be released from the hospital. I'll be in another county, because of the I-Tube publicity. I guess they're worried that good ole Sophie might put a hit out on me."

I felt extremely bad for Cherish. Her situation was all messed up. I had faith that God would intervene on her behalf.

"When your trial is scheduled, I will be there in support of you, and if you need a witness in your defense, I'm willing to testify too."

Cherish took another sip of water. "Javir or rather, Dr. Cavella, you remember him. He has gotten me a good lawyer. I'm hoping to plead out with a decent deal."

"Does he know about your condition?"

"Yes, he knows I have AIDS. He's not holding that against me. He's one of the good guys."

"Did Scott ever participate in the swinger's thing? Did he have any involvement in that lifestyle?" It was a question I desperately needed the answer to but didn't see an appropriate way to ask.

Cherish shook her head. "Never. You have a good husband. Don't put him in the same category as Damon."

I checked my watch. That was becoming a chronic habit. "Well, I'm going to head out of here. You have my address. Drop me a line when you find out your placement."

"Sure. And thanks again for praying with me."

"You never know. One day you may have to return the favor," I said fully believing in that possibility.

CHAPTER THIRTY-EIGHT

SCOTT

The city put a restriction on all outside water use back in August due to the drought. It was November and we still weren't allowed to wash our cars or water our lawns until the restriction got lifted. Anybody caught with a hose in their hands would get between a $100 and $600 fine. They also encouraged residents to limit inside water consumption as well, but they couldn't enforce whether somebody left water running while they brushed their teeth or took too many showers. Considering the low levels of rainfall, the city was talking about imposing those restrictions with 493 penalties until next spring, or possibly longer, if it didn't rain more.

My grass was turning yellow and becoming crisp. It had grown only about an inch and a half since the last time I cut it. The ground was hard as the fertilized dirt dried too.

I had begun to cut the front yard, but ran over a rock or stick. I heard a noise against the blades before the lawnmower cut off on me. I went to the garage for my tool set, which I placed on the side of me as I loosened several screws and lay the green cover on the grass.

Germani came outside and watched me work on the lawnmower. "I should probably let you know that I went to visit Cherish today."

We had driven separate cars to church this morning. I thought it was because she didn't want to ride with me. Since Damon's death a month ago, any conversation we had was strained. It was strained to the point that we could go days without having a conversation.

After service, she handed me Elijah and told me she needed to go take care of something. That's all she said. I brought Elijah home with me. Didn't think nothing else about it. In fact, I assumed that she was going to see her mother, because Mekhi was arrested again.

I shrugged my shoulders when she mentioned seeing Cherish.

"I told her that I would be in court to support her at trial," Germani continued.

"You told her what?" I strained my ears because I couldn't have heard Germani right.

"I told Cherish that I would testify in her defense if she needed me to. I believe her motives were justified. I'm not saying the deed itself was right, but I could understand how it happened. She was going through pure hell because of Damon. You may not like what I'm saying due to your friendship with him. You were too close to see what he was doing to her."

I dropped the wrench on the ground that I was using to fix the lawnmower. I stayed bent over the rusting propeller. "I guess Cherish has no self-accountability. It doesn't matter that Damon's the one dead. You're gonna make Cherish into the victim." It sounded so stupid I almost laughed in Germani's face.

She crossed her arms as she once again tried to make an irrelevant point. "As I said, I don't justify the action, but I justify the person behind the action. She wanted to please her husband and he wasn't appreciative of her efforts. The more she gave, the more Damon took, until she didn't even have her dignity. He sure didn't have any respect for her. I think she felt trapped."

I placed the top back on the lawnmower. "Whatever. It's bad enough that you're on some sympathy kick for Cherish. But did you ever think she had the ability and choice to leave if she was that miserable? Her feet could have walked her out the door at any time. For all the bad you think about Damon, he wasn't the type to keep a woman tied to him if she didn't want to be there."

I used the wrench to tighten the bolts. "Germani, there's this thing called self-accountability. I don't know if you've ever heard of that, but it's when somebody is responsible for his or her own actions, be they good or bad. If they don't have remorse for wrong actions, then there is this judicial system that will force them to be accountable. While you are sitting on the defense side, I can guarantee I will be behind the prosecution, waiting for them to lock her tail behind bars for the rest of her natural life."

Germani huffed. "Scott, you're not even trying to understand where I'm coming from—"

I cut her off. "No, I'm not. I refuse to understand the insane point you are trying to make. You've been jumping down my throat over those videos I watch, but Cherish can plead crazy for killing a man and you are all right with that, quickly rallying to her defense." I could feel myself getting angry. I could feel my voice escalating.

She had another thought coming if she ever took on the notion that we would see eye to eye about Damon's murder. He might have made some bad decisions, like marrying that unstable girl, but he didn't deserve to die for them.

Germani stood there like she was thinking of something else to say and she couldn't.

I pumped the gas button on the lawnmower a couple of more times, then pulled the string, hoping I could finish cutting my grass.

"Before you come up with some other defense on behalf of Cherish, this conversation needs to end." My voice stayed stern.

Germani finally gave up trying to say whatever and she went back into the house.

I watched the front door close, thinking she had too many double standards going on and I'd had enough of all of them.

CHAPTER THIRTY-NINE

GERMANI

At four in the morning, I checked the clock on the night-stand. My husband still hadn't come home.

I held the yellow pages in my lap. *Hospitals-Hotels* was the heading in the corner of page 605. I anguished over whether I should start from the bottom of that page and work my way up, or at the top on down in search of Scott.

It was while I tortured myself over that decision that he walked into the room as if he had just gotten off work. Scott threw his keys on the nightstand and began to undress. His work shirt hit the floor followed by his pants. Not one word passed from his mouth to acknowledge that I was in the room. As he sat down on his side of the bed I could smell perfume and cigarettes.

Things had become intolerably tense since I told Scott that I would support Cherish at trial.

He didn't take my decision well. I didn't want to budge on my principles and he wasn't trying to see things my way.

"Where have you been?" I asked with serious concern as I drummed my fingers against the phone book. He hadn't called to say he would be late or had made plans for after work. He had just left me in a worried daze, wondering if something tragic had happened to him.

Scott didn't respond as he got beneath our thermal blanket and tucked it under his arm at his waist.

I leaned over, pressing my body against the back of his frame. I asked again, "Where have you been?"

The stench of perfume and cigarettes lingered on his skin. I locked my mind from conjuring up assumptions and possibilities while I waited for an explanation from my husband.

When Scott ignored me yet again, the thought of who, where and when, seeped into my mind anyway. Scott and I both knew trust between us was virtually nonexistent. The strain from our differences tightened like piano wire.

"Leave me alone, Germani," he finally declared.

That comment made my head jerk.

"Leave you alone? You come home near dawn and I'm supposed to leave you alone?" I exclaimed incredulously.

Scott kept his back to me, but I heard the rigidness of his tone. "Yeah, that's exactly what you need to do. You need to leave me alone."

Oh, no he didn't.

I sank my teeth in my bottom lip to avoid speaking real nasty and out of turn. I rolled back to my side of the bed and sat straight up. He wasn't going to get the option he thought he had. Not coming into our home smelling like another woman.

The clock on my nightstand read 4:23 A.M. In roughly four more hours, I had a meeting scheduled with Liberty Mutual for a claims division they were opening in the area. With the loss of our biggest contract, Job Track needed all the business we could get. I needed to be sharp for my presentation, but that wasn't going to happen with me functioning on fumes from lack of sleep.

"Scott, you can't honestly think I'm leaving this alone," I said barely above a whisper. I really didn't want an argument.

He still wasn't talking, so I continued. "You need to tell me something, because you can't come in here whenever you feel like it. You're not single and if that's the direction you're gearing your life in, then I think I deserve the right to know that. As your *wife*, I believe you owe me that."

"A *wife* should trust her *husband*." Scott got out of bed, walked across the room and turned the light off as if that would end the conversation.

"If my husband has shown himself to have questionable ways, then I guess trust deserves to be an issue."

"Funny that my ways didn't become questionable until you changed the rule book of our marriage."

The insult came out before I could stop it. The start of an unnecessary tit-for-tat game. "No, Scott, you are shady. We are supposed to have a certain standard of morals and yes, you are correct. It's my job to put things in perspective if you don't know how to act right."

Tit.

"Germani, there you go sounding sanctimonious and ultra religious again. You might want to be careful, because I think those angel wings you're wearing have spikes in them."

Tat.

"Don't hate on me, because I'm trying to get it right and live according to God's design. We get only one chance before we die. I thought you would have learned that lately."

Tit.

"What I've learned is that you're so saved and filled with the Holy Ghost that I can't relate to you anymore."

Tat.

"What? So that gives you the right to stay out all night, doing God knows what with God knows who. At least one of us is acting saved."

"Urrgh!" Scott shook the bee as he flopped onto his back.

I brought up an observation. "You have a high sex drive and we haven't had sex in five months. Five long months."

Scott spat. "I'm so sick of this. Yes, I have a high sex drive and yes, I'd like my needs met. I don't care how saved I'm supposed to act. I will always be a man with manly needs. And you have made it crystal clear that you are not going to meet those needs, even as my wife. I'm telling you right now that I'm not going to stop being flawed and I'm not going to stop being a man. Germani, if you want to be mad at somebody, then be mad at yourself for making me get my needs met without you."

Too much had been said. I didn't get the explanation I sought, but Scott did answer my question.

Our partnership was nonexistent.

He wouldn't make me cry. I wouldn't give him the satisfaction. I got out of bed as hurt bled unwanted confirmation on the inside of me. I quietly left our room and went down the hall to Elijah's, where I crawled into the little toddler bed, curled around my son and rocked myself to sleep.

CHAPTER FORTY

SCOTT

Apprehension stopped me at the door of New Joy Christian Cathedral, where I was scheduled to meet Ahmad for a porn addict's recovery class.

Ahmad had stopped me before church service the Sunday following the big fallout between Germani and me. My wife wanted to believe I was cheating on her, so I let her assume exactly that. She and I were no longer on speaking terms. Our daily routine didn't even require us to have a conversation if we chose not to. My work schedule was attached to a planner board in the kitchen. I made sure to work most evening shifts at the store, giving my weekday hours up to my assistant manager, Craig. He was more than happy to have that time with his family.

I had spent the night Germani thought I was cheating on her at the Playa's Lounge. After more than a month of fighting the temptation to go back and see Pleasure, I stopped resisting. Initially, I had turned down the striptease from Pleasure when I was at the hotel with Damon before he died, out of respect for Germani and our marriage. But she wanted to believe I was messing around on her so badly that I stopped trying to convince her otherwise.

The unrest in my home stressed me out. I needed some relief. Seemed to need a lot more stress relief lately. Ahmad had told me that he saw me leaving the stripper's club on his drive home from a conference in Jacksonville, Florida. He also explained that he didn't know my home situation and he wasn't trying to get in my business, but he could sense I was troubled. I confessed my porn struggles with Ahmad. By the time we finished talking, he had convinced me to attend one Saturday afternoon meeting.

I stood outside New Joy for several minutes before I decided to leave. As I got to the sidewalk I saw Ahmad approaching.

"Good to see you, Scott. I was running a little late, but I'm glad you made it. The brother teaching the class is powerful. You're about to be blessed."

I wasn't convinced by his enthusiasm as we made it into the brick cathedral. Ahmad took me past doors with colored paper signs posted.

LIFE AFTER PRISON in purple . . . DRUG/ALCOHOL ANONYMOUS in blue . . . STREGNTH FROM DOMESTIC VIOLENCE in green . . . PORN ADDICT RECOVERY in yellow.

Ahmad pushed the door open and held it while a stream of men and two women filed into the room.

As everybody got settled in table topped desks arranged in a large circle, hand-outs were passed around by a man Ahmad identified as the session teacher. A tall, lanky, dark-skinned man in a green button-down shirt with black slacks, he looked to be around my age.

I read over the bold letters of the top page: XXXCHURCH.COM THE #1 PORN SITE.

The title alone threw me for a loop. I must admit that I didn't know what to think about the class Ahmad had me attending.

As the presenter noticed the myriad of facial expressions, he burst out laughing. "I love the looks I see on the new people's faces when I first give out these pages. Admit it, you think I'm crazy, don't you?" he walked over and asked a mocha-toned woman with a short afro, who appeared obviously mortified.

She nodded her head.

The presenter told her, "There is a method to my madness." He then addressed the entire room of attendees. "There are quite a few unfamiliar faces in the room. For those of you who are new to the class, I am Myles Corbin. Welcome to Porn Addicts Recovery. Please read over the second handout to make sure you are in the right location before we begin."

I browsed down the list of questions.

Do you use pornography to cope with life?

Do you get angry at anyone mentioning your porn use?

Has there been an increase in volume of porn use?

Do you have an inability to stop using porn, even if it results in a job or marriage loss?

"If you think you are in the wrong room, raise your hand," Myles requested.

No one raised their hands.

Myles further explained as he sat on the edge of a desk, "I am going to say right off the bat that I am an unconventional speaker. What I am not, is a pastor, Bible scholar, licensed therapist or any other label that someone wants to attach to me, as I've heard people ask what right I had to head a counseling class. But you don't need a degree to understand God's love and grace. A label won't determine whether I choose to honestly live by the Bible or not. The reason I bring all that up is because I've gotten used to judgment from whomever. I'm not going to lie to you and tell you I like it, but as a re . . . covered, re . . . newed porn addict, I understand how detrimental judgment from family, friends or the general public can be when you're fighting the weakness within. XXXChurch is a non-conventional Christian based anti-pornography website geared toward helping people with porn related struggles. The creators are on a worldwide mission and have innovative resources for dealing in everyday life."

I was feeling what Myles was saying. My expectations for the class had been limited by my experience with Germani. The fire and brimstone convictions . . . that approach had damaged our relationship.

Myles put his finger to his lips before using that same hand to point around the room. "Here, the focus is on fighting urges and building sexual integrity. The focus is on support in the midst. I'm going to let a few others in this room tell you the benefits of Porn Addict Recovery."

Ahmad spoke up first. "I had been watching porn since junior high. If you would have asked me three years ago if I had any major issues, I would have denied it. Porn wasn't interfering in my everyday life. I could take it or leave it. When my son, Quinn, became a teenager, I gave him access to my video collection. It was a right of passage from father to son, or so I thought, until I received a call from his guidance counselor to appear in the school office. Quinn had gotten caught masturbating in the boys' locker room after basketball practice."

The room was so quiet we could hear the buzz of the furnace. Myles went and sat in one of the empty desks of our circle.

I didn't realize that Quinn had a porn problem. During the conversation, when Ahmad invited me to the class, he had only admitted that he used to watch porn. He didn't mention his son.

Ahmad looked calm and collected, despite his confession about his son. "The principal wanted to suspend Quinn sixty days from school for criminal sexual misconduct. That would have put him behind the rest of the ninth graders. My wife and I stayed in that office for most of the afternoon hashing out other solutions with the principal and guidance counselor. Our parenting skills were placed under a microscope. We spent a great deal of that time defending our son and our morals. The conclusion was that Quinn could get the penalty reduced to two weeks' suspension if my wife and I got him in a rehabilitation program. Quinn's guidance counselor gave me a flyer for New Joy and that's how we ended up here."

A man three desks over asked, "If your son's the one with the problem, why are you here instead of him?"

Ahmad responded, "Because I'm part of the problem. I introduced him to something he wasn't equipped to handle. Quinn completed the required class and went back to school, but his attraction to porn continues to be a struggle. I stop in here every once in a while to keep myself in check on how I deal with him and to encourage anybody else going through."

I never realized that my love of porn could influence my own son in such a bad way. A whole new light was shed.

Someone else began to speak. A middle-aged man with sandy blond hair and a deep tan talked from his chair. "My wife left me because she could no longer compete with the fantasy I was caught up in. I don't blame her. It was a heavy burden to bear. I paid for her to have a tummy tuck, breasts enhancement and dermal abrasion so that she could look like the women in those porn videos, but in the end it wasn't enough. Her self-esteem was shot. We've been divorced for a year now and I miss her, but I respect her decision to move forward without me." He pulled out a tattered note card from his black leather billfold and held it in the air. "I keep this folded in my wallet. It's an inspirational quote from Todd Bolsinger, the author of a book entitled, *Showtime*. It states, *'If your mind is not filled with the Scriptures and your heart is not in the habit of obeying them, then to trust your gut and go with your own insight is to walk a crooked and perilous path.'* It reminds me of how destructive things get when I live in my own will and own desires. It reminds me to not rely on what feels good without questioning the cost."

As others told their stories I found myself comforted by their flaws. And if I was made in God's image, then He was well aware of my flaws whether they were temporary or permanent. I realized that maybe I didn't have things as in control as I previously believed. Maybe my marriage didn't have to keep spiraling from our differences.

As I listened to triumphs and tragedies, I realized that the Porn Addict Recovery class was exactly were I needed to be.

CHAPTER FORTY-ONE

GERMANI

"I am not going to let this be another bad day," I muttered to myself as I pushed open the front door. Things were out of control and there wasn't a thing I could do about it but go with the flow.

The day care charged me forty dollars for picking Elijah up half an hour late, even though I was never late getting him any other time. On top of that, Plas-tech decided to let a majority of our contract workers go by the end of the month after they merged with a Japanese company. Employees were already calling us worried about their next jobs. And worse yet, Scott was treating me like enemy number one. He walked around the house like he was living there alone; didn't want to discuss the murder. It was as if he was the only person going through changes after our discovery. Like he was the only one allowed to grieve.

I played with the light switch. I clicked it on and I clicked it off. I went to the kitchen. Clicked it on. Clicked it off. The time on the microwave was blank. I couldn't get over it.

I lay Elijah on the living room couch. He always fell asleep in the car on the way from the day care. Even with my plantain blinds open, I still could barely see. Darkness was fast approaching due to time being pushed back an hour by daylight saving time.

I picked up the house phone, and like an idiot, waited for a dial tone that wasn't coming. "Real bright, Germani," I said to myself as I placed the phone back on its base.

I pulled out my cell phone and called Scott at work.

Craig answered, "Car Care the automotive specialist for all your repair needs, this is Craig, how may I help you?"

"Hey, Craig, this is Germani. Is Scott busy?"

"Right now he is outside doing a battery check. Would you like for me to have him call you back?"

"No. I can hold," I said.

I sat in the dark waiting for eight minutes before he came to the phone.

"What's going on?" Scott asked in an agitated voice.

Instead of playing into his bad mood when I already had my own, I replied, "The power is off."

He apologized for forgetting the payment arrangement he made with the utility company, then he put me on three-way while he paid the bill. With it being after five in the evening, the electric company didn't know when a technician would be out to turn the power back on. I decided to leave the house and go see Kira.

Nu Taste Café had a calming, yet eclectic environment; the blend of Polynesian and Spanish cuisines that reflected cultures of both Kira and Jayat. They purchased the building three years ago. Brick red covered the walls, while tan wicker chairs lined the small tables. International jazz vibrated from the speakers. The contrasting smell of papaya soup along with saffron from paella lingered in the air as a waitress holding a plate went past me.

"Do you need some money?" Kira asked me as she sat across from me at a corner table.

I helped Elijah play a game on his Leafpad.

"No. Absolutely not." It was embarrassing that she would even feel the need to ask. Her finances were no different than mine. The money they made went back into sustaining Nu Taste.

"You know that pride is man's greatest downfall. Took down more than a few nations. If you need it, then you shouldn't be ashamed to ask. When we were teenagers we used to put our money together for those summer events at the Afro-American Cultural Center, Blumenthal Performing Arts and the Actor's Theatre. This would be no different."

"I'm a grown woman now. It's not your job to take care of me or make sure I have money for household bills. As much as I talk about Mekhi leeching off my momma, the last thing I would do is ask for that kind of help. Besides, it's not that we're broke. The money is in our checking account and Scott carries the debit card for the account. I should have requested my own card when I realized he wasn't using automatic pay for our bills. This wouldn't have happened if I were thinking. Duke Energy gives customers at least ten working days from the receipt of the notice to get the bill paid. Scott made a payment arrangement for three monthly installments. He paid the first amount, but ignored the second notice. It should have been taken care of."

"You two have had a lot happen in the past four weeks. Scott's mind was probably on the death of his best friend. If you didn't have that to deal with, I'm sure he would have remembered."

Kira placed the salt and pepper shakers inside the menu rack.

"Don't get me wrong. I understand that Scott didn't purposely forget to pay the bill. I had forgotten about the bill myself with this whole murder-suicide uproar. But my point is that we would have never received a shut-off notice if he had continued to take care of business like he's supposed to.

"If it weren't for his obsession with porn, we wouldn't have a problem, because our bills would still be paid instead of him wasting *our* money—and I do mean ours, because that's my money in the bank too—on pay-per-view nude movies. Over four hundred dollars worth of porn, if I include the amount from the new bill. Who has that kind of money to waste on pay-per-view movies? We sure don't," I whispered, hoping that Elijah wasn't paying attention to our conversation.

"He used your bill money to pay for sex on television? You didn't tell me that was what happened." Kira sounded astonished.

"I know. We argued about the first shut-off notice on the night Cherish called me and . . ." I flayed my hand in the air. "Well, you know the rest."

"That's serious. I can see why you're so mad. Why would he even need to spend that kind of money on movies?"

"Exactly. That's my question too."

"Germani, he must need something extra in the relationship. Did you ever make it over to Kinky Ways? Maybe buy yourself a cute little French maid outfit."

"French maid outfit?" I scoffed. "I don't need to role play to please my husband. This is bigger than me dipping my body in hot chocolate, doing Chinese splits or spanking him with a leather paddle. Intimacy is a connection between two that goes beyond the physical. Scott should be able to touch my soul when we make love. You can't touch my soul with props."

"Germani, be reasonable, you're sounding like a prude. Why do you think men stray with mistresses and prostitutes?" Kira paused, but she didn't really want me to answer that. "Because their wives are afraid to explore sexual techniques that would keep the love fresh and interesting. I was listening to The Michael Baisden Show the other day and they were talking about this exact subject. Making love work. Several women called to say they are open to try new things. If they didn't keep their homes happy, then their husbands would find somebody who would. No matter how much you love God, you still have to keep Scott happy and interested."

He probably was already cheating on me, but I couldn't handle that subject with Kira on top of everything else. "Scott has a problem . . . a porn obsession. I've been doing research and there are a lot of women out there going through the same thing as me. Scott is going to have to get his sex movie obsession in check, or else."

"Or else what?"

"I haven't decided what the *or else* will mean, but if I have to dish out an ultimatum to get my point across, then I will."

"Okay. Hope that ultimatum thing works out for you." Kira gazed over at Elijah who had bread fries in one hand and his Leaf pad pen in the other. He was completely oblivious to our conversation. Her look made me feel like I was trying to break up a happy home, when my home was anything but.

"Did I tell you that there was a detective at our house asking questions about Cherish and Damon's activities? He wanted to know the extent of our involvement. Basically, what he asked was if we were into the same thing. Evidently, a video surfaced on I-Tube of some prominent figures in compromising positions. They linked the upload of the video to a computer at Cherish and

Damon's address on the night of the murder, and since we were the ones who found them and were their friends, they thought we might have more information about the case than previously stated. You should have seen Scott cut me off before I could speak in our defense. He told the detective that we didn't need to disclose anything. Scott asked them to kindly leave our premises. Kira, it made us look guilty. I didn't have any involvement in their swingers' network, so why the hush?"

"Hmmm. What did Scott say?"

"He told me that Damon was his friend even in death, and the police just wanted information to further smear Damon's reputation and take the spotlight off the rich folks caught on video."

"He may have a point."

I looked at Kira like she fell off a dump truck. "I don't think so. Damon screwed his own reputation. He wasn't ashamed of his lifestyle. What are we hiding it for? Regardless of that, I feel more disconnected from Scott with each passing day. Like we're going through the motions of marriage to save face and—"

The ring tone "Lost Without You," by Robin Thicke began playing.

Scott was calling me. Maybe I should change that ring tone. Even with the croon of a falsetto, I felt more lost with him.

"Hey," I said, rubbing the line of the table with my finger after answering the phone.

"I got a call from the electric company. They won't be able to get somebody out there until the morning. They said the power should be back on first thing. I'm about to close shop and head home soon."

"I don't want to be in the dark. I'll spend the night at Kira's and come home in the morning before I have to be to work." I looked up at Kira for agreement.

She nodded.

"That's who we're with already." Even though it was almost nine at night and I could easily sleep in spite of the power being out, I didn't want to. I didn't want to act like I wasn't mad. I didn't want to undress Elijah or myself in the dark nor vacillate about the electricity not working. And I definitely didn't want to sleep next to Scott.

"Tell Kira I said hello," Scott said like we were okay, like our situation was all good.

"Scott said hello," I told her.

"Hey, Scott," Kira shouted into my phone.

"See you in the morning?" Scott asked me like I had a whole bunch of other options.

"Uh-huh."

What I was giving and what I was getting were far from equivalent. I couldn't keep up the charade.

CHAPTER FORTY-TWO

SCOTT

I cruised down the almost vacant street of a normally well lit North Tryon in Uptown after work. Two patrol officers rode their bikes past me turning down East Fifth, where a man vanished a week ago after leaving the Buckhead Saloon. His story received national attention on *Good Morning America* when his family sent out a plea for any information leading to his whereabouts. I would bet money that they don't find him, at least not alive. If a child goes missing, they may be taken by a disgruntled parent or the child might have run away from home. Worse possibility is they were snatched up by a child molester or some other kind of lunatic. When a grown man goes missing, it is almost always a case of foul play unless that person didn't want to be found. Considering the news hype that he telephoned several people on the night he was last seen, it was highly unlikely that he vanished intentionally.

I wondered how long it would take for the family's denial to fade and the full blown grief to emerge. How long would they keep his picture circulating before public interest faded too?

Damon got his ten minutes of spotlight in two days of news broadcasts. Then it became sensationalized a week and a half later, after a few local doctors were seen streaming bare bottom through the web. Somebody leaked to the press that there was a connection to the murder-suicide in Highgrove. News was only glorified when it was bad.

I wasn't going home yet. I was a little irritated that my wife and son weren't there, although I didn't say anything about it to Germani. In the five years we'd been married, sleeping apart had never been an option.

Further down Tryon Street in the center of the Uptown condos named Ratcliffe, was a three-tier landscaped park with art pieces shaped like fish and a high tech water fountain. I proposed to Germani there in January, almost five years ago. We had come from an art exhibit in the Mint Museum and strolled along Tryon as I held her from behind to ward off the chilly winter evening. She had stopped at Dillworth Coffee on the corner of West Martin Luther King for a hot mocha latte, but they had closed an hour earlier.

She was ready to go find a Starbucks, but I convinced her to walk down Tryon to the Green. There was something special in the park that she hadn't seen before. I remember that she smiled and wrapped herself in my wool trench, my body heat merging with hers as we matched strides in our stroll.

She used to be so agreeable. She used to be easy to love.

After Aquavina, but before the Bank of America Stadium where the street changed from North to South, I parked my car and walked by the Ratcliffe underground parking deck toward international signs, stepping on riddles built into the ground, a hopscotch board several feet away. Right next to the water fountain was where I had gotten on my knee and requested that she spend the rest of her life with me. Her smile, with shivering lips, dropped as I pulled the ring out of my inside pocket. Throughout the evening, I had been checking on the ring, worried that it might somehow slip out without the box to protect it. But I left the box at my apartment so that she wouldn't feel the square bulge when we were close. She did ask me several times why I kept my coat on during the exhibit, but I would change the subject each time she mentioned it. She didn't linger on the subject.

Back when she was agreeable, before the times changed. Now everything was an issue with her.

My daddy once told me that the only thing consistent about a woman is her ability to be inconsistent. He gave me a speech after my sister, Sharon, slapped me for throwing away her raggedy Barbie dollhouse after she flushed my GI Joe. I slapped her back, figured she should be able to take a hit as well as she gave one. She went crying to Daddy, but I didn't expect nothing to happen since she started it.

Daddy came into the room and punched me right below the cheekbone. He made my jaw rattle. Then he took me to the back shed, where I thought he was going to beat me some more. Instead, he explained the rules of man versus woman.

Woman was the weaker vessel. He told me that it was biblical. Women did everything based on emotion. Women had a fantasy expectation of life, while men used logic to solve problems. He told me to never respond to a woman like a woman. The reason he hit me was so I would understand the difference between a woman's hand and a man's fist. Men were stronger physically and mentally, so we had to handle them with cotton mittens, address them like fragile jewels. Think when they don't. Walk away when they don't. If he ever heard about me hitting my sisters or another female, he would break both my legs and leave me with a permanent limp as a reminder of what he said.

Germani should have been my rock, but if what my father said was true, she was incapable of possessing the kind of strength I needed. The newlywed bliss was gone, and as much as I wanted to make things right, I knew I couldn't squeeze water from a dry towel.

I looked at the bronze and silver coins at the bottom of the fountain as I rose.

Headed back to my car, checking my watch.

It was 11:14 P.M. Torrance would be up. He hadn't picked up his last check today. It only had twelve hours, but I figured he still needed his money. I needed to apologize to him. In my stress, I came at him wrong and I was man enough to come correct.

Dillehay Court was one of the older subsidized housing complexes for low-income families. Due to a multi-million dollar urban revitalization Hope VI grant project, most of the properties were given a face lift by the Charlotte Housing Authority. The effort merged families in a residence with various income brackets; kept people without the means to afford the high priced condos like the Ratcliffe in a decent, safe standard of living.

Several complexes got new names to match their new look, but Dillehay remained the same with the exception of the creation of a new computer system in the youth center. It still looked like the projects, the ghetto, the hood.

I turned onto Pine Street and saw a group of kids, teenage boys, standing on the corner. Two of them leaned against a White Cutlass. The brake lights were on as one stood on the driver's side and the other on the passenger side. Bass bumped from a blue Deuce parked nearby; rims with spinners sparkling brighter that the night post on the corner.

I idled my car a couple of minutes, but the boys weren't moving. They acted like they had ownership of all of Pine Street. I pulled my 300 around the Cutlass. I didn't have gas to be wasting. The boy on the driver's side glanced up. It was Torrance with a hoodie on. I watched him from the rearview mirror as I parked on the curb directly in front of the other car. I knew what was up. He'd gone back to the streets, probably peddling crack instead of Jimmies.

I got out and we met in the street.

"Man, what you doing out here?" I asked as two of the boys watched from the blue Deuce.

"I'm doing me, what you doing here?" Torrance's chin was up. His body bucked up like he wanted to fight me. I had tested his manhood before; he wanted to reciprocate the deed.

I pulled the folded paper from my pocket and handed it to him. "I came to give you your check."

"Who dat?" one of his boys with a Phat Farm cap asked Torrance as he approached us. He had a baby face and looked like he should be in bed getting ready for school the next day.

Torrance didn't respond as he unfolded the paper. He laughed as he tapped the paper with his free hand. "Sixty-eight dollars?"

The joke must have passed me by.

"Man, you could have kept this. What I'm supposed to do with this chump change?" He showed baby face the check.

Two weeks ago, sixty-eight dollars would have paid his mother's rent or bought some groceries. Two weeks ago, he would have stretched that money to meet his needs. Two weeks ago, he was grateful for a check.

"Torrance, these streets can't do nothing for you . . . not long term," I told him, shedding a little wisdom.

"Pssh. You can only live one day at a time. I ain't worried about the future." Torrance blew my wisdom off, the vices of a fatherless young man talking.

"If you're not worried about the future, then what about your momma? Aren't you worried about her?"

Torrance's face frowned up. "Dawg, I know you ain't acting like you worried about my momma. You fired me, dawg. Then made sure the unemployment office denied me my benefits. Don't come over here talking about my momma like you care."

"I had nothing to do with your unemployment application getting denied. I tried to tell you before you left that you didn't have enough work hours to claim benefits. I was going to try to get you connected with one of the auto shops for a position—"

"Man, whatever. Go on with all that. I don't need nothing you to got offer," Torrance balled up the check and threw it down. Stomped it with his tennis shoes. Watched the check become ripped and dirty. I stepped forward with no other intent but to get through to him.

He started walking toward the Deuce. "I don't need your advice or suggestions."

"Torrance." I had lost one friend and felt like I was losing a little brother too.

Baby face pulled a gun out; aimed it at my forehead.

I stared at him like he was stupid. "You gonna use it?" I challenged him. He had the wrong brotha if he was trying to scare me.

"Lemon, let's bounce. Those females on Leafcrest still waiting for us to come through," the other boy with Torrance said as they got into the car.

The little punk lowered his gun, laughing.

As I got into my ride, I thought about what I had to go home to. An empty, dark place. It felt like I was losing everything important.

Lord, what are you trying to tell me?

CHAPTER FORTY-THREE

GERMANI

I lay on a camper's twin air mattress, staring at the ceiling in Kira's living room, and for once, it wasn't Scott or his addiction to porn on my mind.

I was thinking about a man other than my husband. I was thinking about Tre. How there was no closure when he dissed me for Africa. Our relationship stopped abruptly, mostly on my part. I had given him an ultimatum after he went through airport security of the Charlotte Douglas Airport. *"Go into that ridiculous war zone to risk your life for nothing and I won't be here when you come back. If you're able to survive."*

He decided that my love wasn't as important as his destination. I stopped talking to him on that day his flight left. Refused to accept his calls, threw away letters without opening them. Did my best to block out my feelings for him.

Nothing seemed to work until Scott took my pain away. I stuffed that need to speak to Tre, to hear from Tre, be close to Tre, in the corner of my heart.

It was the worst decision I'd ever made.

Kira and Autumn were my friends, Scott my spouse, but none of them could replace my bond with Tre.

I rolled over on my side and pulled my arm from beneath Elijah's head. An intense desire rushed over me like a tsunami hitting a small village. I suddenly felt like I was drowning. I couldn't breathe and I thought I was having a panic attack.

Slid on my shoes. Grabbed my purse. I tiptoed down to Kira's room at the far corner, knocking gently. I waited against the door frame. Looked down the hall, expecting my son to awaken. At home he slept like a rock, but we weren't at home.

When I didn't get a response, I cracked open the door and whispered Kira's name. My head lay against the opening, but I couldn't see inside.

She poked her head out, saw me in my coat, "Leaving?"

"I need to get some air," I told her, fanning myself. The house wasn't hot. Her thermostat stayed at seventy degrees, whether winter or summer. It was me. My inner temperature was rising, face flushed from scattered thoughts. "Elijah's still in the living room. He shouldn't wake up, but I need you to keep an eye on him until I get back."

"That's fine. Let me get you my keys." I waited outside her door with a lump the size of a grapefruit in my throat. I had never had a panic attack. Didn't know the feeling.

Kira saw the horrified look on my face as I wheezed like I had asthma. "You sure you okay?"

"I . . . just . . . need . . . air." It wasn't enough oxygen in her apartment to dislodge that grapefruit.

Kira fumbled with her keys, wrapped an index finger and thumb around one oval-shaped key. "Bottom lock, turn twice. Top lock. Pull the door toward you and turn the lock once."

I stared at her. They lived on the ninth floor of a secured building.

"Can never be too safe," Kira remarked.

I shrugged and left quickly. Thought about Damon and Cherish. Seemed to me more crimes occurred by loved ones than burglars on the prowl for free goods.

From the ninth floor on down, I tortured myself with decisions I had made six years ago after Tre got on that Boeing, until six hours earlier when I realized the power bill wasn't paid by Scott.

My life made less sense by the minute, with each labored breath. By the time I stepped outside, that grapefruit had dispersed into a thousand tears. Outside the Camden Grandview Apartments, I cried while the wind kissed my face. I put Kira's keys in my purse and pulled mine out. Needed some time to myself to think things through. Govern a worthwhile plateau. Level my life out. As soon as I got in my car, I knew where I was going. I had to go see him. I had to get some understanding of when my life stopped making sense.

From East Morehead to North McDowell to East Eleventh, stopping on North Davidson. Six years and he still lived at the same address in that small one bedroom studio above a vintage clothing store.

Tre opened the door in an Echo T-shirt with a pair of checkered green pajama pants on.

"Hey." It's been a long time coming.

"Germani, what are you doing here?" he searched the hallway like he was expecting somebody else.

I wiped at my puffy eyes. I knew I looked a mess. "I need to talk to you. I got some stuff on my mind I need to address. That I should have . . . me . . . we.

I don't know," I sighed and closed my eyes as I felt tears soaking my ducts.

"I can't let you come in." Tre rubbed his face. His eyes focused above my head at the swaying trees on the ledge behind me.

"Did I catch you at a bad time?" I stepped back, feeling rejected again. "You know what, I shouldn't have come here. I'm sorry for bothering you. I wasn't thinking." I turned toward the stairwell. Just another bad decision. He couldn't give me closure, if I couldn't give it to myself.

I heard footfalls of bare soles against wood behind me as I rushed downstairs.

"Germani. Wait a minute. Don't leave like that."

I stopped with my leg landing on the third step from the bottom. Turning around, I said, "I was in the wrong for showing up unannounced. It didn't dawn on me that you might have company."

He had said at the store that he wasn't seeing anyone.

"There's nobody up there," he responded. Tre's shoulders were hunched like he was warming himself up. "I just don't think it's a good idea for us to be alone in my apartment."

"Oh." In the three years we were together, only once did we cross the lines of intimacy. If there was anybody that I could trust not to take advantage of me, it was Tre. Unless, that was flipped and he didn't trust me. "Listen, it's cold out here and I don't want to be responsible for you getting pneumonia. I'll go."

"Don't. We can go back up to my place and talk." He sounded reluctant.

"You sure?"

There was laughter and music coming from the club around the corner: the Wine-Up.

"Yeah. Something must be weighing heavy on you for you to show up at my door in the middle of the night." He began walking back up the stairs.

"Do you still go to the Wine-Up?" I asked as I followed him.

We used to go listen to poetry on Friday nights at our main hang-out spot. Sometimes he would do one of his poems. I'd watch him mesmerize the crowd with his prolific nuance, stringing words with unexpected meaning.

"Once in awhile. Not like I used to though. But when the mood strikes me, I go."

"I haven't been in years. Couldn't walk in there without thinking about you."

His head dropped briefly before he pushed his apartment door open.

I bit my bottom lip, regretting that I had said that.

"I was laid out, so I'm going to have to make the place presentable for you."

He moved his furniture. That was the first thing I noticed. His futon was gone and everything in the room was rearranged. The wicker rattan chair was facing a bookshelf instead of the television. The walls were covered with art work he collected from artist friends that used to be stacked in a corner.

"It looks different in here," I told Tre as he pushed in the let out mattress of his couch.

"I sublet the place out to a couple of college students while I was in Africa and came back to a few changes. My futon was missing a leg. They had a chunk of wood holding up the left side. Other than that, everything was kept in good condition. I used their deposit to buy a new sleeping area."

I scrolled through his collection of DVD movies, *Hero* with Jet Li. A Brazilian film called *City of God*. The made-for-television version of *Their Eyes Were Watching God*, starring Halle Berry.

No porn amongst his collection. Porn wasn't something that Tre ever entertained when we were together. Instead, he focused on thought-provoking movies. I appreciated that about him.

I noticed a movie I wasn't familiar with. I pulled out the cover with a boy below marching feet. The title read *Sometimes in April.*

"It's a good movie. Realistic depiction of death in Rwanda. Idris Alba played the heck out of his role." Tre came over and pointed to the case in my hand.

"I'll take your word for it," I said, pushing the movie back in place. It would seem like he had enough violence while over in Africa that his watching movies about the same thing seemed to be overkill.

I wanted to ask why he left me for war, but instead I asked, "What's it like? Darfur?"

"Chaotic. Hundreds of thousands dead. People trying to find refuge amongst the violence. They're scared. Uncertain of the future. What can you do when your country's killing you and the necessary help is just not there? People assume the United States isn't helping with relief efforts because there isn't any oil for us to claim as our own over in the region, but it's deeper than that. There is oil, but China's running that. In fact, China is to Darfur what America is to Iraq. The United States doesn't want to mess with China. They're just as much a super power as we are."

"I read in *Newsweek* that Darfur has become a repeat of the Rwandan genocide. Men, women and children being murdered in bunches like pig slaughters. It seems so senseless. When did life lose its value?" I sat down on his couch.

Tre plopped down on the opposite end. "When Cain killed Abel."

"It was senseless then and it's senseless now."

"It's about perspective. You have people with opposing views, so the militia eradicates the other. Ethnic cleansing."

I placed my arm on the curve of his couch. "I feared for you over there. I thought you weren't coming back. Did you fear for yourself? You were right there. Volunteered to be a moving target." I sounded harsh, blatantly bitter about a past I couldn't change.

Tre glanced at me and shook his head. "I didn't volunteer to be a moving target. I volunteered to help people the same shade as me get out of a distressed situation. We were housed in the neighboring city of Chad. The organization couldn't get in Darfur. Too dangerous. Germani, believe it or not, I wasn't on a suicide mission."

"My daddy died in a foreign land." Some hurts were impossible to let go.

"I know. And you were expecting the same thing to happen to me. I understand why you didn't want to wait for me."

He sounded way more forgiving than I was willing to be.

I closed my eyes as guilt tugged at my heart. I nervously ran my fingers across the back of the couch. "I think I made the wrong decision."

He sat across from me and stared for several minutes. His expression was blank. I couldn't read his thoughts. "Germani, what's going on between you and your husband?" he finally asked.

"It's not working. He's got problems. Big problems that are destroying any chance of us salvaging things."

"Everybody has problems. You have to work through them."

"I've been trying, but he's making it hard to do. He has this addiction. I don't know how to deal with his addiction."

Tre sat up with worry on his face. "Is he on drugs?"

"No. Thank God." I rubbed on my pants leg. "I don't know how much I'm supposed to say. You are my ex-lover."

He sat on the edge of the couch and looked me in my eyes. "Germani, you came to me. You obviously need to talk about it. You know that's something we used to be good at doing: communicating. I can't change your situation, but I can listen."

"Was I enough woman for you? Did you ever feel like I wasn't enough?"

That question jolted him. He frowned. "No, but this isn't about us or what we had or anything like that. You have a husband. Marriage isn't something to be taken lightly."

"Porn. He's addicted to porn." I didn't wait for Tre to respond. "You know what I learned? I discovered that if a man lusts with his mind, then he is an adulterer. That he has broken the covenant of marriage."

"Even a broken covenant can be repaired. Have you prayed about your situation?"

"Yes. I've prayed and prayed, then prayed some more. Futility. That's what it is. I think my efforts are in vain. I'm frustrated and tired. I didn't sign up for all this. You and I didn't have this kind of issue. I married Scott, but I wasn't prepared for this type of issue."

"Germani, you can't base the expectations from one relationship onto another." Tre stood up and walked to the kitchen area. "I'm not going to tell you to leave your husband, if that's what you're looking for."

"I knew you wouldn't," I sighed. "Tre, I just want to be happy again."

"Happiness is relative. That's an inner dilemma. You control that, I don't."

I heard what he was saying, but I needed him to understand my point, understand what I was going through.

"You're the only man I completely trust," I said with honesty. We could be transparent with each other. "I don't think I can trust Scott. You can't be happy without trust."

"*We may handle any how, if we only have a why*. Do you remember that quote?"

I had to smile. "Friedrich Nietzsche."

"Only you understand why you married him and only you can decide how to stay married."

"I disagree. My judgment was skewed. You were gone and Scott made it easier to move on."

"I don't think you married him just to have a warm body nearby or because you were mad at me. He had some qualities that drew you to him; that made it worth ending our relationship so you could be with him." He came over and handed me a cup of steaming raspberry zinger tea.

"Stop giving me Gandhi and give me Tre. The delicate approach is not your style. Tell me how you really feel."

He placed his cup of tea on the table and pushed the wicker chair so that it was facing me. "You made your bed, now you got to sleep in it."

His candor surprised me. "Well, I didn't mean be that harsh."

"Emotionalism will destroy you and everything around you. Your being obsessed about his addiction is just as bad as his having an addiction. You've got to stop trying to control the relationship, trying to fix it. Let God work it out."

"That's easier said than done."

"Only if you make it that way. You can't box people in and expect them to want to stay there. If you focus on your walk instead of his, then life won't be so difficult. God honors your relationship with Him. Your husband has to deal with his own struggles. Either you're going to be supportive or you're not. Just remember that whatever decision you make impacts more than just you." Tre paused as he took a sip of his drink. "Germani, you need to be talking to your husband, not me."

As much as I didn't like his response, I knew he was right.

CHAPTER FORTY-FOUR

SCOTT

I sat across the street from Germani's ex-boy-friend's place wondering how long she would be inside. I couldn't believe she was cheating on me after all her lectures about Christian values. It was all a bunch of garbage to make me feel guilty for her bad deeds.

She played me for a fool.

Instead of going home when I left Torrance with his crew, I decided to go clear the air with my wife. Just as I pulled up to Kira's apartment complex I saw Germani get in her car. I thought she saw me, but she drove right past. I turned around and followed her. Never could have guessed that she was going to see her ex.

I had watched the whole touching scene. Her going up his stairs, only to run down minutes later. Tre chasing after her. Their exchanging words. Him taking her back up.

I stayed in my car for fifty minuets, debating whether I would knock on his door and confront both of them or leave, go get my son from Kira and wait at home for an explanation. Give her time to figure out how to lie to me.

I wondered how long she had been seeing him on the low. Did it start before Damon died? Probably so. That explained her detachment from me, her constant complaining about my faults and the excuses not to make love. It all finally made sense.

After stewing for close to an hour, I got out of my car in a fighting mood.

I rushed up and banged on his door. If they were in bed together, I wanted to make sure they heard me.

When Tre opened the door, fully clothed seconds later, his appearance kept me from punching him in the face. He didn't look like a man interrupted in the middle of getting some. Instead, the brotha was welcoming, smiled at me and stepped aside.

Caught me off guard, but the night was full of surprises.

I stormed in and saw Germani curled up on his couch. She looked too comfortable.

"Well, don't you look cozy. Weren't expecting to see me tonight were you?" I asked Germani as the shock from seeing me settled on her face.

"Scott, I—" She quickly stood up stuttering.

"You what . . . you got a reason for being here? A really good one?" I stopped in front of Germani, wondering what kind of explanation she could give for being in her first love's house at one in the morning. I knew how she felt about him before we got together. If he hadn't left the country, she probably would have married Tre instead of me.

"Scott, we were just talking."

Tre responded, "There is nothing going on between your wife and me. She came to get advice about you, but I told her that she needed to talk with you about it."

I gritted my teeth before asking, "So, you were complaining about me to your ex?"

Germani looked over at Tre. "He's right. There is nothing going on between us. Nothing like what you're thinking. Scott, you know how things have been between us. We don't talk anymore."

The whole scene was too strange for me to handle. I turned to my wife's ex. "Tre, no offense, but there really is no reason my wife should be at your place, regardless of what's going on with us." I then looked at Germani. "I don't want to have this conversation in front of your ex-boyfriend. If you have a problem with me, then we need to go somewhere and talk."

"All right, let's go." She turned to Tre. "I'm sorry for bringing any confusion to your home."

He held up his hand like there was no need for her to apologize.

I walked back out the door just as quickly as I had come in.

Germani met me at my car. "Where do you want to go?"

"Anywhere but here."

"I'll follow you and let you decide the location." For the first time in months, she wasn't being combative.

"All right." I got in my car and drove back down to the Green. I didn't say anything to her until we were back by the fountain.

"What are we doing here?" she asked as she stared at the waterfall.

I sat on a bench. She came over and sat next to me. Germani bit her bottom lip as she listened.

"Germani, I love you. When I asked you to marry me, it was a life long commitment. Lately, it has been sounding like you're looking for a reason to end our marriage, like you're digging for bad things to discredit me as your husband. Things that weren't a problem before are all of a sudden a major dilemma. I didn't get what was going on with you."

"I think I've made my stand pretty clear. I've compromised my values to please you and basically I have gotten tired of it. When I was sitting at that strip club, all I could think about was that environment didn't fit me. You seemed completely comfortable with those naked women surrounding you, and that just wasn't right to me. I felt like we weren't as connected as I originally thought. I felt like you saw women as purely sexual objects and the company you kept only reinforced my opinion."

I took a rock and threw it into the water. Her words made more sense after listening to Myles speak. I hadn't told her about the class I attended with Ahmad. I felt like she was going to judge me on that too. "You should know me better than that. I don't see women as sex objects. I mean, come on; I was raised in a house full of females. And you've seen how protective I am about my sisters and niece."

"Yes, but the people you associated with didn't have that same standard of living. Why would you hang with men that didn't respect women? That makes no sense to me. Plus, you seem to be obsessed with pornography. It all made me question your character. It's as if God was looking down on us shaking His head at our disobedience to His Word."

"Germani, you act like you don't have any struggles. Porn is a struggle for me and has been since way before we got together. Believe me, God knows my struggle. It doesn't mean that I see all women as sex objects. I would think that as my wife, you would be able to stand by my side during my struggle, even if you didn't agree with it."

"No. I can't stand by something I don't agree with. I can't justify what I know is wrong. I desire to get better with time, not deeper in denial. If something doesn't feel right, then that is the case for a reason. As your wife, if I see you are doing wrong, then it is my responsibility to mention it."

"I understand, but it's also both our responsibilities to know when something is not meant for us to control. I wanted Damon to live, but God took him anyway. I can stay mad at God or I can accept that my friend is gone. The same thing applies to you. This isn't supposed to be your battle; it's mine to deal with. You can either respect the place I'm in, or not."

Germani sighed. "I suppose."

Her words didn't sound all that confident about our marriage. "So what's it going to be? I'm willing to work harder on my struggle. Are you able to be supportive?"

She sat there, but didn't say anything. I took that to mean she couldn't be. I stood up and began walking out of the park. Guess it would end where it started. I couldn't force her to understand. She knew what she could and couldn't handle. I didn't want to leave without her, but . . .

"Scott, I love you." She stood up and walked toward me. "I love you enough to make this work. I will not sacrifice my beliefs to have you, but I can be supportive, because I believe God will deliver you from your addiction."

"That's all I ask." I wrapped my arms around her waist and gently kissed her lips.

Relishing in the commitment we had.

EPILOGUE

GERMANI

January 5, 2008

The New Year always brought a desire to change. Many made plans to eat right or workout more. Some became determined to get out of debt or give to charity. While others decided it's the perfect time to stop smoking or drinking. But all change ain't good change. I had read an article in a legal journal that said January was the highest divorce filing month. Supposedly, the holidays caused extra stress and magnified marital problems. Thus, throwing in the towel come January seemed like a logical solution for those in turmoil.

Scott and I had endured so much turmoil in the previous year that I didn't think we would make it as a couple. We'd both been stretched by our extended family obligations. Me trying to help Momma with Mekhi. Scott trying to help Beverly with Alexis.

Fortunately, we were able to put together some money and get the assault charges made by Mishelle's boyfriend, Cyrus, against Mekhi dropped. Child Protective Services were investigating Cyrus for the bruises on Camry. We were all still waiting for Alexis to get a bone marrow transplant, but her name had moved up to number seven on the waiting list. It wouldn't be much longer before she got the help she needed.

Damon's death took a toll on Scott. He had such a difficult time forgiving Cherish. He knows it's something he has to do for his own benefit. I don't even mention her to him anymore.

Cherish took a plea bargain of ten to fifteen years for second-degree murder right before Christmas. The publicity had already been brutal and she didn't want to go through a long trial under scrutiny. She gave her attorney permission to turn over Damon's belongings to his mother, and Cherish also planned to give Ms. Ilene part of the profit from the sale of the Ballantyne home.

For Scott and me, the New Year meant the renewal of our relationship. Biblically, the number eight signified a new beginning, the combination of resurrection and regeneration. We were determined to take the struggles of 2007 and strengthen our new beginning.

I glanced around the packed room at New Joy Christian Cathedral as my husband walked to the center of it.

"I want to tell my wife I'm sorry," Scott said in the room full of people.

Elijah sat next to me in a navy blue turtleneck sweater and dark jeans. His outfit matched his father's. When Scott told me that we would be going to his porn addiction recovery class, I thought it might have been inappropriate for Elijah. Scott insisted that we attend Family Support Day. He had told me about the class on Thanksgiving night. Scott had explained that he needed to sort out his thoughts before he came to me. I was ecstatic that he was doing something about his problem. I listened to my husband apologize. I mouthed, "It's okay."

Scott saw my lips moving and smiled affectionately. "No. I'm sorry. For all the times I made you hurt. For all the words I said in anger. For rejecting your input and denying your beliefs when you saw me getting out of control. I heard you even when it looked like I wasn't listening. I loved you even when I didn't show it. If God had not given you to me, I don't think I could have become the man of integrity I was meant to be."

"Oh, gosh." I could feel tears slide down my face at his admission.

His eyes stayed locked with mine. "With every struggle there is the opportunity for growth. When you're not willing to acknowledge a problem, or in my case, an obsession, you're not willing to grow. I didn't realize how hard I was making my marriage. I didn't realize how I was compromising my walk with God. Thank you, Germani, for staying by my side. I know it wasn't easy. Baby, I get it."

I nodded. Things definitely hadn't been easy. Through it all, I had to reach my own level of understanding. I tried to force Scott to serve God my way. I didn't get that his struggle started in adolescence. That it wasn't something he knew how to just quit. I had to learn to respect the place he was in.

Whatever battles we faced in the future, were battles we would face together.

Reader's Group Guide Questions

1. Germani said early in the story that she agreed to watch porn because she thought it was part of submission. Do you think her intentions were honorable?

2. Both Scott and Germani spent a lot of time dealing with problems of their extended family. Did that prevent them from focusing on their own issues?

3. Scott maintained friendships primarily with men who had derogatory views of women. How does that play into his own actions? Did those relationships hinder Scott's Christian walk?

4. Scott's sister, Beverly, tried desperately to convince Alex to donate bone marrow to their daughter, Alexis. What would you have done in her situation?

5. Mekhi wanted to stay with Mishelle despite their abusive history together? Does the Bible have an answer to abusive relationships?

6. Germani was shocked and hurt that Scott didn't want to give up porn. Should she have been surprised? Should she have responded differently?

7. Today's culture glorifies eroticism and sexual independence. Is the culture a hindrance to Christianity? Why or why not?

8. Germani called Scott unsaved because of his refusal to give up watching porn. She judged him by his addiction. Was she justified? Is one sin worse than another?

9. Germani and Scott sought advice about their sex life from friends, including Tre, Germani's ex. Are there some personal issues that friends shouldn't talk about? Does it depend on the type of friend?

10. How does the story affect your perception of married Christians with similar problems?

Reader's Conversation Questions

BIOGRAPHY

T.N. Williams is the author of the debut novel *Something On The Inside,* which made Black Expressions and Black Christian News bestsellers lists. She has received several awards for recognition and collaborated poetic work in the published collection entitled *Traces of the Infinite*. T.N. Williams graduated from Grand Valley State University with a Bachelor degree in Sociology. She currently resides outside of Charlotte, NC with her husband and three children.

UC HIS GLORY BOOK CLUB!

www.uchisglorybookclub.net

UC His Glory Book Club is the spirit-inspired brainchild of Joylynn Jossel, Author and Acquisitions Editor of Urban Christian, and Kendra Norman-Bellamy, Author for Urban Christian. This is an online book club that hosts authors of Urban Christian. We welcome as members all men and women who have a passion for reading Christian-based fiction.

UC His Glory Book Club pledges our commitment to provide support, positive feedback, encouragement, and a forum whereby members can openly discuss and review the literary works of Urban Christian authors.

There is no membership fee associated with UC His Glory Book Club; however, we do ask that you support the authors through purchasing, encouraging, providing book reviews, and of course, your prayers. We also ask that you respect our beliefs and follow the guidelines of the book club. We hope to receive your valuable input, opinions, and reviews that build up, rather than tear down our authors.

WHAT WE BELIEVE:

—We believe that Jesus is the Christ, Son of the Living God

—We believe the Bible is the true, living Word of God.

—We believe all Urban Christian authors should use their God-given writing abilities to honor God and share the message of the written word God has given to each of them uniquely.

—We believe in supporting Urban Christian authors in their literary endeavors by reading, purchasing and sharing their titles with our on-line community.

—We believe that in everything we do in our literary arena should be done in a manner that will lead to God being glorified and honored.

—We look forward to the online fellowship with you. Please visit us often at:

www.uchisglorybookclub.net.

Many Blessing to You!

Shelia E. Lipsey,
President, UC His Glory Book Club